STONE'S THROE

C.E. MURPHY

D1604019

MKP

STONE'S THROE

ISBN-13: 978-1-61317-179-0

Copyright © 2015, Evil Hat Productions

Cover Artist: Fringe Element (fringe-element.net)

 Created with Vellum

Writing as C.E. Murphy

The Walker Papers
Urban Shaman * Winter Moon * Thunderbird Falls * Coyote
Dreams * Walking Dead * Demon Hunts * Spirit Dances
Raven Calls * No Dominion * Mountain Echoes * Shaman Rises

The Old Races Universe
Heart of Stone * House of Cards * Hands of Flame
Baba Yaga's Daughter * Year of Miracles * Kiss of Angels

The Strongbox Chronicles
The Cardinal Rule * The Firebird Deception * The Phoenix Law

The Inheritors' Cycle
The Queen's Bastard * The Pretender's Crown

The Worldwalker Duology
Truthseeker * Wayfinder

The Guildmaster Saga
Seamaster * Stonemaster * Skymaster (forthcoming)

Take A Chance
Roses in Amber
Redeemer
Magic & Manners
Atlantis Fallen
Bewitching Benedict
Stone's Throe

writing as Catie Murphy

The Dublin Driver Mysteries
Dead in Dublin * Death on the Green (forthcoming)

& writing as Murphy Lawless

Gladiator Shifters
Gladiator Bear * Gladiator Cheetah * Gladiator Hawk (forthcoming)

Raven Heart

1

I am, and have been for the best part of a century, a woman of some twenty-eight or thirty years. There is nothing terribly special about this, no mystery save that which has long since been explained: I, and others like me, born on the first day of the twentieth century, grew from ordinary children into what we came to call *spirits*—spirits of the century, each of us given to embody certain traits and aspects that we believe in, fight for, and hope to shape the world toward. It is as this spirit that I share my story.

I remember my childhood as most of us do, *naturellement*: hazy and indistinct, punctured by moments extraordinary to myself, if not to those around me. My parents were kind but, as I grew to understand, desperate, and it is in their desperation that my story truly begins.

MY FATHER SPOKE the same words he always did when a certain light footstep was heard on the stairs: "Quiet. Quiet, Estelle. Don't sing for him right away. Amelia, go to the kitchen. Go, work on the bread. Your mother and I have to speak to the Benefactor. Go on now, like a good girl."

It was the autumn of 1914, and war raged to the east of us. At times it even seemed to rage within the walls of our own small Montmartre apartment. It had not always been thus; indeed, it had not been thus until the war started and the Benefactor's visits became regular. Before then he was a specter, oft mentioned, barely seen, respected in the way that fear commands respect; even as a child I could see that in how my parents responded to him: warily, as though they were hungry dogs that did not trust the hand that fed them.

Consequently, I had no interest in being a good girl: I wanted to meet the Benefactor about whom my parents were so reticent. I wanted to understand what it was in him that caused them to become stiff and formal when he appeared. But I was not yet quite old, or bold, enough to directly disobey my father, and so to the kitchen I went. Sadly, neither was I in the least suited to baking. Week after week the Benefactor visited; week after week I performed alchemy, making lead out of dough. Week after week I burnt the brick-like bread, and week after week we ate it, because Maman and Papa could not afford to replace what I baked so poorly.

"I do not understand," I finally said to Maman

one night, after some eight or ten months of the Benefactor's visits. That night we gnawed on bread softened by tart jam and sweet wine sauce, because it was not Sunday and there was no meat to be had. Potatoes made a pleasant contrast to the sauce soaking the bread. "How is he our benefactor if we cannot afford bread? What benefit is he to us?"

Papa chuckled, and if it was forced, at fourteen I lacked the insight to hear it. "A benefactor is a complicated relationship, Amelia. He owns this flat. He owns many of the buildings in Montmartre, and it's his...beneficence...that allows us to live here. Your mother sings, and we stay."

I held up my burnt bread. "We sing for our supper, is that it, Papa? Maman's voice is an angel's. Surely it's worth more than a roof over our heads and a crust of old bread. Why do you not sing for the opera, Maman? Why do you not sing at the fashionable clubs, as you did when you came to Paris?"

My parents exchanged a glance before Maman smiled at me, a smile that promised all was well in the world. "I'm not as young as I once was, Amelia. Fashions change. We are fortunate to have the Benefactor's good will. Without it our lives would be very different indeed. Now eat your dinner, *ma chérie*, and do not worry yourself about our needs. They are well enough met."

I set my jaw but lowered my eyes, unable to argue against the injustice I sensed. We ate our blackened bread, and I went to bed as I had been told, but in the morning I stole out to prowl the streets of Mont-martre, seeking a way to redress my parents' poverty.

I was turned away from the clubs, sometimes with sympathetic smiles, but more often with sarcastic ones. No one would tell me why Maman was no longer fashionable. To me she was nearly magical, brave and strong and gentle, the very embodiment of all that was good in a soul. She had left Ethiopia as hardly more than a girl, traveling through North Africa and across the Mediterranean Sea by selling not her body, but her voice. I knew by heart the stories and songs that had bought her passage through Italy, through Switzerland, and finally to the place I was born: *la Ville-Lumière*, the city of lights.

There was no doubt that she was beautiful, with large black eyes and the long, slender bones of the Ethiope people. Her hair she wore in a *shuruba*, many braids along her finely shaped skull, loosening at her nape; it was a style of her country, and decades in Europe had not inspired her to adopt a more conven-tional style. Her skin was a shade of brown and red, as if gods had mixed together the colors of earth and sunrise to make her. Yes, she was beautiful, but—as if thinking the job only half done—those same gods had then mixed together *la Nil*'s songbirds to give my Maman her voice. And yet not one club would have her sing for them, nor explain to me why.

Even when I dared travel farther afield, going so far as to implore the opera house for an audition, I was turned away. I might have thought it was my age making me a laughingstock, save that every person I spoke to caught their breath and murmured, "Ah, Madame Stone," or "the voice of an angel," before remembering themselves. Even with these accolades escaping their lips, they would not hire her, nor offer me more than furtive excuses before their swift retreats.

I had no further recourse beyond the opera house; I had chosen it for last because it was both the greatest prize and the most unlikely seeming to my young self. Denied its glory, I stood on its broad shallow steps, hands fisted at my sides, and scowled at Paris to keep myself from crying.

That was how the Benefactor found me, a slight creature outgrowing a little girl's dress, but unable to afford something more suitable to my age. I did not remember being introduced to him, but he stopped his swift climb of the opera house steps and examined me. "Mademoiselle Stone, *oui? Je suis* Monsieur Laval, a friend of your parents."

I replied, "*Oui,*" stiffly, and curtsied even more stiffly. I did not want to see the Benefactor then, when I was at a loss and close to tears, for reasons of youthful vanity if nothing else. He was *very* handsome, the Benefactor, very handsome indeed, even if shockingly old; at least as old as Maman and Papa. His eyes were like Papa's, bright and intensely green, and his hair as black as Maman's. He was taller than Papa, though, and narrow through and through, like a knife cut of black shadow, for he wore black all the time, even in the bright spring sunshine that day. Always the finest wool, the finest linen, always with a splash of color at his throat or pocket: a cravat or kerchief in blue or red or green. His shoes shone even when he came in out of the rain, and the hem of his coat was never dirtied.

"You look unwell, Miss Stone. May I be of assistance?"

"No one will answer me," I replied, and to my horror, the confession flowed from me then, as did tears. I told him everything, how Maman could find nowhere to sing; how we were still poor despite his support; how I had tried for days to find employment for her and had been turned away everywhere without explanation. The Benefactor listened with gratifying attention to my woes, and I hardly knew that we had left the opera house until we stopped beneath a shady parasol and he bought me a sweet ice to calm my histrionics.

"And your *père*?" he asked as the lemon flavored treat stung my tongue.

I laughed with a bitterness I had not known I contained. "Maman and Papa think I don't know, but I have deduced it on my own. No one wants Papa, you see, because he is American, and the Americans have not joined the war. It is their way of punishing a whole country, though it is only we who suffer. He comes from a banking family and knows a great deal about finance. I can think of no other reason he should not be successful, than his nationality is held against him."

I did not tell the Benefactor the rest, that Papa could not return to his banking family in America because he had been disowned long before my birth. Papa, broad-shouldered with thick gold hair and intelligent green eyes, had been sent to Europe to finish his education and to find a wealthy Parisian wife. Instead he had found my mother, an Ethiopian lounge singer, and not even my birth a few years later had softened his father's heart toward him.

"You may be right," the Benefactor murmured thoughtfully, "but you are not entirely right, Miss Stone. You forget who holds Montmartre in his hand."

"*Le Monstre*?" The sweet ice made me bold, and I scoffed. "*Le Monstre* is a fairy tale, monsieur. He is a name given to the injustice of wealth and poverty and to the barons who do anything in the name of profit with no care for the lives of the less fortunate. He is a shadow used by crime lords to demand tithes from the poor as a pretense of providing their safety. He does not lurk around dance halls and opera houses refusing singers jobs any more than *la bête* holds *la belle* in a castle in the woods. My parents have nothing to fear from stories, monsieur, and if you were the benefactor they call you, they would not have poverty to fear, either."

Vivid amusement danced in the Benefactor's direct gaze as he looked down upon me. "You are opinionated, Miss Stone. Where did you learn to speak such radical thoughts?"

I gaped at him, struck dumb in search of an answer. *La vie de bohème* was the world in which I was raised. Revolution and social justice were topics for passionate discussion amongst my parents' friends; they feared little, being hardly divorced themselves from the criminal underworld, so close in hand did artists and darkness run. They proclaimed allegiance to truth and beauty and named *le Monstre aux Yeux Verts* —the Green-Eyed Monster—as the very antithesis of all they loved. He was the very soul of jealousy and loathing, of pride and profit. He was the world we lived in personified, a cruel master who held these *artistes'* throats in his hands, and their defiance to that cold world was to pursue song and dance and art as if they did not fear it.

"My thoughts are not radical," I finally said, "to the poor. Which you would know, monsieur, if you had ever been poor. If you are our benefactor, I beg you to act as one. Speak to the opera house on Maman's behalf; perhaps they will listen to you where they would not listen to me. You are wealthy and must have influence; find a position for Papa at a bank. Otherwise you are no good to us, and should leave my parents in peace."

Amusement sparked in his eyes again, glittering through the most intense gaze I had ever encountered. "I will think on what you have to say, Miss Stone. I confess I have found this to be a most enlightening discussion, and I hope to continue it one day soon. For now..." His smile was as striking as his eyes. "For now, enjoy your ice. I shall visit your parents at the usual time next week."

2

A week of cowardice and dread followed. I slept little, ate less, and startled guiltily each time my parents spoke to me. I had gone far beyond the bounds of propriety and—too late—knew it. I still did not understand what amenities the Benefactor offered my parents that they felt so reluctant to trouble him, but I knew that neither of them would have said the things I had said to him. Although it would be better for them to hear it from me, I had been unable to gather the courage to confess my conversation with him to my parents. And then there was the light, familiar footstep on the stairs, and my father's familiar command for me to retreat, and it was too late for courage.

I went, but I did not pretend to be a good girl, or to work on the bread. Heart rattling my chest, I pressed myself into a ball against the kitchen wall and peered through a crack as the Benefactor entered my parents' domain and, as always, dominated it.

For the first time in nearly a year of visits he did not ask Maman to sing. Instead he said, "You have a daughter, do you not? I would like to meet her," and for the first time in my life, I knew my father to tell a lie.

"Amelia," he said easily. "She is not here, monsieur. She rarely is, in the evenings. Friends keep her occupied. They write letters of support to the soldiers at the front, and find it romantic. You understand how young women are."

I blinked against the crack in the wall, as nonplussed as the Benefactor appeared to be. I had friends, some of whom, indeed, wrote romantic letters to boys gone off to war. I was more inclined to pore over the responses, trying to understand the personal toil and cost of the battles they fought. Answers were sometimes found between the lines, in the things not said, and the pain I saw there woke in me an urge to fight and protect, too. It was difficult to bear their sorrow without wanting to alleviate it through sharing it myself. I did not, however, write to those young men, as I was unwilling to form attachments for what were suspiciously voyeuristic reasons on my part.

"Of course I understand," the Benefactor responded. "A pity, though. Some other time, perhaps. Estelle, you will sing later. Now, there are things to discuss with you, first of which is that I would like to trouble you for a glass of wine."

The wine was in the kitchen, with me. If the door opened, my father's lie would be exposed. Breath held, I leapt to my feet and ran on tiptoes to the window, which I threw open silently and escaped through just as my mother opened the door. I glimpsed her upright posture sagging slightly as she saw me gone, and then I scrambled quietly down rough-mortared stone and windowsills until I landed lightly on cobbled streets.

I remained there a moment, looking up at the home I had abandoned and afire with curiosity about what the Benefactor had to say. But I could not stay without risking discovery, and so, reluctantly, I fled.

Montmartre's narrow streets were as well known to me as my mother's smile, and the spring sunshine stretched the length of the days. It would not be dark for another hour, and the Benefactor would be at my home for at least twice that. I stole through the curves and twists, watching old men flirt with younger women at cafes and, as it grew darker, watched those same old men find their way toward the Moulin Rouge and other clubs of its nature. I took refuge a little while in a church, using its welcoming quiet to imagine how I might explain myself to my parents once the Benefactor had gone. I could only conclude that I must offer to find work myself, for I doubted his generosity, limited as it might seem to me, would continue after my ill-conceived behavior. Finally, as the bells struck the penultimate hour of the day, I rose to return home.

I did not at first notice what I should have: that all the city sounds were distant. Music played from the dance halls, vehicles and beasts could be heard down-hill nearer the river, but the neighborhood's usual traffic was absent. However, preoccupied with my own thoughts, it was not until someone's running foot-steps slapped loudly on the cobbles and echoed from the walls that I realized how quiet it was around me.

Sensible alarm burst in my chest, for although I had laughed away stories of *le Monstre*, there were footpads and villains enough without fairy tales to fear. I did not quite run, but I walked more quickly, gaze alert to anything moving in the shadows, of which there were many.

Still, I was unprepared when a hand seized my hair and pulled me backward. My scream of surprise was muffled by another hand clamping over my mouth as the first released my hair and instead closed around my throat. An instinct awakened in me and I threw my head back, trying to smash my assailant's nose with my skull. He was too tall: my head met with his collarbone, and my efforts earned nothing more than an ugly laugh from my captor. The hand over my mouth slid to seize my jaw and squeezed my cheeks together in an iron grip. It hurt more than the hand over my mouth had, and was still effective in silencing me: I could scream, but the sound was strangely throttled by the crushing of my face. "Scream all you want," he suggested in a voice like pitted steel. "No one will come."

I believed him. Even if I could cry out loudly enough to garner attention, the silence in Montmartre was a deliberate one: the denizens had known trouble roamed their streets tonight, and had closed their shutters and locked their doors against it. No one would come; they were all too afraid to act on behalf of anyone caught out on the street on such a night. Rage seized me as surely as fear did: I would *never* turn away from those in need.

Fueled by anger and by the same instinct for self-preservation that had caused me to attack once, I struck at my assailant again, this time driving my elbow backward. It sank into the heaviness of his coat, scratchy wool absorbing the power of my blow. His breath left him in another mocking laugh, but, not yet daunted, I stomped my heel into his instep. The sturdy leather of his boots was nothing to my own light shoes, and he laughed a third time. "You have spirit, if not sense."

His hands were gloved with the roughest leather, too hot for a spring evening but superior for brutal work, and so coarse as to leave an impression of violence by their very texture. His woolen coat scraped my cheek as he held me by the jaw. "Idiot child. Who do you think you are, petitioning every dance hall in Paris on your pathetic mother's behalf? Did you think no one would tell me? Did you think you could challenge my laws in my territory and come out unscathed? I *own* those miserable souls, every one of them. Your sort, you deplorable romantic artists and revolutionaries, you'll always sell each other out, for fortune or fear, one or the other."

He released my jaw and spun me so quickly that I became dizzy; all that kept me from falling was his grip on the bodice of my dress. He dragged me forward, close enough that had he features to make out, I would have been able to. But all I saw was a hard, expressionless face: a pig-iron mask, its eyes dark slashes across the dull metal. My assailant's eyes showed no hint of color within the mask's depths, and I knew I had been a fool a dozen times over. I did not believe in fairy tales, and yet I had somehow thought that, should he truly exist, this creature would have the eyes he was named for. *Le Monstre aux Yeux Verts*, the green-eyed monster. But green eyes were only a code, a way of implying jealousy, avarice, haughtiness—all things that *le Monstre's* role in the fairy tale stood for.

"I am not afraid of you, *monstre.*" Every part of my body cried out that the words were a lie: my quavering voice, my cold hands, my weakened knees, and the twisting sickness in my stomach. But I would not, *could* not, allow myself to falter before this shadow-clinging monster, even when his grip on my dress's bodice changed. He ripped it open, not salaciously, but so that he could press a small, cold suction cup above my wildly beating heart. The cup was attached to a thin tube that wound toward one of his coat pockets. For a moment my astonishment defeated all other emotion within me. Then, as amazement faded, I realized that my fear, too, was draining away. I thought I saw liquid swirl through the tube between us, and, before the suction cup could prove to have a needle buried within, I ripped it away from my body and cried, "I am not afraid of you!" with greater certainty than before. I *was* no longer afraid; I felt no depth of emotion at all, and wondered if that was courage.

Le Monstre seized my face again, drawing it closer to his own, and from so near that he might have kissed me, he whispered, "You will be." His hand covered my face and drove my head back to connect brutally with the wall behind me. Light erupted in my vision, edged with red pain, and though I braced my knees, I could not remain on my feet. I slid down the battered wall, hardly feeling the scrape of stone against my spine. When next I became fully aware, my fingers lay against my collarbone, not quite touching my abused throat but lying near it, offering comfort without increasing my distress. Each breath I took was ragged and tasted faintly of iron, as if blood vessels had been bruised or broken inside. My hand drifted a few inches lower, testing the space where the suction cup had attached to me. It felt a little rough and raw, but had none of the sensitivity that suggested I had been pierced with a needle or otherwise violated. I lowered my shaking hands and sat pressed against the wall a while longer, hardly able to think beyond the gratifying fact that I was alive.

The bells tolled midnight and I realized through my discomfort that my parents would be worried. Stiff with uncertainty, I rose and tested my skull for visible injury. My hands came away clean: no blood had been shed, and my throat would not yet show bruising. It was enough that I would have to admit to having met the Benefactor at the Opera House; I did not also have to tell my parents that I had met *le Monstre* in the Montmartre streets.

Maman took me into her arms with a glad cry

when finally I arrived home, mumbling apologies about having fallen asleep in the church. And then, with her forgiveness in hand, I could not help myself, and asked, "What did the Benefactor want to talk about, Maman?"

Hope came into Maman's dark eyes. "He has found somewhere for me to sing, Amelia. Not at the opera house, not yet, but a studio to make records in. To preserve my voice, he said. To share it with the world. If it is well received, *ma chérie*, I will sing...everywhere, he says. Maybe even travel to America!"

Astonished, I looked to Papa, whose face held wary stillness. "Europe is more friendly, Estelle. Even the most sophisticated cities in America..."

Maman dismissed his concerns with a graceful wave, though I saw hurt flash in her eyes. She did not wish to imagine what Papa said to be true, that her Ethiopian heritage would deny her an honored place in America's entertainment. I shared her wish, but I also read the newspapers and listened to the radio, and feared Papa's judgment was all too correct. But Maman would not let that tamp her excitement, not tonight. "It doesn't matter now. It might never. But I will sing for the studio, Amelia! I will be heard everywhere!"

Her joy was infectious. I captured her in an embrace, then pulled Papa into it as well, and for a moment it seemed all was right with our world.

3

The Benefactor did not ask to see me again, and I did not dare search for him in the city. It was enough—more than enough!—that he had acted. Maman sang for the studio, and they, captivated by her voice, recorded her and began to find outlets in Paris where she could perform. I believed the Benefactor acted as her agent, but I knew that to me he was a hero, a man who had taken up the mantle expected of him and become a true benefactor to those who needed him. Maman's spirits lifted weekly, until it seemed she might fly away with joy, and then at the end of the summer, a little more than a year after the war started, Papa found work, improving our lot even more. I believed that, too, was the Benefactor's doing, but I could not ask, only hold the hope to myself in secret and relieved joy.

My parents flourished, and I, my secrets intact, began to find reasons to steal away for hours at a time. I had faced *le Monstre* once, and his threat lingered: I believed I would face him again, and that he would try to instill fear in my heart. But I would not be so unprepared the next time. Montmartre was the hub of many questionable activities, and even a girl of fifteen could find an instructor in the art of *Savate*, if she was determined enough.

I was determined. I learned to hit with open palms, closed fists, with canes and sticks, and most of all I learned to kick: high and fast and deadly, for my teacher cared nothing for the niceties of formalized fighting. The only rule he respected was survival; the only one I cared for was serving justice. Never again would I be caught unarmed by the likes of *le Monstre*. Between my parents' happiness and my training, the winter rushed by. Yet each week, when the Benefactor visited, I was banished to the kitchen to watch an adult life unfold through cracks in the wall, tantaliz-ingly near and still untouchable.

He seemed less old to me as my parents blos-somed: *they* seemed less old, as though the years fell away through the gift of song, for Maman sang more joyfully now than ever before. The Benefactor glowed with pleasure to hear her voice while Papa, more reserved, sat with steepled fingers, behind which I could not discern his expression. But it was not Papa whom I watched, mostly; it was the Benefactor, whose vivid gaze and sharp features seemed larger and more handsome than life to me. My baking attempts grew worse, but even above the scent of burning bread I could smell his cologne, subtle and rich. When he left I would slip to the coat stand and breathe in the lingering bouquet as I pretended to tidy after his visits.

Each time Maman would watch me at my invented chores, standing as she had sung, alone in the middle of the room with a brightly colored scarf wrapped tight around her slender shoulders. Each time she would take me into her arms and kiss my forehead and murmur her thanks, always spoken in her native tongue, for me being a good girl. Each time I would think guiltily of my *Savate* lessons, and of the heart-hammering lightheadedness I felt when I saw the Benefactor, and return her embrace without meeting her eyes.

Each time the importance of staying out of sight seemed increasingly absurd, until one winter night just after my seventeenth birthday, I slipped out of our small Parisian apartment and followed the Benefactor into the city.

I do not know if he always stopped on *le Pont des Arts*, perhaps to admire its nine iron arches bending gracefully over *la Seine*, or to stand in the heart of Bohemian Paris, with *la Louvre* upon one bank and Notre Dame visible in the distance, or if somehow he knew that I crept after him through snow-damp streets, not quite clinging to the edges of electric light shadows. I only know that he stood waiting that night, gloved fingertips making indentations in the slowly building snow on the bridge's rail, and that he did not look around, not even when I came to stand beside him. The snow did not melt on the leather of his gloves, though it turned to water in an instant on my own fingers, pressed much more deeply into the rising flakes of whiteness. Snow settled on my eyelashes and cheeks, too: I had not been wise enough to wear a scarf or hat when I had escaped our house, and so in no time at all I was a thin shivering thing beside him.

Finally he chuckled instead of speaking, and swept his cloak off to wrap around my shoulders. It had a velvet collar, high and soft, that brushed my cheeks as warmly as his laugh did, and the intoxicating scent of his cologne was strong. I felt a hot sharp pain of excitement in my bones and struggled not to tremble.

"You are Estelle's daughter through and through," he said then. "She also believes that the African sun of her childhood could not have abandoned her, and that she can walk through wintery Parisian streets to no ill effect. It is Amélie, is it not?"

"Amelia," I whispered, for my father had chosen the name and my mother had accepted his American way of saying it.

"Amelia," the Benefactor said thoughtfully. "I have not seen you properly for years. Not since you so passionately petitioned me on your parents' behalf. I had thought we might see each other again after that."

He turned me toward him as he spoke and tipped my chin up with a finger. Laughter lines crinkled around his eyes, reminding me that he was ancient, as old as my parents at least, but age enhanced, rather than diminished, his beauty. I drank in his smile and the greenness of his eyes like a woman denied water across a desert march, and forgot completely to speak.

I could not have, even if I had thought to: the breath in my lungs was squeezed away, not even a trace of steam to linger on the cold air.

"Why did you follow me, Amelia?"

"Amelia," he repeated when I did not, could not, speak, "why did you follow me? Your parents wouldn't approve."

"My parents think I am still a child!" The answer burst out childishly, and mortification burned my cheeks.

"All parents see their children *as* children, long past the day they should know them as adults." The Benefactor—Monsieur Laval; I struggled to think of him that way and failed—the Benefactor offered me his arm, clad now only in his beautifully made suit, though he showed no sign of chill in the cold night. We began to walk, although I had no confidence that my feet even touched the ground. On his arm I thought I might be flying, and was loathe to look down and discover I was not. "I am sure your parents have many names for me, Amelia, but you may call me Paul-Gabriel."

I whispered, "Gabriel," though to a Frenchman, to use only part of a name was an oddity. But my father was American and, as Maman said, besotted with nicknames. "Gabriel is the angel who whispered to Joan of Arc. The angel of voices."

"As I hope I have been to Estelle," he said with gentle self-deprecation. "Does it please you, then, this name? Gabriel?"

I nodded, mute with the power of my heartbeat,

and the Benefactor stopped at the bridge's corner to lift a gloved finger to my lips. "Then it shall be my secret name between us," he murmured. "You shall be my Amélie, and I, your Gabriel. Do not let your mother see that you wear my cloak, Amélie. She would fear for you, when you and I both know that is hardly necessary."

Then he was gone, taken by the quiet night, and though I spun and searched, I saw no footprint to follow in the snow.

4

M aman did not see the cloak, but neither did she long think I was without a beau. I could not contain my delight, nor keep stars from shining in my eyes. She and Papa teased me, and asked when they would meet my young monsieur, and laughed when I blushed. I was not so dark of skin as Maman, and at times even she blushed so that the eye could see. I had no hope of hiding the condemning changes of color.

I was careful to go out in the day to meet this imaginary youth, though in truth there were few enough young men to be found in Parisian streets in the long years of the Great War. Maman and Papa speculated to no end. Was he an *artiste*, too fragile to fight? Was he returned from the war, injured or emotionally scarred? Perhaps I had taken up nursing, though that gentle art was more suited to Maman's temperament—or even to Papa's!—than mine. I had grown up amongst revolutionaries: it was the dream of the battle that caught my breath, even then.

And that, perhaps, was why my Gabriel was such a dear and exciting secret to me. Maman and Papa could not approve, and so he was in his very self a fight, a stand, a way of etching my own mark in the earth. He was as circumspect as I—more so!—and we met only after he came to visit Maman and Papa, and asked Maman to sing for him.

But he came more and more often.

I saw but could not, with the callowness of youth and the flush of first love, understand that his visits took their toll on my parents. They were happy: Maman sang, Papa had employment, and all of it could be laid at the Benefactor's feet. I could not understand why his visits did not inspire them with joy, when I could only barely keep from flinging myself into his arms when he arrived, or deny myself the chance to shower him in kisses that he gently and agonizingly spurned. He seemed more beautiful to me each time I saw him, more vibrant, more knowledge-able, more fascinating. My bread baking efforts grew worse still, until Maman forbade me from even trying and instead sent me to sit and practice our silent piano, the long sheet of butcher paper upon which she had drawn a keyboard with a grease pencil.

Had I practiced the silent piano with one tenth the passion with which I pressed my eye to the crack in the wall, I should have been a virtuoso, and my life a very different tale indeed. And yet it was those frac-tured efforts which changed my life after all, for as

Gabriel and I walked through Paris one evening he led me into a music shop that ought not have been open, and asked if I could play.

Cold-fingered and with racing heart, I gave the shop's owner an apologetic look, and played. Well enough for a girl who rarely practiced, but, desperate to impress, I raised my voice as well. To my own ear, I lacked Maman's gift of song, but I had spent my life in the arms of her music, and I could sing. I chose a saucy piece at first, hoping to make my beloved laugh, but the rising passion in his eyes led me to sing another, a simple hymn with depth and power.

He did not move at all as I sang to him, my beautiful green-eyed man. He barely seemed to breathe, and I could only think that I dreamed it when I saw tears glimmer in his thick dark lashes. As the final notes came to a close, he sighed and almost bowed, a curve to his spine and shoulders that I had only ever seen offered to my mother at the end of a song. Beyond him, I saw the shop owner, a white-faced man with hunched shoulders and wringing fingers, whose gaze never seemed to leave my Gabriel's back. But then Gabriel straightened and offered me his hands, and when I took them, he drew me to standing and for the first time touched his lips to mine.

All thought was lost beyond that moment. In the tangled aftermath of tumultuous lovemaking, I could not even recall how we had left the music shop for more appropriate quarters, but neither did I care. I did not return home that night, nor for many months after. Our love was no longer a secret; my Gabriel took me everywhere with him, showing me, showing us, off to the world. I had visited *la Louvre*, of course, but doors that had been closed to my family and me were opened when I was on his arm. Art, music, theatre, beauty, love: everything that the Bohemians I had grown up with most desired was laid before my feet, and all he asked in return was that I sing for him. In his presence, I was allowed to forget that a war raged around us; that there were those who went without; that crime carried on even as my world became breathless and magical.

He even ceased to visit my parents, and in so doing, let me forget that I had been swept away from troubles and hardship. I chose not to visit my parents, knowing they could not approve. That was unbecoming of one who had believed herself ready for battle, but those pangs of guilt were easily buried beneath the unebbing ache of desire and the thrill of being an adult on my own. And I was an adult, or felt I was; at Gabriel's side, I was as cosmopolitan as any Parisian could hope to be. No one had known love like this, not in all humanity's history; no one could ever have felt such excitement, such joy, such wonder, in the arms of a lover, else the world itself could not know hatred and anger and war.

The new leaves of spring deepened to the same green as my lover's eyes, summer green, before I returned to my Montmartre home to once more visit my parents. The narrow streets seemed shoddier, more worn and less careworn; the leaning brick buildings grayer and shabbier than they had been. The men and women who crowded the streets there were less familiar and more distressing to my eyes. I feared that my shoes, as polished as Gabriel's, would stain with the offal on the streets, and could only be grateful that hemlines had risen so that my silk chiffon dress would not be damaged. That was as far as my thoughts went: only to myself, and how far I had flown above the ugliness from which I had come.

I went up the long and narrow stairway, hearing as I never had before the creak of old wood, seeing as I never had before its dull, unstained color, and wondered how Gabriel had even brought himself to visit, despite the richness of Maman's voice. My dress, frothy green; my lips, strawberry red; they were the only colors of note as I entered the flat in which I had grown up. I came as a peacock, preening, ready to be admired. But there was no admiration to be found, and my surprise at that was so great that at first I could not even see what was wrong.

My eyes expected Maman and Papa, one at the piano, the other at the table doing sums. My heart waited on the strength of her song, and beneath it the faint scratch of Papa's pen against thin-scraped paper. I breathed in, ready to laugh at the scent of burnt bread, though it was I who burnt it time and again, not Maman. Each detail was etched in my expectations, so sharp that they might have been real.

But my dress was not the only color of note: it was the only color at *all* in a ransacked home. Maman's brilliant scarves and shawls lay dull on the floor; Papa's pens were broken, the ink soaked into dry floorboards. The piano lay in shambles, as if an ax had been taken to it, and the windows that let watery sunlight shine through were broken and unshuttered.

I flew through the four small rooms that made up our home: kitchen, sitting room, a bedroom carved in two so that Maman and Papa, as much as myself, might have a hint of privacy. There were no clothes missing save what they must have worn; no notes left to scold or warn a wayward daughter should she return. Arms and legs of furniture lay broken, some of them shorn in half just as the piano was, as if they had been used in defense.

I did not remember leaving again, only that outside in the street I knelt at a wretched man's feet and begged to know where my beloved Maman and Papa had been taken. Begged to know *who*, and felt long cold fingers of fear grip my belly as the man averted his gaze and whispered the words I knew he would: "*Le Monstre.*"

I do not fear you, I had said to him years ago. *You will*, he had replied, and I had armed myself against that. I had learned to fight, I had learned the lay of the district in ways I had never before known, understanding where the criminal element gathered and discovering the places they moved and hid wares. I was too gently raised to come by this knowledge natively, but my *Savate* teacher knew more than how to fight, and I learned it all from him in preparation for facing *le Monstre*. But he had never shown himself. His threat had been left fallow so long I had nearly forgotten it, and yet now it rose up inside me, cold and terrible. He had been a prophet after all: I did fear him now. Not for my own sake, but for my parents'.

In a flash I understood, too. I had been nothing, a silly girl with a trembling voice, and I had thought he had forgotten me over the years. He had not forgotten. He had *waited*, a long and deliberate game, until I was complacent and happy. Only then could fear truly be awakened in my belly. Only then could his promise come true.

Hate twinned itself with fear, building an unbankable fire in my breast. Later, looking back, I knew that a girl had gone into Maman and Papa's apartment, but that something else left there that day. Even then I knew I was changed, that I walked away from that broken flat with more weight and certainty than I had had, but it was years before I understood that that day, my spirit awakened to its destiny.

A carriage awaited me. I walked instead, feeling the streets change under my feet from cobbles to pavement; feeling what I had let myself forget: that I had come from a place where a madman, a monster, could steal a family away, and that no one would raise a hand to stop him. I had met that monster, and yet I had done nothing to stop him. Instead I had left my parents to that haunting fear while I danced on clouds and drank the finest wines. No one had known love like I knew; no one could have felt the self-disgust that I felt.

"Amélie," my Gabriel said to me as I entered the vast foyer of his Parisian home. Horror made his voice light in the single word: horror, concern, love. All the things he *should* voice, but shame writhed in my belly like a snake and I could not go to him. "Amélie," he said again. "Tell me what has happened."

"*Le Monstre.*" I spat the words and he flinched, though my rage was as much for myself as for the creature who had taken my parents away. "I have to leave you, Gabriel. I must find Maman and Papa. *Le Monstre* has stolen them from me." *Just,* I could not bring myself to say, *just as you have stolen me from them.* But that was unfair; he had not forced me to follow him that winter night, nor much had to coax me out of the gutters and into the light of his sun.

Shock whitened his lips and made tension around his vivid eyes, as if he had heard my unspoken accusation. But no: he came forward to clasp my hands, and his own were as cold as mine. "Estelle? She is missing? Let me help you, Amélie. Your mother has been so important to me for so long. And your father," he added, though we both knew it was because of Maman's voice he had chosen to become their benefactor. Even now he still played the records of her singing, often when he thought I could not hear, but still, he played them, and it seemed to me that he was revitalized each time he did, as if her voice lent him strength and power. "I know many people. Let me call them, my love. Let me help you find Estelle."

I unwound my fingers from his to put my hand against his cheek. He was pale, as pale as I had ever known him to be, and the brown of my own skin beside his was startling in comparison. "You know many people," I agreed, "but not this kind of people, Paul-Gabriel. *Le Monstre* is where I am from. From *le dix-huitième*." The eighteenth district, where lay Montmartre, Pigalle, the Moulin Rouge; all the places I had known growing up, and which had not, until I returned, seemed desperate and ugly. "You, your beautiful home, your wonderful food and your amazing artists, you do not belong there. Your friends will not know where to find *le Monstre*."

"Paul-Gabriel," he murmured, and a hint of a knowing smile played at his lips. "You are very serious, then, my Amélie, to use all of my name."

"I am."

"And you know where to find this *monstre?*"

"No. But I will." I kissed him, looked into his eyes once more, and left his palatial home with the memory of his beauty burned into my mind like a brand.

5

I could not know whose motorcycle I borrowed from the Parisian streets, but I could be grateful to him for it. A soldier, I imagined: a boy back from the war, a messenger boy who had perhaps loved a German girl too near the front; who had wooed her with the rumbling engine of a Triumph, and lost her when the army called him home. The girl was gone, but the pursuit of that memory lent me this roaring black beast.

It was easy to steal, easier to drive, and put a love for machinery into my loins that was as intense and throbbing as any I had ever known for my Gabriel. Its grumble announced me long before I saw the warehouse, and it spat stones at the unadorned walls when I spun it in a circle to stop and take stock of the heart of my enemy's territory.

Empty warehouses, noisy railways: this was territory beyond the edges of old Paris, a wasteland squirreling up and around *la Butte*, the hill upon which

Montmartre was built. Thieves and bandits had once peopled these places; now, where the warehouses were occupied, it was by their heirs: thugs and brigands, all in the employ of *le Monstre.* No one warehouse was easily distinguished from another; they all had broken or blacked out windows with no signs of life within.

One, though, had men outside; wary, watchful men. I counted six and suspected more: burly men with gnarled arms and thick necks, hired for their size rather than their wit. They wore the casual clothes of dock workers, broad-striped shirts and denim pants over black leather boots. Most wore caps; those who did not sported stubbly hair on their ill shaped heads. One carried a crowbar, but dropped it loosely at his side when he saw who approached.

I knew the picture I made: an African girl in a sea foam dress, loose sleeves brushing the elbows to show strong, not soft, arms. The skirt was hitched high to show an unseemly length of leg wrapped around the black belly of a motorcycle. I had not even changed my heeled, lambs-leather shoes, knowing that the clothes, taken together with the motorcycle, would paint me as a harlot. That, I judged, was more useful than being seen as a threat; my reputation, should I survive the next hours, could be repaired.

Two of the men exchanged grins, then sidled glances at the crowbar-bearing man, whose leer encouraged them to leave their posts and step my way. I waited, smiling, and did not think of the chill in my hands or the racing of my heart. I could not be afraid now, even if fear consumed much of my mind; of such stuff was courage made, acting despite terror. I braced my toes against the street and saw the workers' hungry eyes follow the shape of my calf as it flexed. They were not looking, then, when I withdrew the pistols strapped to my other thigh.

The weapons had come from the same place I had learned the location of *le Monstre*'s warehouse: through my *Savate* teacher, though he would himself not give me the guns. Instead he had—disapprovingly, for why had he taught me to make weapons of my hands and feet if I only chose to resort to guns?—sent me to a disreputable man known to deal in cash and lies and the things they bought. Even if I was not my teacher's student, I was Paul-Gabriel Laval's woman; I had both coin and stories to spare. If I had not had those things, the weight of a favor owed by one so close to the Benefactor still would have purchased me all that I needed to know.

I had never fired a gun, but the disreputable man had told me what I needed to know. A willingness to do harm was worth more than a sure shot; marksmanship did not matter if the trigger could not be pulled. He had not believed I could pull it, but his belief did not matter: the astonished pair whose gazes drifted back upward to find themselves in my sights believed, or were at least cautious.

Not cautious enough: one smirked and stepped forward, a meaty hand extending toward me. "Don't," I suggested. "I will shoot."

His smirk broadened and he took another step. Only a fool would allow an adversary close enough to seize her weapons, and I had had enough of being a fool. I lowered the pistol a little and shot him in the thigh.

The report was the loudest thing I had ever heard; the scent of gunpowder stringent and intoxicating; the kickback, a surprising thrill. This was power, extended beyond the human hand, beyond mortal reach. I had never dreamed that guns would appeal to me; now I knew that I would carry one into adversity for the rest of my life. For the rest of my life, however long that may be. Long enough, I vowed, to free my parents from *le Monstre*'s grip; anything beyond that was a gift.

My assailant had not yet fully realized that he had been shot when I kicked power back into the Triumph's engine, spun its rattling beauty again, and roared past the crowbar-wielding thug and the other workers to burst through the warehouse doors.

Voices cried out behind and before me, startled men racing for weapons with reach: chains, staffs, and guns. The latter were in great supply, and heat flushed my skin. I was a fool after all, if I had thought *le Monstre*'s warehouse would be filled with lace doilies and the stiff-armed stuffed bears called *Teddy* after the beloved President of the United States. No; there were stacks of munitions, clearly labeled, and I could only imagine that he supplied the Central Powers, lining his own pocket to the detriment of the Allies.

But it was not for the weapons I had come. The Triumph's engine rattled and roared, echoing off the warehouse's tall, windowless walls. I crouched low over the handlebars and gunned the beast, its leap of

power driving us into the warehouse's heart. I had
pursuants, but I did not look behind myself to see
them: my quarry lay ahead. I wanted Maman. I
wanted Papa. And I wanted *le Monstre* himself.

A chain clattered against the Triumph's wheel,
entangling it. The wheel seized and I flew forward,
regretting in that instant my decision to wear a gown
rather than borrow my father's leather coat to protect
my tender skin. Pallets and straw broke with my
impact, cushioning me somewhat from an otherwise
disastrous landing. I rattled to my feet, discarded my
shoes, and ran without taking stock of my injuries.
They were not debilitating; that was all that mattered.

The warehouse was poorly lit and overfull, though
mercifully without dust, and those hunting me were
entangled in the clattering mess created by a spilled
motorcycle. For long seconds I ran uninhibited, until a
man rose up from between boxes without warning
and I ducked under the Tommy gun he pointed
toward me. I did not shoot him, but only hit his belly
with the butt of my pistol, which had the satisfying
effect of dropping him to his knees. I used the pistol a
second time at the base of his neck, rendering him
senseless, seized his machine gun, and ran the way he
had blocked, believing that a guard there meant some
degree of importance.

We were very close to the Seine in this warehouse; I did not expect to find a door with a
stairway leading down, and yet its very unlikeliness
gave me confidence that it was the direction I
needed to go. I crept down the stairs rather than

catapulting, grateful for my silent bare feet even if the stone steps were clammy beneath my soles. Water dribbled down dimly lit walls, distant torches offering guttering light. I emerged, in time, into a chamber ringed by small glass boxes with brightly colored tubes rising from them. Liquid pulsed through those tubes, a few bubbles bursting within them as steady drips of the colored *liquo* fell into the boxes.

At this chamber's center were welded two pig-iron chairs, terrible to envision. Leather straps slashed the pitted metal, holding the chairs' occupants in place. Their hands clawed the ragged chair arms, their bodies strained and thrashed with tension, but their faces were hidden beneath vast metal helmets from which wires and suction cups dangled.

"Maman. Papa." I did not need to see their faces, *bien sûr*, to know their tortured bodies, and my whisper was lament and apology both. A second glance around the room told me we were alone, and I slung the machine gun to my side as I ran to save my parents.

The wires were a desperate tangle, some seeming to carry electricity to the nodes attached to Maman's head, others draining away the bright liquid that pulsed into the glass boxes. I hesitated, fearing to do even more damage by tearing at the contraption without discrimination, but Maman's grey skin and dull eyes brought ruin to my uncertainty. I seized a handful of wires, whispered another *désolée*, and yanked—

"Do you like it? I call it the Emotion Extractor. It's taken me years to perfect it."

The familiarity of that voice sent spasms through my arm, weakening its strength. A wire or two, no more, came away from Maman's skull, and it was with sick horror that I turned my gaze whence the voice came.

A gaping black hole in the wall: a door, unseen until it was opened. Within it, the bane of Paris, the criminal underlord to whom I now knew my parents had owed their every success...and failure. My lover, my beautiful angel, my Gabriel...*le Monstre*.

Such emotion rose in me I had no single word for it. It chilled and heated me all at once, weakened my knees and soured my stomach, sent me trembling even as I could not move. No air passed my lips; no useful thought formed in my mind. My heart was an emptiness inside me, rent open and left to bleed on the cold stone floor.

Le Monstre came toward me, stopping to caress Maman's careworn face. He did what I could not: plucked free the wires and cups, loosening her from her bonds. "Emotions," he said, almost gently. "They command us, *ma chérie*. Would it not be better if we commanded them? If they could be bottled and sampled, used when we need courage or fear? Awakened only when we wish to feel love, or require hate's fire? And what if we could inspire those feelings—if we could inspire loyalty, trust, obedience, creativity, anything you might imagine!—what if we could inspire those in the moment that we needed them most?" The last of the wires came free from Maman's shorn skull and she slumped, drawn, drained, with no spark of life in her dark eyes. I moved without grace, trying to catch her; *le Monstre* caught my wrist instead, and discarded Maman from the chair.

The horror that held me in place shattered, giving me control of my limbs again. Unfiltered rage exploded in my breast, and with my free hand I reached for the pistol at my thigh.

Gabriel lifted a vial with soft gold liquid within an atomizer, as if for perfume. He sprayed it once into my face: it was sweet in flavor but somehow unscented. I breathed it in unwillingly and he spoke a single word: "Sit."

I did, with utter and instant compliance. I took my mother's place in the chair even as my muscles fought and trembled against the action. "Obedience," murmured Gabriel. "The first of my Distilled Emotions, or Behaviors, if you will; there are so many actions and sentiments that can be commanded with my concoctions. It will last for days, perhaps weeks; your parents have tasted only a single dose, and still they do as I demand. Sing for me, Amélie. Sing, because music heightens emotion, and I wish only the purest emotion possible for my distillations. Your mother sang until she could sing no more, and from your father I drew helplessness, regret, anger, all magnificently pure. Your mother's were more splendid yet: the depth of her regret will be bettered only, I think, by yours..."

I sang as he spoke. I could not help myself, though

he had not commanded a particular music and so I could, and did, sing songs of war and rage and hate. My chest felt as if it might tear in two, so wretched was my broken heart, and that too I sang, even as I began to understand what I offered him with the music. Once I tried to change my tune, but he *tsked* and told me to continue as I had begun. "I have you to thank for all of this," he said then, with a certain sly pleasure. "That day you pled for your mother's career, for your parents' happiness—I could not help but think, that day, *what if I could capture this passion? What if I could distill it, make use of it?* You were even the first of my experiments with the distillations, my dear Amélie. Your fear that night in Montmartre was potent enough to bottle, and gave me the first promise that what I desired might be possible."

Sickness rolled through me as I recalled that night three years ago. I remembered how the fear had drained from me. I had thought, of course, that I had found my courage, but no: he had taken my fear, not for my benefit, but for his own.

"I have always had an interest in the alchemical," *le Monstre* murmured. "I've sought, as many men have, an elixir of life, a way to defeat death through alchemy or science—or both!—and while that has as yet still slipped through my fingers, these potions offer me a greater command over humanity than any mere long life might do. I am grateful to you, Amélie. You have been a delight, even if you were too young to truly love, of course—"

I knew he might well lie in order to waken fresh

emotion in me, but I could not batten down against betrayal, against sorrow, against love spurned, for I had loved him truly. My voice broke before my rage did, and when my song no longer hid the sounds of the suction cups and tubes and wires, fear finally took its place in my breast, all for *le Monstre*'s terrible distillations. He waited some little time, then said to me, "Sing," and I opened my mouth to try again.

A wretched croak came forth, but of vastly greater import was the startling realization that I felt no compulsion this time. I could choose not to sing: the Obedience had faded, and Gabriel did not yet know it. It had been hours, *oui*, but certainly not days, not weeks. I thought his distillations were less powerful than he imagined; it did not occur to me that perhaps it was *I* who was *stronger* than he thought.

I sang regardless, sang while I worked at the leather straps around my wrists, and when they were free, at those around my ankles. *Le Monstre* was not interested in watching me, so long as I tried to sing; instead, when I stole a glimpse around the edge of my chair, he worked with great intent on the vials and boxes of emotions, distilling them into more bottles topped with atomizers. They were beautiful, shimmering in every hue and shade with more subtlety than the rainbow. Even the darkest emotions shone, blacks with such clarity that I could nearly see through them, and the indigos and violets were translucent.

I was nearly free when finally he thought to look again. I sat back in the chair, leather wrapped around, but not bound to, my ankles and wrists. My eyes crushed closed, honest tears leaking from them; there was no shame in crying now, and *le Monstre* would find the distillations of my sorrow a triumph.

"Your voice," he said, sounding so sympathetic, so like my lover, that I could not help but open my eyes. He stood above me, beautiful features creased with sadness. "Stop singing, Amélie. Let us not destroy that instrument."

"Let them go." I could hardly speak, my throat an aching ruin. "Let my parents go, Gabriel. I'll stay with you. I'll sing for you, but let them go."

"Can I trust you?" He caressed my cheek as he had done my mother's. "I wish I could."

"For their freedom, you can." In the moment, even I almost believed myself. I turned my face away, though, and said, bitterly, "How can you not trust me, when my obedience is yours to command?"

"Then why would I free them, my Amélie? Oh, the hate. It flows from you, *ma chérie*. The Essence I distill from your hate will be the strongest I have ever made. I thought as much, the night you first followed me. I chose then to encourage you in hopes of bringing about this very moment."

I ought to have waited, but with that confession I could no longer hold myself still. I did not know where the strength came from: perhaps that too was distilled, and wafting in the air, or perhaps it was inborn. Perhaps it was simply that the pig-iron chair in which I sat was poorly made, with crackling dry wood holding joints together. It did not matter; what mattered was that my grip was strong and the chair weak. I ripped upward and the chair's arm came with me, the bludgeoning weapon I required.

The side of my beloved's face dented with the impact, his cheekbone breaking under the power of my blow. He screamed as I tore free the wires from my head, and he flung his arms up to protect himself as I rained my fists down upon him. I saw nothing but his face, the greenness of his eyes; the world around us was a red and angry blur. Ichor spat across his broken cheek: undistilled emotion that absorbed into his skin and sent him wild with rage.

His strength was suddenly as great as mine. Greater, for his frame was more powerful. But rather than strike back, he ran, a gift of the fear that had so recently been sucked from my soul. I hardly understood how I myself felt anything; surely I had been drained empty of emotion, as my listless mother and still trapped father seemed to be. Gabriel leapt Maman's boneless form as he ran, and chose not the hidden doorway through which he had entered, but the stairway that I myself had come down.

But of course: there were weapons and men above, and a girl who could tear an iron chair apart with her bare hands should be met with both, rather than alone, and yet I could not give chase in the hopes that I might catch *le Monstre* alone. Cursing, I knelt to gather Maman into my arms, and wept that she did not seem to see me. I stood, still wondering at my own strength, and took in the parts of Gabriel's lair.

The chair in which I had been a captive was on

fire. Electric wires spat and sparked, while the undistilled emotion itself seemed to burn of its own volition. Papa's chair was not yet alight, but I feared the
fire might spread. Still bearing Maman's weight, I
freed him, then in desperation, sought a vial of the
soft golden Essence of Obedience. Spraying it into
their faces, I whispered, "Escape, Maman. Escape,
Papa. Leave this place as quickly as you can, and
return home. I will come for you soon. I am so sorry."

Like automatons, they rose and stumbled toward
the exit: toward the hidden door, as if they somehow
knew the way from there. Perhaps they did; perhaps *le
Monstre* had brought them in through his secret
tunnels, rather than through the warehouse. That was
to me a relief: they would not be endangered by what
would go on above. I waited long enough to close the
door behind them, then finally gave chase.

6

I had weapons: my pistols, the machine gun, and the righteous need for justice burning in my breast.

Le Monstre had more. Many more: I burst back into the warehouse at a run, only to be faced by a ring of surprised men with guns. I raised my hands, pistols dangling uselessly from my thumbs, and spoke: "My only interest is in *le Monstre*. Allow me to pass and no harm will come to you."

These words, spoken by a barefoot girl in a wracked and ruined dress, won laughter from most of them; only the man with the crowbar, whom I had faced on my way in, did not find humor in my offering. His gaze locked with mine and his hand lifted, ready to give the signal to fire. He would do so if I did not act, and I could not, from this position, defeat them all. That I believed I could defeat *any* of them was a wonder, but not one to dwell upon in this moment. I had other weapons at my disposal too, and chose to use them instead.

I dropped my pistols, let tears flow, and staggered in misery to the closest of my enemy. *"Non, s'il vous plaît,* I've done nothing wrong, please don't hurt me...!"

Startled beyond thought, the man dropped his weapon and embraced me. I let him take my weight, making certain that it pulled him around so he stood between myself and the other men. Crowbar's protest echoed sharply into the high warehouse walls, but it was by then too late: I slipped free of my savior's grasp and ran, using the stacks of pallets and boxes to hide myself between. Commands followed me: *Spread out! Search high and low! Don't let her escape or you'll face* le Monstre *yourself!*

Munitions lay ahead of me. I oriented myself by the windows and searched for them, finding other items of use along the way. Matches here, a discarded gun there, straw everywhere; these things and more offered all a woman might need in the fight against evil. More than once I evaded capture only narrowly, but evade it I did, until a quiet scramble up rough crates put me atop the munitions pile with, I regretted to discover, a splinter in my bare sole. Wincing, I withdrew it and tossed it away, then stood with my trophies in hand. *"Messieurs!"*

Gunshots rang out before wiser heads prevailed; I was not standing on material a clever man would choose to shoot. *"Messieurs!"* I called again, and this time lifted my prizes.

The matches, yes, of course; dangerous enough, where I stood. The tin of gasoline, though: that was the challenge. I held the matches clearly in my fingers as I twisted open the tin's top, then with careful concentration began to pour the flammable liquid in a circle around myself. The dry crates drank it down greedily, but much fell between slats, staining packing straw and dripping onto the guns, bullets, and bombs that made up the mountain of munitions beneath me. "You may run, *messieurs*," I said then, "but I will find you, and I will not be gentle when I do. If you wish to survive this evening's bonfire, I suggest that you step outside, arrange yourselves tidily, and await my arrival."

Most ran. I watched with a smile, heady from the fumes of gasoline, and wondered if any of those who fled now would await me outside. Three remained: Crowbar and two of his compatriots, their gazes torn between my apparent madness and their master's imagined ire. Still smiling, I struck a match, and two of them fled, leaving only Crowbar behind. "Do not be a fool, *monsieur*," I said to him, and even at the distance heard the disbelief in his exhalation.

"*Moi*? I am not the one preparing a ring of fire to die in, mademoiselle. How do you think you will escape?" He sounded cultured, like my Gabriel. Like *le Monstre.*

I dropped the match.

Even as I did so, I jumped. I had faith in the strength of my body and faith that unserved justice would not allow me to die tonight.

I also had gauged the distance to the next stack of crates, and—had I not suffered a sting of pain from the splinter damage to my foot—I might have made it.

I knew almost before I took wing that I would not. Too late, in any case, to stop; the flame was falling, the petrol igniting, the straw turning to ash. The power of sudden blooming heat pushed me some small distance farther than I might otherwise have flown, and yet it was not far enough. My palms hit; my arms and belly scraped as I fell; my fingernails turned to blood as I struggled for purchase. Then I was upside-down, bouncing, barely able to protect my head as pallets and crates broke beneath me. The warehouse floor loomed, hard and deadly. My faith in justice had been ill placed: I had no more time than to think that, no more time than that to regret.

Gabriel caught me.

Where he had been, I did not know. Why he did it, I could not understand. But he was there, my lover, and I, safe in his arms. For no more than a heartbeat I looked into his face, into the green depths of his eyes, into the twisted darkness of his soul, and I believed all over again that he had loved me. That he loved me still.

The roaring flames took him and he thrust me away, out of danger, into safety, even as his own flesh screamed and melted in boiling heat. Afraid for my own life, bitterly aware that my vaunted justice had been served, I turned and ran from his visage and the sound of his screams.

HIS MEN WAITED OUTSIDE. Not for me, but for *le Monstre*. When it was I who emerged from the inferno, they, white-faced and shaken, submitted to the demands I had placed before: they lay down together to be bound, just beyond the edge of where the warehouse blaze might harm them.

I took promissory notes and threats for the poor, invoices for the Central Powers—all the written material on their bodies—and with a certain gleeful vengeance, gagged them with them, and left them for the police to find.

Le Monstre's warehouse was not the only thing to burn that night. So too did my innocence, and as it burned, it left behind a wish to protect those who could not save themselves. I was not long for Paris, after that; I was not long for any one place in the world, not when oppression was to be found in all its corners. I burned now with new energy, with the joy of righting wrongs, and with the spirit of justice.

My darling daughter:

It is September of 1934 as I write this; I make note of the date because I write to you in care of the Century Club, whose return address is the only one ever cited on the many letters and postcards you send me from around the world. I have confidence that your extraordinary brethren will make certain this letter finds its way to your hands in a timely fashion.

I must not prevaricate, Amelia. I am an old woman now, and my fears may be no more than an old woman's fears, but there is too much familiar in a story being told in la Ville-Lumière today, and I think it is a story you may wish to hear.

There is a woman here, a woman whom all the world knows: Madame Josephine Baker, whose beauty and boldness are as renowned as her vaudeville acts. Although American by birth, she has long been a Parisian favorite, and although always beloved, of late she has taken on a new voice master, a Sicilian by the stories, and has been, they say, transformed from petite danseuse sauvage to la grande diva magnifique. I have heard her sing, Amelia. Heard her before and after this voice master's attentions, and what they say is true. Before, she was delightful; now, she is tremendous.

I know that it cannot be, and yet I also know that in all my long years I have only perceived one singer undergo such transformation, and only under the tutelage of one man. That singer was myself, and the voice master none other than our terrible Benefactor, le Monstre aux Yeux Verts.

Come to Paris, Amelia. Visit and set an old woman's heart at rest. Come, and discover for me that le Monstre is dead as we have long believed him to be, and that Madame Baker is not entrapped as we once were.

with love,
ta Maman

7

I knew of Josephine Baker, *bien sûr*; surely there was almost no one who did not. A great and talented beauty, acknowledged by all but the country of her birth, which could not see beyond the color of her skin—a color which was not so far at all from my own. I had heard records of her voice, which was powerful, and I trusted beyond measure my mother's judgment of its improvement. I trusted, too, her fears, even though I had watched *le Monstre* stumble into the flames of his burning warehouse and could not fathom how he might have escaped.

Still, there had long since been rumors of his return, the Green-Eyed Monster, and more than once in my world-scouring adventures I had visited Paris in search of those rumors' truth. It had been some years now since I had been home, and to return was more joy than hardship though my palms itched, as they always did, with the hope that I would find and settle *le Monstre* once and for all. Josephine Baker was to

open a new opera, *La Reine du Nil*, and it was my
delight to take a seat in the boxes as the orchestra
began to tune.

All of Paris seemed to be there that night. One
or two of the dignitaries, artists, and scientists I even
knew and was pleased to be greeted by; others cast
curious glances at me when I shook hands with *le
Colonel* du Gaulle or laughed with Kandinsky. One
woman, all too flatteringly, wondered aloud if I
might be Madame Baker's sister, and I spent the
next minutes entirely delighted with my choice of
gowns for the evening. Cobalt blue and fully
sequined, the bodice was fitted but breathable and
the skirt gored to allow freedom of movement. I had
a wrap of white fur against the autumn's chilly air,
but within the theatre I forewent that in favor of
showing the gown's sleeveless straps and plunging
back. I could not, in truth, hold a candle to
Madame Baker, but neither did I do myself any
shame, and after the woman's charming comment,
more than one eye roved over me in approval. I was
therefore happy and ready for the evening's entertainment when finally, to thunderous applause, the
curtain rose.

It did not, to my surprise, rise on Madame Baker,
but instead on a set scene that, in swift and grand
gestures, told the story of Egypt's most famous
queen's rise to power, with an aristocratic young girl in
the role of the child Cleopatra. Two queens and a
king died as she ascended, none by her own hand,
and yet the closeness of death—even theatrical death

—held the audience in a near frenzy as the girl knelt to be crowned.

Light erupted on the stage as the crown settled on her head, and in the brilliant confusion, Josephine Baker rose center stage as the last Pharaoh of Egypt.

There could be no singing, for even her great voice would never be heard above the tumultuous roar within the theatre. She stood still, arms uplifted, face noble and with a secret smile, and let adulation roll over her. For over one minute she held that pose, allowing us all to take in her glory, and glorious she was: dressed in gold so sheer over her bodice that had it not in places reflected the light I might have thought her nude. It snuggled close into glittering, glimmering gold at her hips until it flared wildly at the knee, creating a skirt that lay across the floor in such quantities that, by its very nature, the costume afforded her more space upon the stage than any other three people might consume. It was masterful in conception.

It was also wholly unnecessary: no other creature upon the stage, upon any stage in life, could draw the eye as did Josephine Baker. Her uplifted arms were ringed with golden bangles, her beautifully extended hands were wreathed in shimmering snakes of gold. Her eyes, so large and dark and known throughout the world, were lined in kohl that made them depthless pools, and upon her head she wore an extraordinary golden headdress, looking like nothing so much as a bowling pin set into a scoop-backed chair; at the brow, two cobras rising as if to strike. I knew it for what it was, of course: a *pschent*, the double crown of ancient conjoined Egypt.

I had not yet had my fill of gazing on Baker's astonishing presence when finally she lowered her hands and fixed the audience with a look so fierce that it seemed she could see into our souls, each and every one. Silence fell as if she had commanded it, and into that silence, unaccompanied even by the orchestra, she sang.

From that moment on, the world fell away. There was nothing in it, *pour moi*, save Josephine Baker's beauty and song. Cleopatra's tragedy spilled across the stage and my heart spilled with it. I was transfixed; I, who had met dignitaries and performers, artists and scientists, and had never stood in awe of them, could not breathe past the wonder and joy that Josephine awakened in my breast. I had not known such an intensity of admiration since my indiscreet youth in Paris; not since I had fallen desperately, foolishly, in love with *le Monstre aux Yeux Verts*.

I found myself obsessed with Baker's eyes as she sang, gazing at them time and time again to assure myself that they were not green. It seemed somehow to me the thing that all my future happiness relied on, though any spark of native wit left to me would have known differently. It was no matter: each time I looked, her eyes remained dark and deep pools of promise, no hint of treacherous green within them.

In her reign as Pharaoh, Baker commanded her people to rise in worship. As one in our devotion, the audience did, hands extended in supplication and adoration. I believe in that moment the great lady nearly forgot herself: her smile became other than the ancient queen's, more mischievous with pleasure. She even spoke, the first ordinary words to pass her lips as she stood upon the stage: *"Asseyez-vous, vous imbéciles!"*

And sit we did, like the silly fools we were, all of us laughing and sheepish without any hint of true humiliation. Along with the rest of a captivated audience, I watched enraptured. Had I the ability to think clearly, I might have told myself that my enthrallment was only for one whose remarkable vocal skills could lead me to *le Monstre*, should he still live. Listening to Josephine Baker sing, I believed that he did, and that he had brought forth from her the most talent, the most beauty, that her voice could ever achieve. A Sicilian voice master: no. That tale could only be a disguise, nothing more, for the Green-Eyed Monster who had once haunted my dreams. But it was not the tenuous thread to *le Monstre* that held me mesmerized, and I could not pretend that it was. It was Baker herself, and I had been struck by Cupid's arrow.

Had I not been so thoroughly stung by that shaft, I might have taken note of the Nazis before they attacked.

8

They came out of the shadows, clad all in black, save the brown shirts tucked beneath long coats and the stark red band around their upper left arms. Their silhouettes could not be mistaken, not even by the most casual observer, not in *la Ville-Lumière*, not in 1934. But as taken by Baker's performance as we all were, not one of us saw them until they were upon us.

Not *us*, but indeed, nearly upon the stage, their square-shouldered shapes descending upon the spectacle of Egypt's final hours of glory. Once again the audience came to their feet, a rumble of excitement and confusion rushing through. This could not be part of the performance—or it *could* be a daring commentary on the fascism rising to our east reflected in the fall of one of history's most opulent empires. On a Parisian stage, anything was possible, and in that thin space of possibility appeared hesitation for all but one.

Not for nothing had I chosen to sit in the boxes.

Curtains and cords hung heavily around me and those I sat with, offering us privacy from outside view if we so wished. I had other desires, and in leaping to my feet also smoothly slipped a knife from the thigh-sheath beneath my cobalt gown. Beauty was one thing; going unarmed was another. With the razored blade, I struck free a cordoned rope and yanked to see how and where it attached above me. I was in luck: it wound upward and around the curtains of other boxes, and a few quick twitches loosened it from the grips above. I wrapped its dangling end solidly around my wrist and, in silence—for I never understood the impulse to run into battle screaming; it seemed wiser to me by far to surprise my enemy than warn him I was coming—I leapt over the box's balcony lip and swung toward the stage.

I discarded my shoes as I swung, sparing an apologetic thought for the patrons whom they hit before my wild flight came to an abrupt halt with my heels slammed into the kidneys of a Nazi soldier. He collapsed with a scream of pain and I, momentum lost and still seeming miles from Madame Baker, spun to find what materials I had on hand to make use of.

There were many: a Roman sword of heavy dull steel in the hands of a gaping extra, bludgeoning tools of every sort in the form of set pieces, and, if necessary, the extras and stagehands themselves—though it was my preference not to throw them into the fray. I released my box seat rope at once and seized the Roman sword, disappointed to discover it was painted wood, not metal at all. There was no time to prevaricate, though; the audience was beginning to understand that this was not bold commentary but a Nazi incursion, and panic would soon rear its ugly head.

Wooden sword set distastefully in my teeth, I caught a nearby rope—I had landed downstage left, beside the curtains—and slashed that rope's other half forcefully. It parted, and from off stage came the sounds of counterweights careening toward the floor. I flew upward in an instant and was jarred to a tooth-rattling stop—the sword bore the shape of my teeth as a scar for the rest of its brief existence—as the counterweights finished their plummet. I reached for the next looping rope, cut it, and soared toward the stage with such vigor that I took a moment's relief that my legs were well-shaped and the skirt's cut ensured I did not entirely dispose with my modesty. Madame Baker had no time at all in which to prepare for my arrival before I swept her from her feet. Together we shot up again in a glorious arc of blue and gold to land solidly upon the prow of the magnificent Egyptian scow that made up the set's triumphant back piece.

Under the audience's roaring approval, I set Madame Baker on her feet and removed the sword from my teeth to offer a swift smile. "Amelia Stone, at your service. Do remain here, madame, whilst I deal with these ruffians."

With that, I sheathed the knife and leapt from the ship's prow again, the curtain rope offering me the ability to skim well across the stage from *la grande dame*. As it should have, Nazi attention turned to me: I was a danger to their nefarious plot, whatever it might be.

That it involved Madame Baker was clear; perhaps those who sought to build a master race also sought to learn how a colored woman could bring the elite of Paris to grovel at her feet. I shuddered to think what experiments might be performed upon her in order to release those imagined secrets. Another uniformed thug fell beneath the strength of my wooden sword, and a third from the power of my swinging kick. As he collapsed, I hit the stage and rolled, reluctant to loosen my grip on the curtain rope; it seemed that it might somehow save me, or at least offer a weapon beyond the dull blade in my hand.

Three Nazis converged on me, not yet fully realizing, perhaps, that I was no part of the evening's entertainment. They did not withdraw their weapons to threaten me, and I, thinking fondly of my *Savate* instructor, handily dispatched them with the sword.

The next three were wiser, and not men to rely on fists when guns would do. I dropped low, feinting with the blade at their ankles, but as one danced away the other two took aim, while others still began to close in on me with deadly intent written on their snarling features. My hand snaked toward the knife again at my thigh; if I were to die on this stage, I would not be the only one. But just before my fingers closed on the small blade, tension came into the rope wrapped about my wrist. I had only an instant to understand, and swiftly spun the rope around my hand, giving myself better purchase.

To the stunned and shouting audience, it must have looked choreographed: I burst upward from a ring of Nazis, one hand extended above me, the other wielding a shining sword as I kicked upward with violent force enhanced by the rapidity with which I rose. Three Nazis fell as one, and the cheer that went up from the audience was echoed by the stagehand whose quick wits had sent me soaring.

Nor did he abandon me: I rose and fell, dancing about the stage with the practiced skill of an acrobat. My skirt flashed and glittered blue, an always moving target as I did battle with evil men. Gunshots were fired; Madame Baker screamed, and that vibrant, reverberating voice silenced the entire theatre for a shocking span of heartbeats.

But in screaming, she brought herself back to Nazi attention. They had, in their pursuit of me, forgotten their objective. Now it was foremost in their minds, and a man with commander's bars on his shoulder barked orders that he never dreamed I could understand. But I had grown up with three cradle tongues and had learned many languages with ease as I had traveled the world: *Forget the flying woman,* he demanded. *Get to Baker!*

The race was on, a convergence of black-uniformed hooligans against myself, all of us scrambling the set to reach Madame Baker first. I had the advantage: the moment my unseen stagehand supporter realized my desired destination, he flew me upward and my running momentum carried me angel-like toward *la grande dame.* My left arm ached from the endless hoisting, but I dared not complain, nor even think of it: a helpless woman was in danger, and I would not let her fall beneath the Nazi scourge.

Baker, whose pride was in this instance perhaps greater than her wisdom, stood above us all with a look of scorn that would have done well on the queen whose part she played. Had I been one of the jack-booted thugs, I might have hesitated, but they feared their master more than any woman's scathing disdain. They swarmed the scow, and it was only by good fortune that I arrived in time to knock the first of them away.

The commander, a giant of a man, seized one of his own and bodily hurled him at me. I met him with the broad side of the sword, staggered back, then threw him off. He fell with a shout, but the seconds dedicated to that act were enough for the commander to take the scow and reach me. I wasted no time watching his compatriot fall, and yet in the instant it took me to recover, the enemy landed his first real blow against me: a full punch to the face, mitigated only by my swift action in leaning back.

None the less, stars exploded in my mind as the bitter flavor of iron filled my throat. My backward lean became nearly a fall, but confident hands caught my spine and thrust me forward again: Madame Baker, assisting in her own rescue! What a woman she was! Though I could see almost nothing through pain-stunned tears, I lashed out, hoping my opponent had not yet moved to press his advantage. Remembering his size, I went for the ribs, swinging my wooden sword as if it might cleave him in twain.

As fate had it, it was the sword that broke in two, not the Nazi commander, though I heard a satisfying crack of ribs and his yowl of pain. I dashed tears from my eyes and swept blood away from my nose as I leapt, bearing him to the deck in a blur of elbows and knees. We writhed and struggled, his strength and size to his advantage, my litheness and size to mine, and neither of us gaining the upper hand.

The broken sword came to hand and I clobbered his temple with its hilt. He collapsed against the scow, and I, triumphant, raised my gaze to receive Madame Baker's accolades.

To my unending dismay, she was instead staring enraged after a few escaping Nazis, her lovely head divested of its magnificent crown.

9

" A moment, madame, and I shall retrieve your headdress for you—" Forgetting that I did not wear my usual leather jacket and fighting togs, I wiped my nose across my arm a second time and was dismayed to discover blood smeared along my forearm and dripping onto my cobalt gown. My drycleaners would require upfront payment, and at least half an hour of my time in which to lecture me. I sighed, but such was the cost of my chosen lifestyle. To Madame Baker, I smiled apologetically for my appearance, then wrapped the stage rope around my wrist a final time. With only a touch of fortune, I could catch the escaping thieves in a single swing.

A steel grip grasped my bloody arm. "Like hell," said the fabulous Madame Baker, in raw American English. "You're not leaving me behind, Madame Stone. First, you've just saved my bacon and I want you near me if any of these thugs wake up. Second, *that's my hat!*"

I stared at her, dazed with bemused admiration. I could argue; I could lay her out and make good my chase; I could bind the unconscious Nazis so they could not trouble her.

Or I could waste no time, and offer her a dashing smile. "As you wish, Madame Baker."

La grand dame's answering smile was ferocious, and I recalled that she was known to keep a cheetah called Chiquita; I thought she had learned that sharp smile from the wild animal, and also thought she would do well at my side in a fight and perhaps in gentler arts. I clenched the rope and made to pull her close, ready to swing, but a change of her weight made me hesitate.

Madame Baker took perhaps one half of a step forward, putting herself just ahead of me on the prow of the Egyptian ship, and took a long, deep, glorious bow to uproarious applause and appreciation from the scattered, standing audience. Her fingers dug into my forearm, pulling me into the bow as well. I joined her, though less gracefully and without the depth or duration. When she stood, it was to await further, forthcoming accolades, but under my breath I murmured, "Madame Baker, I must insist. Come with me or remain for your adoring audience, but the choice must be made now."

She released my arm so that she could wrap hers around my neck. I, in turn, tested my grip on the rope and snugged her against my side with my free arm. What a picture we made, she in gold, myself in blue, whooping wildly—hers inspiring mine—as we swung from the scow. The audience's roars of delight followed us in waves. We came to the backstage floor as one, laughing at the madness of it all as we clutched hands and fell into hot pursuit of our quarry.

Black-uniformed men swarmed ladders reaching for the catwalks high above. They were nearly impossible to see, until a clever stagehand—perhaps the same one who had helped me before—illuminated the backstage with harsh electric lights. I was grateful to be in Paris for this adventure; nowhere else had so many electric lights as to deserve the name *la Ville-Lumière*. I released Madame Baker's hand and dashed up a ladder, now able to move more quickly than my Nazi prey. I had gained on them by half when the first threw open a door leading to the rooftop and they slipped out into the night.

I was behind them in a moment, gasping at night air so cold and fresh on my bare arms that it seemed to buzz and hum. I had, I realized too late, been a fool: instead of seizing Madame Baker, I ought to have taken a gun from one of the fallen fascists. *C'est la vie*; I would simply have to defeat them with my wits and my fists, which had never yet failed me in battle. To that end, when Madame Baker flew through the door behind me, I caught the outrageous skirt of her gown, issued an apology, and tore its delicate fabric until her legs were exposed to above the knee and I had a shimmering length of material to twist into a rope.

The rooftop of *le Palais Garnier* was a vast, flat thing centered by a huge green glass dome lined with copper. The whole of the building was cornered by gold angels who bore instruments and lifted their arms to the sky in musical supplication; behind them both lay the rest of the building and its less dramatic rooftop. We had emerged near the dome; the fascists were already approaching the roof's edge, where they would no doubt slither down and away like the snakes they were. I bound a lasso into the rope as we ran after them, judging the height of an angel's wing for ensnaring. It could be done, though perhaps not by Madame Baker.

"What *is* that?" she demanded as we ran, and I realized the soft buzz I had felt upon exiting the warmth of the opera house was not simply cold, but indeed the air itself vibrating with the sound of engines. In front of us, our Nazi game flung themselves from the rooftop without care; I did not even see them catch hold of ropes to rappel safely to the ground. We were nearly upon the rooftop's precipice ourselves when finally we saw the answer to their reckless actions.

Slow, low-flying biplanes roared past *la Palais Garnier*. Painted as red as the infamous Baron's and decorated with the spiderlike swastika, they caught their falling comrades in flybys. Offended outrage rose in my chest. They had been very certain, these Nazis. Biplanes were old, used in the Great War and replaced now with faster, single-winged aircraft. But for tonight, for an incursion into France to steal a headdress from a singer, surely the Nazi commanders had concluded that their old planes would suit, and sent a bevy of them forth to drop off and collect their troops. *Naturellement,* they had not anticipated my presence, nor that any single person could foil them all. Ah, but they had never met a Spirit before; I knew from adventures past that those of us born to shape the century had gifts beyond the ordinary.

I was not ashamed to admit I put some of those gifts on fine display as I leapt from the rooftop with my golden lasso in hand. I knew an exhilarating handful of heartbeats wherein I had no mistress save the wind: I was free of all constraints, unable to feel even gravity's call. This was flight; this was the thing that humankind had longed for since time immemorial.

I landed on the curved upper wing of a biplane with grace and elegance: on one knee, the other foot and both hands planted firmly against freezing metal, with my skirt blowing around me like a cobalt storm. It was my dearest hope that Madame Baker saw that glorious and dramatic landing, for no sooner had I accomplished it than I was obliged to fling myself face down and cling to the wing like an insect afraid of being blown away. The plane banked sharply at my arrival, then spun upward into the sky, trying to shake me off. I was thrown back and forth, my grip loosening with every wobble, but I soon had the rhythm of it: when the pilot drove the wing opposite me toward the earth, the air itself pinned me in place before I was nearly flipped headlong upon the reversal of that tilt.

When, for the third time, the pilot drove the opposite wing downward, I let my golden rope unfurl.

Roaring wind captured it and snapped it down and back, around the plane's upper wing. I lurched for the free flying end, seizing it in cold fingers just as the pilot realized what I was doing. He flung the plane to the opposite pitch, trying to dislodge me, but now I was effectively bound to the wing—so long as my grip held. Eyeing the city lights speeding below and the terrible distance there was to fall, I vowed that my grip would not fail me, and did my best to perform an unconcerned wink and smile at the pilot.

Rage contorted his features as inventive invective spewed forth. Only then did I truly notice that a second man sat in the plane's passenger seat, whence the guns could be operated. Indeed, he was struggling to bring them around to an angle from which he could fire at me, and I dreaded that he might carry and soon remember a sidearm. The pilot became secondary in my concerns, and as the plane pitched again I made no effort to hold on to anything but my rope. Its silken length zipped down the wing to catch violently on struts, the freedom of play it granted allowing me to meet the plane's passenger with the flexed heels of both feet. He was not secured and the force of our encounter wrenched him from the plane. Screaming, he made the very fall I was trying so conscientiously to avoid.

The pilot leveled the plane again, which threw me away from him, but the silken rope did its duty and held me to the wing. I scrambled up, buffeted by wind, and realized the pilot dared not tilt the aeroplane again for fear of depositing me atop him. I had no such concerns, and, cat-like, began to creep toward him. He turned a look of savagery on me and withdrew a pistol from the cockpit.

He could not hit me easily; I had the advantage of movement, though I wished that I had tied the rope to something rather than trust my own strength. I doubted I would be afforded the opportunity now. The first shot, fired in anger, flew wild, but the second was more carefully aimed. He sighted along the pistol and I, crouched on the wing, waited to determine which way to fly. But then surprise wiped rage from his face and I, more fool than I knew, followed his glance upward.

A crash heralded the arrival of another player in our performance, and a woman leaned over the wing's trailing edge to hit me in the face.

10

S he missed. I was not to take a blow to the face twice in a week, much less twice in a single night, and my silken harness on the plane's wing allowed me to slide a fair distance from her striking hands without endangering myself. Then, because the plane was now level and the pilot no longer inclined to incline— indeed, he had slowed his speed with the woman's arrival—I swung myself to the top wing and crouched to meet my adversary.

She was younger than I by some considerable margin, and while by the moon's light I could tell that her eyes were light, I could not determine their color. Her cap had been blown away as she fell—the plane she had leapt from buzzed above us, one of many in the night sky that blotted out stars and made shadows in the moonlight—and her lush dark hair quickly lost its shape in the wind. I had never before seen a woman dressed in the SS uniform. It suited her as it suited everyone: strengthened her shoulders, narrowed her waist, made intimidating what might have otherwise been insignificant, as did the command insignia on her lapels; she outranked the officer I had felled at *la Palais Garnier*. At her hip was her sidearm, visible when the wind whipped her long black coat aside for a moment. A satchel lay over her back, its single strap snugged against her breast. That was not standard for the uniform, and a smile crept onto my lips. "You should have left that in your plane, mademoiselle."

"*Commander* Knapp," she snapped with high pride.

"Are you sleeping with the *Führer* to have received such rank?" I wondered aloud, in as deliberately insulting a tone as I could manage when conversation had to be shouted in order to be heard at all. It was true I wished to antagonize her: *she* was dressed for the cold speeding winds of flight, whereas I was rapidly losing feeling in my extremities, but it was also true that curiosity had me in its grip. I had traveled the world, and knew well enough that women soldiers peopled nearly every war front, but in the skies above Paris was not a place I had expected to encounter a female SS commander, particularly one of such tender years. "How disappointed he will be, when you fail to bring him back the crown."

"The crown is ours!" Against all sense she disregarded her sidearm and surged at me, as if my words were so personal an insult that I must die at her hands, with my life crushed between her fingers.

But I had been fighting since I was fifteen and knew better than to strike in rage. To succumb to emotion in battle was often to lose, even if at the time it seemed to be success. This I had learned at the knee of *le Monstre* himself, and his spectre, living in Josephine Baker's voice, reminded me of it. I stepped to the side, unwilling to engage with this girl if I did not have to. The force of her approach threw her past me. I inserted a foot before her ankle and laid her out, belly down, on the plane's wing. My own hair finally began to loosen from its tight-pinned waves as I knelt with my weight against her spine, and withdrew the knife that had so long been resting in my thigh-sheath. With a single slice, her satchel came free. My weight still pinning her, I bound the satchel in place against my own back, using the golden silk rope to secure it, then turned the girl onto her back and held her with both fists. "You're young and foolish, mademoiselle. Return home. Better yet, go to England, to America, away from the poison that is the *Führer* and his ambitions. Do not die for one man's ugly dreams. The world is a better place than that."

The wretched *enfant* shrugged her knees to her chest and kicked me in the belly hard enough to knock me back. She had not thought it through, though: I retained my grasp on her coat, and thus pulled her with me as I fell. We bounced once on the plane's wing, then flew free, myself breathless from the blow and her face white with terror.

But she rallied well, fear lending her speed: one

hand shot out, capturing the lowest strut on the plane as we were swept below it. The strain showed instantly: she could not long hold both my weight and her own. She fumbled once for the buttons on her coat, but gave up as the effort threatened her precarious grip on the strut.

"*Surtout, ne bouge pas.*" To my relief, she did as instructed: she did not move as I used all my strength to haul myself up her lapels and hook an elbow around the strut. Dangling there, I seized her coat more firmly and hoisted her onto the strut before me.

She did not try to dislodge me, but rather went immediately for the satchel I had tied to my back. I made a fist of my loose hand and hit her. She shied back, then, teeth bared, accepted that if she lost me, she would lose her prize as well. With that thought clearly in mind, she scrambled up the biplane's side to swing into the second seat.

I, still dangling, looked at pilot and Commander both with a disbelief bordering on laughter. She offered a hand, and my laughter broke free. "I think not, mademoiselle." There was no grace in hitching my legs around the strut, nor any beauty in humping myself around until I could scramble to the wing, but it was effective, and little else mattered. The pilot bucked the plane once, but Knapp's sharp soprano rang out to stay his hand. Perched between wings, cold as night, and beginning to tire, I wondered what the *pschent* represented to the Nazi cause, that it was so worth pursuing.

They would not answer even if I asked. Knapp clambered over the pilot, pursuing me onto the wings. I swung upward, leaving the comparative safety of the lower wing for the upper's room to move; if it was a fight she wanted, a fight she would have.

All thought of battle was swept from my mind as I stood on the upper wing and an unparalleled vista spread before me. We had traveled a fair distance in our struggles, and *la Tour Eiffel* rose up before us, presented to me at an angle I had never dreamt of seeing it from. It glimmered in the moonlight, a paean to architectural grace and beauty. Stars shone brilliantly behind it, the moon caught in its highest spires. *La Ville-Lumière* spread out below, no less glittering or fair than the stars themselves. *La Seine* glided through streets silenced by distance, its black ribbon steaming here and reflecting the lights of delicate bridges there. Smoke rose in thin lines from chimneys, but no scent of ash was carried to me at this height. The only disruptions in those smooth streaks of smoke were those caused by other biplanes, some distant and some near, as they too roared through the sky. Even their red, swastika-marked wings, though, could not diminish the awesome sight of Paris from above. I forgot all else: cold, battle, wind, fear faded into a simple and sublime joy, that I should be so fortunate as to stand here now and see this beauty stretching before me.

My admiration came to a harsh end as the aeroplane suddenly bobbled in the air and Knapp struck me from behind. Or rather, fell upon me: her intentions of slashing the satchel from my back were made clear by the flash of silver blade that flew past me, and though her weight bore me to the wing, her own startled grunt implied that the wind-induced dip of the wing had thrown her.

As well for me it had; she might have succeeded in her endeavor, so rapt was I in Parisian beauty. But no more: the battle was once more at hand, and together we rolled, thumping and kicking, across the entire breadth of the upper wing. My spine did not take kindly to rolling over the *pschent*, which had sufficient weight and solidity that I dared think it was truly made of gold. Knapp, having had enough of precarious rolling, seized the shoulder twists of my golden rope and hauled me to my feet; she was smaller than I, but strong.

And, I feared, foolish: her hands were now wrapped around my straps, and mine were free. "Stop this now," I pled, genuine emotion trembling my voice. "One or all of us will surely die if you cannot give up this madness."

Her eyes, so large and wide that my heart demanded that I see her as an innocent, seemed for an instant conflicted, but rather than succumb, she released me to strike a blow.

Too late: I had moved even as I spoke, preparing myself, and when I knew she could not be reasoned with, I threw a right fist that connected with her jaw at speed. The sound was audible even above the engine's roar. Knapp's eyes rolled back, unconsciousness all but claiming her, and she fell backward. She was close to the wing's end, and even with her faculties dulled by the power of my blow, enough awareness remained within her mind for rigid terror to shape her face.

I lunged forward, my hand extended. Her fingertips brushed mine, and she was gone.

11

Horror struck me, but I had no time to mourn; no sooner did she fall than the pilot pitched the plane as if to follow her. I flew upward, screaming merrily all the way, and through no more than the grace of fortune did I seize the upward wing as the plane passed below my soaring self. I am not too proud to say I gibbered, teeth rattling and body shaking with fear that could only be expressed through nonsensical babbling as I crawled in a terror down the wing while the pilot chased Knapp.

I reached him first, seized his goggles, cut his restraints, and threw him after Knapp. Without hesitation, I swung into his seat, then faced a grim and unavoidable truth: I could not fly an aeroplane.

Motorcycles were my transportation of choice; they were simple things, a few gears, a brake, and the body's own weight to help it corner. I was not of sufficient mass to guide an aeroplane by leaning, nor, I thought, were most pilots: there was not enough room

in the cockpit for a person of tremendous size, and so
there had to be another answer.

The blocks under my feet provided that answer. I
pressed one and the plane banked sharply; releasing it
sent me back on a steady keel. The other tipped me in
the opposite direction, leaving me to face the next
uncertainty: gaining and losing altitude. Principally,
losing it in a controlled and calm fashion until I
landed somewhere wide, smooth, and untrafficked
enough for a novice pilot to survive a first landing
attempt. *L'Avenue des Champs-Élysées*, perhaps; I cast a
nervous glance beneath me, trying to place myself in
regards to its location.

It was behind me, and so were half a dozen Red
Barons, as I had started to think of them, all closing in
on my location at far greater speed and with vastly
more confidence than I had in my own flying skills.
Gulping down worry, I pressed forward on the yoke
before me, trusting that forward meant down.

It did not. My plane climbed and almost instantly
began to choke and sputter: the acceleration was
insufficient to the rise. I pulled back and leveled out
again, a relief that was all but secondary to my frantic
search for speed. Bit by bit I accomplished it, though
the old plane had no chance of reaching the speeds of
a more modern vehicle. If it had, *bien sûr*, I no doubt
would have been unable to fight on its wings while it
flew; it had been difficult enough to keep my feet as
it was.

With my lead, if not growing, at least no longer
shrinking, I squirmed out of the bindings that held

the crown against my back. There was suddenly more room to breathe, though the satchel was awkward on my lap. I checked my pursuit, then hastened to lean over the back of my seat into the one behind me, where I tied the satchel so firmly in place that I doubted it would be removed without a knife's help. Then I slunk back to my own cockpit, tied myself in as best I could with the tattered remains of Madame Baker's gown, and turned the plane to meet my enemies.

It was not blood lust, but pragmatism, which drove me to do so. I believed I could safely land on *des Champs-Élysées*, but I was not at all certain I could so much as find an airport or field that would be otherwise suitable; I was not accustomed to seeing Paris, much less navigating it, from the air. If returning to territory I knew meant facing down an oncoming Nazi scourge, so be it; the world did not need their sort terrorizing it anyway.

The flash of gunfire against the city-lit night came before the sound of guns rattling, before the sound of bullets whistling by. I lifted my plane higher before the projectiles zipped by, but a tight smile pulled at my lips. They had begun the aerial battle. I would make certain to finish it.

Mastering the controls for the mounted machine guns was less difficult than flight, and flight had been simple. Landing, I trusted, might be another matter entirely, but should the enemy prevail, it would be the least of my many worries. Staccato bursts of light flew from my guns, spattering lead toward oncoming aeroplanes. They were warning shots, nothing more: the crosshairs etched into my window-shield did not contain any enemy planes, but it seemed only sporting to announce my intention to fight. A few bullets clanged against the Eiffel Tower's elegant struts as we came around it again, and I made a silent apology to Monsieur Eiffel even as the thrill of a fight stretched a grin across my face. I had always said that my fists were the only weapons I ever needed, but that did nothing to diminish my enjoyment of the roaring power of gunfire.

I banked sharply, taking a turn around the Tower again, and found one, then two, Red Barons bearing down into my crosshairs. Gunfire exploded toward them, and the first of the Nazi planes screamed and plummeted toward the earth.

Instantly a bullet shattered my windscreen, destroying the crosshairs that had been of such use. I fired in return, only slowly realizing that my survival was thanks to my last flurry of bullets hitting not one, but two marks: not only the plane I had meant to fire at, but the one behind it had fallen to my bullets. The Nazi shot that had shattered my windscreen had been its last, lucky volley.

Lucky indeed, that it had shattered only the glass and not my breastbone as well. I was not afraid, but healthy respect for my enemy's skill made my next sally less rash. Rather than a frontal assault, I gained altitude again, watching the Barons as they roared upward behind me.

Their formation was a tight V, five remaining of

the original eight—two I had shot down and the third
I had absconded with. Given the state of my windscreen, I could hardly hope to defeat all of them in
direct combat; wit and wisdom would be required.

I had seen barnstorming tricks performed, and
without daring to think hard on my actions, brought
the aeroplane's nose up at an alarming angle. I knew
too little: that a plane would stall out in the air was
certain, but at what altitude, at what inclination; these
things were a mystery to me, and yet the risk had to
be taken. Up, up, up and over in a mighty loop so that
I might catch my enemy from behind and send them
from the skies in a blaze of righteous fire.

Up, up—and panic seemed to seize the fuel lines
themselves. From the engine's steady roar came a
missed beat, then another. Up, and I lay pressed
against my seat, heart in my mouth, gaze tipped to see
the wide open sky with all its glittering stars and the
brightly watching moon. Up, and in an exhilarating
moment, momentum carried me over. The earth itself
curved above me, Parisian lights becoming a man-
made reflection of the distant stars. *La Seine* ran
through them, a black, winding, dark reflection of the
Milky Way. But I could take no more time to admire
the city as the five Red Barons began to climb toward
me while I fell back toward them, back toward the
earth, guiding my aeroplane out of its arc and into
pursuit of the Barons.

They, finally understanding my tactics, broke off
their own rapid climbs too late. Three fell in a hail of
bullets before any of them had righted themselves to

face me; the fourth I met headlong, both of us blasting away at one another as if rage and determination could win the day. My plane shuddered and twitched with the impact of bullets. I hunched low, barely seeing over the dash, and aloud whispered, "*S'il vous plaît, mon dieu*, perhaps I will begin again to believe in you if I should survive the next few moments—!"

We passed so close to one another, my opponent and I, that I saw the stricken fear that crossed his face as he realized he had lost our confrontation. Whether it was his voice or the aeroplane's final scream that sounded as they fell, I could not know, but it seemed to me that it was the plane, and not the man, that shouted its last defiance before it hit the earth.

I ought not to have allowed myself to become so distracted: there was a final Baron left. But as I searched the Parisian night sky for it, I discovered it had chosen flight over fight: already it was some distance away, heading for the countryside rather than Paris's center. The impulse to hunt it down seized me and the decision hung in the balance until I remembered Josephine Baker standing bold and beautiful atop the opera house. The depth of her dark eyes called me back to my duties, and I turned my winged vehicle to the streets in search of a landing strip.

12

"Amelia! What splendid good fortune to hear from you! Of all our brethren, there is none I could have more need of in this hou—good heavens, Amelia, what has happened to you?" The exuberant greeting of my friend and compatriot, Professor Khan, became a trumpet of concern and alarm as he took in my appearance as I stood in the doorway of his professorial suite at *la Sorbonne*.

I had Madame Baker in one hand—speaking figuratively, of course. She had not so much deigned as to take my elbow when I offered it, although, given my state of dishevelment, she, nor anyone fit for company, could not be blamed. So: Madame Baker in one hand and the gold-wrapped crown in the other, and me between them in a gown that had only hours earlier been long, sparkling with sequins, and fit for the *Opéra*. Now it stopped above my knee, had nary a sequin to be seen, and appeared—with good reason—to have been in a series of fistfights.

"And," Khan went on, his dismay dissolving into admiration, "do my eyes deceive me, Amelia, or do you bring the divine Mrs. Baker to my humble offices? Madame, it is a genuine honor." With this accolade, Khan swept a bow and, with dark hopeful eyes, extended a hand to Madame Baker.

Had I not admired her before, Madame Baker would have won my affections forever with her next actions. Without visible hesitation she stepped forward and placed her hand in Khan's—and this time I did not prevaricate, not even within the confines of my own mind—in Khan's enormous *paw*, for my friend and fellow Centurion was a great ape.

The greatest of them, indeed: a gorilla, gifted with intellectual superiority by his warlord father, also called Khan, but my Khan had foresworn violence in all but the most extreme of circumstances, preferring instead to devastate his enemy with his mental superiority and extraordinary wits. Tonight, as most days, he was clad in garb suitable for a being who went among men as their intellectual equal: a kilt that left his magnificent torso bared while according him the basic tenets of modesty. In no way could he be mistaken for human; in no way was he anything less than a person, and Madame Baker treated him as such from that first extraordinary moment of meeting. Khan bowed over her hand, and she graced him with a blinding smile as he released the hand that was so small and delicate in his own.

"Professor Khan," she said with evident unstinting

pleasure, "the honor is mine. How wonderful that you're in the world."

Khan could not, to my knowledge, blush, but there was something of that attitude to the rumble of his voice as he stepped back to allow us full access to his office. "No more wonderful than the fact that you are, Madame Baker, and perhaps less so, for your voice brings joy to the world whereas my countenance has been known to inspire fear. But discussion of our various virtues cannot be why you are attending me at this late hour, particularly given Amelia's unusual attire. My dear," he said to me with all due humor and rue, "I should have liked to have seen you *before* you saw fit to go adventuring in that evening gown. I imagine you were a candle to match Madame Baker."

"Josephine," that worthy said with imperious pleasure. "She was, Professor Khan. The whole of the Paris *Opéra* had the opportunity to see it tonight. She rescued me from a Nazi attack and did battle across the wings of biplanes in the sky. If only that could be staged, I would draw audiences from every corner of the world." Madame Baker threw off her fur stole, an item which she had acquired sometime between my leaving her on the opera house rooftop and my return, to display a long-waisted day dress of layered sheer fabric bound with burgundy under her bosom; all in all a far more practical item to wear than Cleopatra's gold gown. The stole was flung over the back of a green velvet chair before she sat, regally, in that selfsame chair.

Both Khan and myself were silenced by the

dramatic nature of her behavior. It was as if every action she took was meant for the stage, larger than life and drawing all attention. She did not so much diminish the objects around her as made them her own. Khan's office, with its mahogany shelves and vast, paper-covered desk, with its burning electric lamps and the scratchy, musty scent of ancient manuscripts, seemed as though it had been deliberately prepared not for the large gorilla professor, but for the slight American singer. Her chair with its heavy padding, large curved arms, and high back, seemed as though it was meant to be the center of attention. We gazed upon its occupant with all appropriate supplication, until one of her thin painted eyebrows twitched upward in curious amusement.

"Madame Stone," she said to me, her tone prompting, and I replied, "Amelia," rather suddenly.

"Amelia," she repeated obligingly before turning the devastating effect of *both* lifted eyebrows upon Khan. "And if we're all going to be on a first name basis, Professor...?"

"Khan," my eloquent friend said as abruptly as I had done, before clearing his throat. "Ah, that is to say, I have no other given name, no Jonathan or Charles that I might be known by. I'm afraid Khan is the sum total of my appellations; it is all that I am."

"Oh," said Josephine Baker with a delighted smile, "I doubt that. Amelia," she prompted again, and finally, shaken loose from her spell, I began to unwind the *pschent* from its golden bindings as I quickly related the adventures of the evening just gone by.

For all the depths of his eyes and the leathery dark wrinkle, despite the protrusion of his muzzle and the slashing incisors, Khan's expressive features were no more difficult to read than any human's. Horror, delight, dismay, admiration: they all shone as I told the story. Madame Baker—Josephine—as fine an audience as she was a performer, laughed and clapped and gasped, fingers pressed against her lovely lips, as my tale and the *pschent* were unwound.

The entirety of Khan's uttered response to the adventure was thus: "If only your dressmaker had known," but his massive mitts were eager and delicate as I handed over the golden *pschent*. Fiery interest lit his black eyes as he turned it this way and that, and he spoke to both of us, though he might well have been speaking to the ancient past. "You know, of course, that this is the double crown of Egypt. The Pharaohs who wore such crowns ruled both the Red Nile and the White, the Upper and Lower Kingdoms, and controlled—oh, much more than modern Egypt. The Upper Kingdom stretched much deeper along the Nile—"

"Wouldn't that be the Lower?" demanded Josephine, but Khan waggled a finger with professorial authority.

"To our minds, accustomed to our north-is-up mentality, yes, but remember that the Nile flows backward; its source is deep in the jungles of darkest Africa, and it wends its way not south, but north to the Mediterranean. For ancient Egyptians, the Upper Kingdom was the upper Nile: south, toward the river's unknown source. But as I was saying, the ancient conjoined kingdoms of Egypt controlled access to the Red Sea. That, of course, is irrelevant here; what is important and interesting is *this*."

With hands that could tear a man apart, he touched the two cobra heads rearing from the crown's front, then with particular delicacy, tapped only one of them. "This, my dear Amelia, my divine Mrs. Baker, is typically a vulture, the symbol of Upper Egypt. *Two* cobras aren't unheard of, but they *are* legendary. No one has even seen an artistic representation of this crown, Amelia. Stories are told about the double cobra crown, but not even in the images of Hatshepsut does she *wear* this."

I was quick to speak: "Hatshepsut?"

"Queen—well, technically, king. All Pharaohs were kings; they had no other word for their divine monarchs. King, then, of all Egypt. Ancient stories suggest she wore a *pschent* with two cobras, said to lend her compelling powers, even greater than one might expect of a god-on-earth. It was said no one who heard her speak when she wore this crown could defy her, or even want to. In this crown, Hatshepsut was said to have absolute, iron control over all of Egypt— but it was also said that any ordinary mortal who donned it would lose their minds in a swift and terrible way."

Josephine drawled, "Oh really," with such inso- lence it broke Khan's spell and we all laughed, but a slow chill slid down my spine as I looked from *la grand dame* to the gold crown.

"Wait. *Pardon*, Professor, but are you saying this crown itself is mystical in nature?"

"Well, to be wholly scientific about it I should like to run some tests, but frankly, Amelia, we live in a world of wonders, do we not? Myself, if I might be so bold as to say so, included. So I shall look at what evidence we have available, which is as such: firstly, it matches an item of legend. Secondly, it is of evident interest to a fascist regime whose explicit intentions appear to be international domination. Thirdly—"

"Because it grants the wearer Commanding Presence." I heard myself shape the words with importance, though I spoke in no more than a whisper. "He who wears it can sway anyone to anything, *non*, Professor? Do I understand that correctly?"

"Yes, but—"

Now cold throughout, and not because of the sad state of my attire, I turned my gaze to Madame Baker. I had come to Paris on Maman's suspicions; I had believed immediately when I heard the stunning quality of *la grande dame*'s voice. But belief and evidence were not, as *mon ami* Khan would rightfully argue, the same. Evidence, though, was nearly at hand; I was sure of it. "Where did you get the *pschent*, Josephine?"

Eyebrows furrowed in curious confusion, she gave the answer I dreaded: "It was a gift from my voice master, of course, to be worn when I played Cleopatra on the stage."

13

Had the world itself come down around my ears in the next moments, I would not have heard it, could not have stopped it. Cacophony reigned inside my head, all the certainties and horrors of youth replaying themselves, all the inevitable ramifications crashing down with the sound of cymbals in my ears.

No voice master save *le Monstre* could care that his protégée should wear a mystical crown of command when playing the role of a queen—the role of perhaps the most famous queen in history. Not only playing her, *non*, but *singing* her, in the voice trained by his care and talent. Singing, to waken the greatest height of emotion, of passion, of obedience, in those who listened. Rendering them vulnerable to command, opening them to the machinations of induced emotions, preparing them to generate more emotion for *le Monstre* to distill and bottle and use.

And in this modern era, Baker's vocals would be recorded, extending *le Monstre*'s reach not just to those who attended the *Opéra*, but around the globe, to anyone who might ever listen to *la grande dame*'s vocals soar and demand.

Had I any doubts, they were settled. *Le Monstre* was alive and had taken Josephine on as his student. I had failed as a youth, and *la Ville-Lumière*, perhaps all the world, was endangered again thanks to my failures.

Because worse even than *le Monstre*'s plans for the crown could be the *Führer*'s. If *le Monstre* had not survived to find Hatshepsut's crown, then it might have remained forever hidden and not an item of interest to a growing fascist regime. This single item could win the *Führer* unchallenged command over Egypt, over the very land from which Moses had led his people, then everywhere might indeed fall to his reign. *Le Monstre* then would seem a pittance, a laughingstock against the injustices meted by a madman on the throne of the world. In failing to kill *le Monstre* half a lifetime ago, I had failed more utterly than I could have comprehended.

"Amelia? Amelia." Distantly, as if I watched someone else and felt what they felt from a remove, I knew Khan's hand fitted itself around my elbow; knew that he guided me to a chair and sat me down, then wrapped something warm and soft around my shoulders. A hint of perfume drifted from it: Josephine's stole. I buried my face in it, eyes closed, as

if that soft sweet scent and the wild woman who wore
it could somehow save me from the errors I had made
long ago.

"Forgive me my enthusiasm and the distress it's
caused you," Khan said in clear concern. "It clearly
can't be real, Amelia. Circumstantial evidence aside,
if it was truly Hatshepsut's crown, Madame Baker
would have lost her mind upon donning it. Unless, of
course, it requires a certain awareness to trigger its
mystical powers—"

"No." My voice and the world came back to me
all at once. "I felt it in the theatre. We all did. She
sang and we rose up as the Egyptian people might
have, had Cleopatra commanded them. The compulsion was overwhelming. I thought it was only the
performer, the performance—"

Baker sniffed, elucidating her opinion of it being
anything else with that tiny derisive sound. Could I
have laughed, I would have, but the magnitude of my
mistakes and the task to set them right was too great
to allow for humor now. I went on with a bleak
conviction lending my words weight. "She is no ordinary mortal, Khan. She is Josephine Baker. She has
been extraordinary since her first steps on a stage. She
is a performer, larger than life, known around the
world. What else might a queen be, than that?"

"But to what end, Amelia? Why give a performer,
even a superlative one, the crown of Hatshepsut?
Who is this mysterious voice master?"

"*C'est le Monstre, Khan. Le Monstre aux Yeux Verts.*"

The Centurions—my brothers-in-arms, the others also born on the first day of the century and gifted with certain traits to help us defend the changing world from extraordinary threats—had known me long enough that no more explanation was necessary. Khan's comforting hand fell from my shoulder, and I heard him lean heavily into his chair, its joints creaking and complaining with the sudden weight. "Oh. And foolishly, I thought you had come for the race."

"*Le Mon*—the green-eyed monster? Who is the green-eyed monster? My master is Giuseppe Abatino—"

"Your master is a crime lord," I said as swiftly and harshly as I could. "I know it will seem unlikely to you, but I knew him in my youth. He has always been besotted by music, searching for the most powerful voices in order to work alchemical magics. My father died at his hands and my mother, who was a singer, nearly did as well."

"Oh." Josephine, too, sat back into her chair, and gazed at me as if unseeing for a little while. I could not guess at her thoughts, save to imagine she thought me mad, but in time she spoke again, more subdued than I had become accustomed to. "He teaches from shadow, like *le fantôme de l'opéra*. Of course I saw the parallels, but it seemed romantic and charming and theatrical, and his skill was indisputable. He moves—" She took a breath, as if steeling herself. "He moves short on one side, as if he can't stretch himself to a full stride or reach. All of his gestures come from the left, where his range of motion is easier. It could be that he's disfigured. I suppose I thought he was. Like the Phantom."

"Did you never wish to rip his mask away?" asked Khan softly.

"And expose myself to the horror of his face? I've seen the film, Professor. I know what happens to the eager *ingénue*. I am not that young." Josephine examined the backs of her hands momentarily, murmuring, "Perhaps I never was." As if her hands had told her a story she did not wish to hear, she closed them again and lifted her gaze. "I've never seen all of his face, but I've seen the color of his eyes. They are green. How will I help you ensnare him?"

"You will not," I said with unnecessary ferocity. "He is a matter for me to deal with, and I will risk no one, least of all you, Josephine, to his machinations. I shall bring you to my mother—"

"While I would adore to meet the woman who raised a swashbuckling daughter," she said in so dry a tone I could not determine whether she teased me or not, "you will certainly not hide me away from the world while you pursue a madman. I have not worked this hard to disappear in the hour of my crowning glory, and neither you nor your impressive friend will succeed in forcing me to."

Khan cleared his throat and, when we both looked to him, appeared abashed. "My dear Amelia, I must stand with Josephine on this, though I confess my reasons to do so are manifold. First, although I am as loathe as you to lead her into danger, I might point out that she is uniquely suited to draw *le Monstre* into the light. Surely, if he's taught her, he won't be able to resist seeing her perform at least once? So our goal must first be to keep her safe in daylight hours, a task for which your mother's apartment might indeed be eminently suitable. She, more than anyone, knows the risks of succumbing to him, and would certainly bar her doors against all strangers if required."

Despite having been the one to propose my mother's home as a place of safety, I muttered a sour, "Bars would not stop *le Monstre* should he suspect where Josephine had gone to ground," and my next thought was interrupted by Josephine's simple suggestion:

"Then perhaps you ought to remain at my side, Amelia. I have never seen anyone so well suited as a bodyguard, except perhaps Chiquita, and the authorities don't care for her being unleashed in public."

I gazed nonplussed at Josephine, unable to decide between delight at the prospect of spending my days in her company and offense at being compared to the world's most famous cheetah. "Madame, the authorities also do not care for *me* being unleashed in public."

Josephine showed no regret at all over the comparison, though her dark eyes sparkled enough to tell me she had made the jab deliberately, wanting, perhaps, to see if I would unsheathe my claws to scratch at her. She sounded pleased that I had. "After this past evening's performance, I can see why. Come home with me, Amelia. I'll introduce you to Chiquita and we'll see which of you is the more dangerous."

"Ahem." Khan shifted with discomfort as we both looked to him. "The trouble with this plan, Amelia, is that I, er, am in quite dire need of your assistance on the morrow."

14

D awn had not yet begun courtship with the horizon when I revved the engine of my beloved Indian motorcycle and took my place on a starting line crowded with riders and bikes of all shapes and sizes. Even before the race began, I could not keep the grin from stretching my face, and there were those who met my eyes with that selfsame expression of joy, with the readiness of life preparing to be lived at its fullest.

How I had come to *la Ville-Lumière* and not known of the three-day street race was a mystery beyond my ken, save that I had been somewhat distracted by the task Maman had set to me, and more distracted yet by Josephine Baker. I had the Indian, *naturellement*; I had not traveled without it since its purchase six years earlier, though it occasionally incurred great expense if speed demanded I fly, rather than sail, between continents.

Not, it seemed, as much expense as *mon ami* Khan

had incurred, though. As engines tore early morning silence and wakened the ire of Parisian residents, I thought back on the predicament he had explained only a few hours earlier—the predicament that had landed me here, eyes on the horizon, waiting for the sun to break through as our signal to ride.

I wore his colors pinned to my leather jacket: black and green, jungle colors, though I would not swear Khan had intended that when he chose them. Those around me wore different colors, and often emblems of racing companies—or rather, the motor-cycle aficionados who had developed entire compa-nies to justify their adoration of racing. Yesterday another man had worn Khan's colors; an English boy, no larger than myself, who had placed well in the first day of racing and then, terribly, had fallen beneath the wheels of another racer careening out of control.

Khan was not so hardhearted as to continue a race when his rider clung to life by a thread. He now sat at the boy's bedside, reading to him and, I trusted, even now tuning the radio that they might listen to the illegal broadcast of the unauthorized race.

For unauthorized it was, but the prize was of such magnitude that there were men here willing to risk their entire companies for a chance to win. I had not yet even glimpsed it myself, but Khan's descriptions had left me eager to see it: *lighter than light,* he had said; *faster than fast, and so sleek as to be another machine entirely from motorcycles as we know them.* So extraordinary was it that he, who had no interest in motorcycles, had been drawn into its history and development, all by a

Signor Ignatius Panterello who had once worked for the Gilera company, whose racing cycles went back a quarter century. But Panterello's secrets were well kept, and only the winner of this race would gain inside knowledge of its design—and win the motor-cycle itself. Khan had sunk not only his own savings but, it seemed, a substantial portion of the Century Club's finances, into supporting and developing the English lad's racing kit. I was racing today to assure his investment paid off; but *en vérité*, I now wanted to see Panterello's creation for myself and intended on winning for my own sake as much as Khan's.

I would not, however, ride their motorcycle. I knew my Indian better than any other. It would stand me well in the race, and even if other machines were smaller and lighter, few of them had a rider with nearly two decades of experience.

Stars began to fade from the sky as a blue blush crept up from the world's edge. I took a final look at my opponents, choosing from among their expressions and stances those whom I thought would offer the greatest competition. Three struck me as particularly driven. Two were men, one probably Italian and the other perhaps an Englishman. The Englishman was relaxed, confident, comfortable: for him, this street race was akin to home. I liked him at once, though that would not help him to win. The Italian was harder and more intense, but if he had the reflexes to go with his intensity, it would be a tight race to the finish line.

The third was another woman, both younger and

blacker of skin than I, who sat on her blue Harley with the confidence of a longtime rider. She felt me looking at her and turned to grin, and with a gasp of delight, I knew her: Bessie Stringfield, America's most famous black motorcyclist. Overwhelmed by the prospect of riding with her, I touched two fingers to my forehead in a sign of such respect it could only be called a salute, and Madame Stringfield gave me a broad wink in return.

My childish pleasure at being acknowledged nearly cost me the first moments of the race, and later I wondered if Madame Stringfield had known precisely what she was doing. I had, after all, counted her among the most promising of my competitors, and it seemed only likely that if they were the best of the best, she would have no compunctions against distracting me as the sun's golden tongue finally tasted the horizon.

I was prepared, though, even if my eyes were not cast forward, and I accelerated as much in response to other bikers surging forward as in awareness of the waking sun burning night from the sky. At once the race was on, dozens of bikes jostling for their places. As soon as we began, half a dozen riders fell, their wheels catching cobbles or gravel or deliberately placed sticks that choked and slew them. Those that survived spun forward, too many at once to fit the narrow streets, for we could not begin this race somewhere so obvious as *des Champs-Élysées*. Instead we were pressed into tracks meant for foot travel amongst houses that sprang up straight and tall; laundry blew above us and cats scattered in our headlamps. A few more of the racers fell to disgruntled householders with the wit to wait until the race had begun to express their displeasure: rotting fruit and hard bread pelted down, splashing under wheels and sending the less certain wobbling into nearby walls. There were no significant injuries, as no one had reached enough speed to be more than stunned by these minor collisions, but it was not those who fell who were my concern. Only those who leapt ahead, handling their bikes with surety and suavity, held my interest; if I hung back at first to observe them, it was a tactical decision, and not fear, that compelled me to do so.

The Italian was very good, taking corners more closely than a wise man might choose to. He braked rarely, but hard, his thick black mat of hair swinging forward abruptly when he did. Other times it blew back in the wind, as if he had no concern for the state of his skull, or perhaps a great dislike of the slight limitations in visual acuity caused by helmets. I, having greater respect for my brains, wore my helmet loosely, as did Stringfield and the Englishman.

Of those two, the latter rode in the Italian's wake, if less cozily in the corners. It seemed as though the Italian pulled him along; the Englishman's riding was effortless and casual. Stringfield also had no apparent need to take an early lead, though from her deft handling down the chalk marked streets that showed us our route, I had no doubt she could overtake both men easily. The greatest test would be on the home stretch, and the question would be whose bike was the faster: my six-year-old Indian Scout or Bessie's hot-off-the-line Harley.

But the answer lay miles and hours away yet: the track we followed was long and complex, racing through Parisian streets and along the river, avoiding angry police and angrier passersby, all with the wind smearing laughter across my face. The pack was left far behind; the race was between we four, and the rivalries began to define themselves as we reached more open streets and bridges that allowed us room to maneuver. The Italian hungered for the lead; the Englishman, happy in his wake.

Bessie and I exchanged a single glance: if either of us was to lose, we determined with that look, it would be to the other woman. Her smile flashed, and without need for discussion we moved as one to overtake the Italian, whose rash corner-cutting tendencies made him the most dangerous of us. The Englishman saw what we were doing and fell back, happy to allow us the opportunity to remove one of his rivals and trusting, no doubt, that he could catch and surpass us at his leisure.

It was a decision that saved him; he, of all of us, had the most time to react. I, being quicker than most, survived as well, but both the Italian and String-field were taken in the chest as a rope—a rope, not, *grâce à dieu*, a wire, which might have cut them in half at the speeds we were traveling—jumped up across the end of the bridge we crossed. Both of their motorcycles careened wildly, the Italian's into and through the thin stone railing, Stringfield's turning on its side and skidding across pavement. Sparks flew, and the shriek of metal promised that the fresh blue paint would be scarred when she righted it.

Of the two, Stringfield herself fared a little better than the Italian. He had already stretched the rope forward with his impact, offering her the barest instant to respond. Rather than being thrown backward as he was, she caught the rope under one arm, saving herself from bouncing across the road as her Harley did.

The Englishman and I, ducking below the twanging rope, each took a breath to look behind us in dismay and horror, then to meet one another's eyes as Bessie and I had done only a moment earlier. There was challenge in our gazes, to be sure, but also concern: making certain that the other was unharmed, that the sabotage had not ended the race. Once we were certain it had not, collusion became part of our strategy as well: together, the Englishman and I raced on, determined that we would best this course. For my own part, I was also determined that I would search out and bring to justice those who had threatened both the race and innocent lives.

15

There were no further mishaps, or at least not of the deliberate and malicious kind. I saw other racers make errors as they tried to catch the Englishman and me, but my sensation was that, having thinned out the forerunners, our adversary had done all that was necessary. The rules of the race were clear: each day's course was worth a certain number of points, offered in descending order depending on time elapsed and placement across the finish line. To ride away on Signor Panterello's new motorcycle, its patents in hand, the winner not only had to place highly each day, but attain overall what an auctioneer might call a reserve bid: in his determination that only the very best and most deserving would win the bike, Panterello had declared there would be no winner if fewer than three hundred course points were assigned to the first place rider. In exchange, I was given to understand that he had grudgingly conceded that the sponsors could bring teams to the race, allowing them to choose the best rider for that day's course. Had it been otherwise, I would not have been allowed to ride in the English boy's place.

In a moment of retrospect offered by a clear stretch of street, I was offended that Khan hadn't asked me to ride for him from the start. It was true, perhaps, that as a Centurion I was somewhat more difficult to locate and draw into a plot than a speed-loving youth who could be found at any racetrack. But we were comrades, brothers-in-arms, and I would have gladly come at his call.

Of course, had I done so, it might be me with the broken leg and shattered ribs now lying in the hospital bed, with no one left to finish the race on Khan's behalf, for he could never hope to ride himself. His weight was too great even if one did not consider the inhuman strength that would undoubtedly wrench the handlebars and front wheel off the motorcycle at the first enthusiastic twitch of muscle. Regarded that way, it seemed the fates knew their business and should be left to it, as I was left to mine.

In my moments of reflection, the Englishman moved ahead of me, though not to a dangerous lead. The sun was high now, less than an hour from its zenith; we were meant to be finished with the race before the noon hour, or all who completed the course would be docked a certain number of points. The Englishman and I had only a little distance left, and those behind us would have to make haste, for it seemed our destination was *la Louvre*, where the police would certainly congregate once it was realized the finish line lay there. More than fifty riders had started with us today; I wondered briefly how many had begun yesterday only to be met with disappointing arrest after the morning's ride, and how many fewer might meet at the sunrise starting line on the following morning.

It did not now matter. I gunned the Indian and she leapt forward, making up the inches I had lost to the Englishman. Together we roared around street corners to alarmed shrieks and enthusiastic curses. Suddenly, though, we were in the clear: passersby had taken to the sidewalks and vehicles of all other manner had pulled aside, offering us no more traffic to dodge through. Relief and dismay pricked me in equal parts: I did not wish to see anyone accidentally harmed, and yet the thrill of darting through traffic, adjusting for its flow and for the unexpected gifts and difficulties it caused, was a not-inconsiderable part of the joy of riding. But in the last few hundred yards it seemed it would be only about the speed of our bikes and the skill of their drivers. Wheel and wheel, the Englishman and I raced onward, each of us grinning with violent intensity.

I prided myself on the quickness of my reflexes; anyone who uses her fists and wits for her living must. Yet it was the Englishman who sensed that something was once more amiss, and acted before I so much as saw what threatened us.

He thrust out his right arm, impacting my left with astonishing strength. A bloom of pain was muted by astonishment, and instant retaliation only foresworn by the need to twitch the Indian's handles into alignment again. But I was already off course, losing precious inches that would cost me everything in the race to the finish line. Moral outrage seized me, for I had not imagined my opponents would resort to such blatant cheating—

—and then horror drowned outrage as the Englishman's front wheel hit the oil slick I had not seen; the oil slick that he had saved me from, judging his own course already too set. I watched him, not the so-close finish line, in cold-bellied terror as he lost traction and slid at desperate speeds across gleaming oil. *Clear* oil, oil with the sharp sweet scent of kerosene, not the dark and easily visible stain or pungent scent of motor oil. We had not been meant to see it at all; only a fortunate ray of striking sun and the Englishman's quick wits had saved me from the fall he now took. And fall he did, terribly, with the weight of his speeding bike crushing one leg while the wildly spinning wheels threatened the other as he tried to kick away.

A match arced in the air, hardly visible in the bright light of day, and flames roared before *la Louvre.* The width of the oil slick became clear: it went on for many yards, farther than the Englishman's speed would carry him. Farther than speed would carry even his bike, which he kicked free of and which carried on, its weight helping it slide as much as it hindered it. The Englishman, less weighty, slowed more quickly and came to his feet just as the inferno reached him, his face set with nothing but raging determination to survive.

I could not stop. I could not stop in time: the finish was so near and my speed so great that even as I slammed a foot down to pivot the Indian around, even as I wrested the handlebars sharply to the side to spin her, I crossed the line in record time, albeit facing the wrong direction.

The whole of the oil slick was alight already, the Englishman barely visible in the licking orange heat. I crushed my eyes closed for an instant, envisioning what I must do. Then, never one to take my eye off the target, I returned my gaze to the Englishman, begged a favor from the Fates, and plunged into the flames.

16

The heat was tremendous, snatching greedily at my clothes, my skin. Khan's silken colors, pinned to my leather jacket, blazed and clung to the coat; it would burn through in moments, if I could not escape the fire and fling myself to cooling earth. I was grateful beyond reason that I wore leather—the helmet, the goggles, the gloves and jodhpurs, the boots that were my usual footwear—for without all of those things my desperate rescue attempt would be dashed before it even began.

Knowing the oil lay beneath me was perhaps half the battle; it could be accounted for, adapted to. Strangely, the fire offered some assistance: in places it had already burned away the fuel, leaving drier patches of stonework beneath my tires. But knowing was not enough, not with flames licking what skin was bared to it; not with the Indian's weight wobbling and trying to spin out of control as I rushed through the gates of hell to save an innocent man.

He had not moved, when I reached him, as if he realized that I came for him and that I could too easily lose him in the flames should he leave his post. The nerve of the man, to be able to stand within the fire...! I counted myself amongst the bold, but did not know that I could have been so stalwart at the heart of an inferno. And yet there he stood, waiting. I even thought that I saw his lips shape numbers, as if he had counted the seconds until my arrival, and then, expecting me, moved as fluidly and certainly as any Centurion might have: a long leg swung out and over the Indian's tail, and he was with me, face buried against my shoulder, arms knotted around my waist as we rode through the flames. With his added weight, the Indian was more stable, and in no time we shot free of the fiery lake.

Only then did the Indian betray us, finding a final unexpected splatter of oil that caught its front wheel and sent us flying. The earth was up and the sky down, cloud-scattered blue and stone-patterned pavement entangled in a flail of leather-clad legs and elbows. We landed together with a crash; the Indian, largely unharmed, skittered to a stop some yards away, its back wheel whirling madly in the air.

For the space of three gasps, my opponent and savior lay atop me, both of us wide-eyed and stunned at our survival. Then, with two swift movements, he stripped from me my helmet and goggles, and flung his away as well.

A shock of golden hair fell forward to brush my forehead—that was how close we were, as close as lovers, and in the aftermath of rescue, equally intense. His deep-set eyes were vividly, sharply blue and his features bordered on the attractive side of ungainly: a too-large nose and a thin, expressive mouth that suddenly twitched in a smile and rendered him inexpressibly compelling. He spoke with the cultured vowels of an educated Englishman. "My thanks, good woman. I hope that someday I might be able to return the favor."

He cast one look away from us, seeming to assess some situation there, then sprang upward as though the flame had given him new vigor. He offered me a hand; I took it and he pulled me to my feet, his gaze locked on mine. "You will, I think, know where to find me should such an occasion arise. Until then, goodbye."

He strode away—across the finish line!—and left me gaping at the edge of a pool of flame, my heart beating wildly in my chest and my feet commanding me to move, to follow him, as I had never been compelled to follow anyone in my life. I knew the signs of instant infatuation; these were not those, though they were not unlike that delightful sensation. I also knew the strength of attraction in the aftermath of fear, but that was not this either. I believed that, had I seen him on the street and locked eyes with him, I would have been equally impelled by a desire to be near the fire that burned within that man, to warm my hand at it, and, I knew with raw and startling simplicity, to die in it if he should so require.

"Madame Stone!" Reporters—reporters who

ought not have been there, given the race's secrecy and illegality, but reporters who were none-the-less there, and whom, it now seemed, the English motor-cyclist had seen and intended to avoid—reporters swarmed me, showing the press's usual idiotic lack of fear for dangers such as the still-burning fire beside us, and thrust cameras into my face. "Madame Stone," came their shouts, "Madame Stone, how does it feel to have saved TE Lawrence's life? Tell us, Madame Stone, did you know it was Lawrence when you went into the fire? Madame Stone, are you intimate with Lawrence—?"

Their questions faded into insignificance as I turned, stunned, to watch one of the most famous men of my lifetime hasten away from the notoriety he had never wanted to pursue. He looked back once, not at the reporters, but directly at me, and I felt again the overwhelming strength of his presence as he offered the briefest wink and smile, then disappeared so swiftly into the crowd that even his height and astonishing persona were swallowed by it. It was all I could do to not run after him myself, and had my attention not been drawn elsewhere in just that moment, I might well have done.

But a new roar silenced the reporters, the crowds, even my own racing thoughts, and like those around me, I sought it eagerly, and finally saw the beast we were all racing for.

My breath caught in admiration. Signor Panterello had approached its design with innovation and an eye for streamlining. Its front fender flared as it approached the body, creating an elegant flow to guide rushing air; in fact, everything about its shape was intended to let air spill past easily. The engine was encased, with intake valves and pipes to ensure it would not overheat, and the paint—if it was paint; somehow it seemed to be the metal itself—was two-toned, black with bold white lines that lent themselves to the idea of speed. A low, deeply angled windshield had been added, creating a space in which a smaller rider could huddle, reducing wind sheer even further. A black leather seat nestled at the machine's waist, and nestled in that seat was Josephine Baker, adorned in black and white herself, as if she had always meant to ride Panterello's motorcycle.

I could not help myself. After the race, after the fire, after encountering Lawrence of Arabia himself in such a way, discovering Josephine—who was meant to be hiding—jauntily displayed atop the extraordinary motorcycle was more than I could bear straight-faced. I burst into laughter, glanced at her confident pose again, and laughed until the tears came.

I could not recall meeting in two years two people whose very presence was as intense as the fire I had just come through, and yet now in two days I had met two such people. I wished dearly that Lawrence had not so swiftly absconded, for I might have liked to see the world shift and tilt on its axis, trying to accommo-date the weight of those two meeting, but it was not to be. Instead, feeling as though my own world had taken on an unexpected shift and tilt, I was allowed through the crowd of reporters who now turned their attention to the new notorious star amongst them.

She was accompanied, I eventually saw, by a slight and swarthy man whose beard could be bettered by a teenage boy. He had a nervous look about him, and stroked one hand over the motorcycle's chassis as if reassuring it—or perhaps himself. Signor Panterello, I presumed; his evident tension ratcheted as I approached, then suddenly soothed away as Josephine flung a glad hand toward me and caroled, "Amelia! What a race! Amelia, we have to find a zeppelin before tomorrow so I can watch the entire thing from above. I've never seen anything like it, my darling! You were fearless! And the fire, Amelia! My God, how could you ever dare?" She drew me into her arms for a fierce and wonderful embrace. I was only distantly aware of the cameras clicking and clattering around us as she set me back again and turned, as if presenting a special and prized possession, to Signor Panterello.

"Monsieur, the winner of your race today, Amelia Stone. Amelia, Monsieur Antonio Panterello. Didn't I tell you that Amelia would win the day, Mister Panterello? Though I thought that fella there at the end—but Amelia had it in the bag all along! And he didn't even stop to say thanks, the yellow-bellied coward!"

Either Josephine did not know whom I had taken from the fire, or—I suspected—she preferred not to know, so that attention might be entirely upon herself. I had read Lawrence's biography and believed he might have been happiest left in Arabia to do great things without outside notice, so I did not try to dissuade her, only took Panterello's hand in a firm grip and was unsurprised that, though he looked like a wet fish, his handshake was solid and strong. "Signor. Yours is the most beautiful motorcycle I have ever seen."

Pleasure could not make him handsome, but it gave him some life. "*Gratzie*, madame. Your riding today was, how do they say, exemplary, and your speed in the flame's aftermath—Signor Lawrence owes you his life."

Curiosity piqued within me. "You knew it was he who rode?"

"Madame, motorcycle *aficionados* have come from all the world over to try their hand for my creation, and Signor Lawrence numbers himself amongst such lovers. I know many of the riders here personally, and more by sight. I had even expected you."

"*Moi?* Surely I am not well known—"

"*La Stringfield de France,* I believe they say, though it is known that you, like Signora Stringfield, travel everywhere."

"I had no idea you were famous, Amelia." Josephine, with a sparkling smile, tucked her arm in mine. "I've been talking with Mister Panterello while you raced. These accidents, Amelia—!"

"They are no accidents. Pools of kerosene do not simply appear before the Louvre—" Finally I looked to that grand museum, having not thought to worry that it might have seen damage. It had not; nor was it much in the way of a finishing line, for smoking oil still lingered in its foreground and masses of crowds littered the space racers were intended to come through. Now that I thought to listen, I could hear the remaining competitors as they approached, and wondered at their slowness, given the terrible length of time since Lawrence and I had first arrived.

A glance at the sky sent a shiver of surprise and confusion down my spine: it had, *en vérité*, been a scant five minutes since that wreck of a showdown had begun. And a wreck it had been: with a sudden jolt I remembered my Indian, to which I had given no thought since the moment my eyes had met Lawrence's. But it was nearby, righted by motorcycle lovers who inspected it and, when my gaze found their own, reassured me with nods and smiles. My shoulders sagged and I gathered my thoughts before speaking again. "Nor do ropes spring of their own volition at the ends of bridges," I continued. "Signor Panterello, there were desperate injuries yesterday, too. Who are your enemies? Why attack the race rather than you, assuming, as I must, that they want the prototype?"

Panterello's smile was thin. "Because without me, the machine is useless. They must assure they win the race and my services along with it. There is a reason, Signora Stone, that I have made this difficult to win. As for my enemies—"

Before he could say more, the Italian rider, with Bessie Stringfield hot on his tail, appeared on the stretch to roar across the finish line in third and fourth places. The Italian swung off his bike almost before it had stopped and began pushing his way through the crowd toward us. Face ashen with alarm at their arrival, Panterello seized my arm and whispered, "I beg of you, Signora Stone, only take me to safety and I shall explain all."

17

"Amelia." My mother spoke with muted surprise, concern and curiosity all in the single word, though her smile and, perhaps to untrained ears, her voice offered nothing but pleasant delight as she opened her door to my extraordinary little band of companions.

My own smile was genuinely happy, though I too had certain concerns, foremost among them for her health. She was slimmer than she had been last we visited, her skin seeming to stretch more thinly over her magnificent bone structure than ever before. She was dressed beautifully; she always was in the height of fashion, and even a plain housedress looked elegant on her long frame.

I stepped into her apartment, embraced her and kissed her cheeks, then invited my companions in behind me. Though no other eyes would be so well trained as to see it, I knew spots of color appeared on my mother's dark cheeks as Josephine Baker stepped over her threshold. "*Maman, mes amis,* Josephine and Antonio. *Mes amis, ma mère,* Estelle Stone."

Signor Panterello had not the ease or charm that one might hope upon making introductions, but Josephine more than made up for it by clasping Maman's hands and drawing them upward until they rested over Josephine's own heart. "Madame Stone, *enchantée de faire votre connaissance.* I've wanted to meet you from the moment Amelia burst into my life. *Merci* for taking us in during our hour of need."

Maman's eyes strayed to mine and I saw the barest hint of laughter there, though she was nothing but grace and sweetness as she smiled at Josephine. "Any friend of Amelia's, Madame Baker. I'm overwhelmed to have you in my humble home."

"Nonsense," Josephine proclaimed. "There's nothing humble about a house built with love." She released Maman's hands and gave herself permission to examine the premises, while Panterello lingered uncomfortably near the door until Maman offered him a place to sit. Even then, he looked askance at me, but I gestured for him to do so.

"We have been half the afternoon getting here secretively, signor. The motorcycle is well hidden in the garage below, and my friend Professor Khan will see that it goes into even better hiding. Please, let me get you some tea and then you must share your story, for I admit to untoward curiosity."

"No!" Panterello twitched so violently I paused on my way to the kitchen to peer at him in consternation. "No, it's bad enough to have it out of my sight in the garage, signora. I can't allow someone else to take it away. My patents—"

"Are safe in Khan's hands," I assured him. "He has the ethical core of a saint; no matter how curious he might be, he will not examine your machine until I've won it for him fairly." I was not actually sure this was true, but I spoke with conviction.

Conviction that did nothing to assure Panterello, it seemed. He twitched to his feet again, miserable with discomfort. "No. I must insist, no. In fact, I'd better go down to it. I don't like leaving it alone."

"Might there be a discreet way to bring it into the apartment?" my mother wondered with gentle curiosity, to all of our surprise.

"It is a five hundred pound machine," Panterello said with stiff offense. "I don't believe so, madame."

"I could cause a distraction," Josephine offered with rather more enthusiasm at the prospect than I might have hoped, and refused to be quelled when I gave her a despairing glare.

"The purpose of bringing you to Maman's apartment, Josephine, is that no one will know where you are. Ridding ourselves of the reporters at the Louvre was ordeal enough. Displaying yourself on the street now will do us no good at all. No one will make off with the machine, signor; no one knows that it is here. Now, please, your story, while I make the tea."

Even Josephine sat down then, not, I thought, because she was happy to cede the limelight, but because she sought in Panterello's tale an emotional connection she could later use to her best advantage on stage. Given that his sniveling and weak persona was wholly at odds with her own boldness and strength, for her to achieve his likeness in a performance would be skill indeed. I could not say which of them I was more interested in as his tale began.

"I am from Arcore." Panterello announced this as though he expected it to resonate, and for me, it did: Arcore was the town whence Giuseppe Gilera came, he who had first built Italian motorcycles for racing and whose patents had grown into one of Italy's most famous motorcycle brands. Satisfied with my nod of acknowledgment, Panterello continued directly, speaking only to me; Maman and Josephine might have been window dressing, or storefront mannequins, for all his interest in them. "You understand my interest in building—and improving upon!—motorcycles stems from childhood, then. I worked directly with Gilera for a time."

"I would think he would be loathe to let you go, from the prototype below."

Panterello's mouth turned downward. "You would think, but he proved a jealous master, signora. He wanted to take claim for my advancements, while offering to share neither credit nor cash."

As in any starkly competitive field, this was not surprising, if, as always, disappointing. I nodded and he carried on. "So I stole my own designs and left. He claims they're his, because I developed them while working for him, but I worked on *his* designs at the factory, signora. The machine below I designed entirely on my own, developing the metals, the compact engine, the new look. No one can prove otherwise."

"Is it Gilera who is after you, then? Trying to retrieve his—that is to say, the designs he perceives as his?" I had no intention of discussing the particulars of legality, for I did not much care if the hours had been Gilera's or Panterello's own: the radical design departure was sufficient, in my uninformed opinion, to make the project entirely Panterello's own, regardless of whose time it had been designed on.

"If only. It's possible he and I could settle it like reasonable men." Panterello's tone suggested otherwise, but once more, that was not my battle to fight. I spread my hands in expectation, asking for elucidation, and my mother rose to serve tea as Panterello went on. "Mussolini is my problem."

He might have struck a bell, the silence that reverberated after his words was so loud and ringing. Not one of us—not myself, jaw agape, not my mother, frozen with tea in midstream, not Josephine, who had never yet been without words—could speak after that astounding confession. Panterello was not, to my mind's most wild imaginings, a man whose problems could be laid at the Italian dictator's feet.

Finally the tea spilled over onto the plate. Maman jolted, righting the kettle, and this ordinary action brought life back to all of us. "The prototype," I said finally, foolishly, as Maman poured us all tea and offered small cakes she had baked herself. I tasted one; it was light and delicious and reminded me, inevitably, of the hard lumps I had baked as a child.

Despite the topic at hand, Maman and I shared a small smile before I returned to the conversation with Panterello. "He wants it. If its speed, its lightness, its strength are not exaggerated—"

Panterello, offended, snapped, "They aren't."

"—then your motorcycles would be an invaluable resource to his ambitions." It made sense after all, once the ice of astonishment had fallen away from me. "Have you—have you fled Italy, then, signor?"

"Fled and am in search of funding from a source that will not then steal my patents and sell them to the highest bidder. Hence the reason for this race, signora: the buy-in is considerable, never mind the hopes I have for appropriate sponsorship. But Mussolini is reluctant to let the patents go." Panterello was still thin and weak, but he at least had the courage of his convictions; that, I had to admire him for. "Ten riders yesterday crossed the finish line in good enough time to earn a century of points or more, putting them in the lead after the first day. It is possible to gain ground on the second and third days, but easier, of course, if the previous days' riders are...indisposed. I suspect a man in the top fifteen of having done harm to Mister Khan's first rider, for example, in hopes of improving his own place today. As he did."

"And that rider was...?" I had my suspicions, but would not voice them myself; this was not my tale to tell.

"Bernardo Viccini. The Italian who was so very nearly strung up in today's race."

A certain worry suddenly took root in my gut.

"Signor. I must ask. Are you responsible for the accidents today?"

Shame flooded his thin face. "The rope, I will confess to. The flames, no. You must believe me, signora, I wished only to slow him should he take the lead. I would never resort to burning a man, even for the safety of my patents. And had you not been there today, if I had been in any way responsible for *that* man's death, even by simply sponsoring this race——!"

Maman's curious gaze flickered to mine, but I shook my head ever so slightly; there would be time for that story later, when I could share undistracted the extraordinary presence I'd encountered, for such a narration required full and rapt attention. I looked back upon Panterello with more censure than before, though. "Even if he escaped unscathed, Bessie Stringfield was as caught by your trap as the Italian, and her loss would have been as great."

My mother's eyes widened again at that name, but Panterello looked as though he meant to argue. I quelled him with a glare, and only after a judicious sip of tea did he dare to speak again. "Signora Stone, I'll do anything to keep my machines out of Mussolini's hands. You must help me, signora. You must win tomorrow's race, for all of us."

18

Panterello's plea lingered as I took my seat in the opera house a few hours later. I had every intention of fulfilling it, but Josephine came first—Josephine and *le Monstre*. At least the race was tomorrow, a daylight event; it could not, by its very nature, interfere with the activities at the opera house.

If the opera house had been filled the night before, it was beyond capacity now; that much was clear from my box seat. The story of the previous night's Nazi incursion had spread like wildfire, and not a soul in Paris wished to miss the riveting follow-up performance—or whatever deviations from the script might manifest.

I cared for it not at all. Had I my druthers, Josephine would be safely ensconced far away from dangers offered by Nazis and green-eyed monsters both. I was not, though, to have my way; even if Josephine had not been the consummate professional, determined that the show must go on, she was also the surest way I had of drawing *le Monstre* out. It would be nearly two weeks before *Queen of the Nile*'s run ended, and I did not expect to see him before the final performance, but neither could I allow Josephine to go unattended each night as she risked herself on the stage. To my reckoning, she would carry the crowds to new heights with each show, working them toward a frenzy that would culminate on closing night. The only way to intensify the experience any more would be to have the same audience night after night. Of course, the less fortunate would find themselves without tickets, should a wealthy patron wish to see the performance again and again. Perhaps Josephine *would* be casting her spell on the same people every night.

I did not watch the patrons; instead I studied the ceilings, the floors, the very seats themselves. In my youth, *le Monstre* had made use of his pig-iron chairs to extract emotion, but he could surely not have so crude a plan in place for the opera house. Neither, though, did I think he could pluck emotion out of thin air; certainly some kind of conduit must be necessary, and I had only to find it. With an absent *désolée* to my fellow box-mates, I crouched and examined the undersides of the seats there and investigated the arms. Nothing seemed untoward—nothing save me, crawling about on the floor in my jodhpurs and leather jacket, because I had no intention of facing a second night of histrionics in an evening gown—and I returned to my seat with a frown. My greatest talents lay in fisticuffs and gunplay, not investigative work. I would return here tomorrow in daylight with Khan and together we would take the opera house apart, if necessary, to discover *le Monstre*'s secrets.

Until then, I allowed myself to become entranced by the show. I imagined, knowing the source of Baker's tremendous presence—and knowing that the crown she wore tonight was a replica made by Khan's deft hands—that her second performance as Cleopatra would not take me in the same way the first had.

I was wrong, *naturellement*, so wrong as to make me weep. Perhaps knowing that she did *not* wear the true crown brought out the greatest of her talent and presence, but I thought not: Hatshepsut's crown only gilded Josephine's lily. Long before the curtain fell for the interval, I—and I dared say everyone else in the theatre—would have done anything she asked, and it was with a tremendous sigh that I finally tore my eyes from the stage as the lights came up.

Had a spotlight swung to illuminate the box across from me, I could not have seen it more clearly. Someone—two someones!—had slipped into that box after the performance had begun, and I had noticed them no more than anyone else. But now I saw them, a man and a woman, sitting together with expressions as rapt as mine.

She was the Nazi commander with whom I had wrestled the night before: petite, dark haired, wearing a gown of changeable green silk that shimmered and caught with every breath. A white stole wrapped her shoulders, softening her considerably from the warrior of the night before, but there could be no doubt of it.

At her side sat my beloved angel, my Paul-Gabriel, *le Monstre aux Yeux Verts.*

In profile, as I saw him, he was perfect, his beauty untouched by fire. He wore black with touches of green: green shot silk, as Commander Knapp wore. His hair touched his collar, unfashionably long, and even across the distance I saw the shape of a mask lining his nose.

He must have felt the weight of my gaze; surely it had weight, like an anchor pulling us both down to depths whence there was no return. He looked at me suddenly, far too suddenly for me to look away, and I saw the fire in his green eyes, still fierce and brilliant despite the years, across the intervening space. But the entirety of the right side of his face was hidden beneath pitted grey metal: pig-metal, the same rough-cast stuff he had made his dastardly chairs from.

I shuddered to think of the damage done to that beautiful face, though my horror was tempered by the memory of Maman's slack jaw and dull eyes; it had taken her months to recover from *le Monstre*'s ministrations, and my father had only survived, not lived, for years before slipping emotionlessly into the grave. Some of Maman's reclaimed passion had gone with him; she was an entirely quieter person than she had been in my youth. Remembering that, I was able to cast aside my pity for Paul-Gabriel Laval and remember him only as *le Monstre.*

But I could still read him, whether I wanted that

skill or not. He moved twice, both times so minimally as to be hardly visible. The first was a nod of acknowledgment: he saw and remembered me as clearly as I saw and remembered him. The second was a tip of his head: an invitation to speak in the lobby.

I wished, with fierce, youthful pride and stupidity, that I had worn a gown, and I stood to meet my enemy on the field of his choice.

19

H ad it been anywhere else, anyone else, I should
have said that it was only my imagination that
opened a pathway between *le Monstre* and myself as
we came our separate ways down opposite staircases
within the opera house. Hundreds of people
enthralled by a stunning performance could not be so
aware of their surroundings as to part, as had the Red
Sea for Moses, to allow three people unimpeded
passage.

Three, because Commander Knapp was on *le
Monstre*'s arm as they came down their sweeping stair-
case. I had only myself as accompaniment, but then, I
was the only one at the *Opéra* dressed as I was;
perhaps my thick leather boots and beaten white shirt
beneath a battered leather jacket were enough to split
the seas for my own part, and *le Monstre*'s mask was
enough to send anyone a step backward. The cunning
thing was that many of them moved without seeming

to see him, as if he had an aura of warning about him.

We met alone in a crowd, in an empty circle greater than my own doubled arm span. Conversations rose and fell, loudest from those closest to us, who strove to prove their disinterest with false joviality. *Le Monstre* carried a walking stick now, silver-headed black wood, and wore black leather gloves over hands I had once known as elegant. I could not help but look and wonder, and was taken aback when he spoke.

"It seems you will have no need for my cloak tonight, Amélie. You are warmly dressed now."

His scent, the weight of his fine cloak, the lingering heat of his body: they came back to me as if I had donned that cloak only yesterday, but I would not let such sentiment show. "I am not here to be charmed or romanced, *Monstre.*" He flinched to hear that name from my lips, and the satisfaction of leaving a palpable mark warmed me more than any memory or cloak might do. "I will keep Madame Baker from your clutches. I will not let you have another one."

Mademoiselle Knapp breathed in at that, a short and sharp sound that brought my attention to her. Her eyes, I could see now, were green too, though not the same vivid green that *le Monstre*'s were. There was barely controlled fear in those eyes, and a spark of hope that had, I thought, been born from my bold words.

Convictions fell into place. I knew already that *le Monstre* had trucked with fascists in the past; that this girl was his pawn in attempting to retrieve the crown should it fall into Nazi clutches suddenly seemed clear. That explained, without a doubt, how she had gained commander ranking; a favor from one monster to another.

"I will not let you have any innocent," I said to *le Monstre*, but the words were a promise and an offer to Knapp. The faintest flicker pulled at her lips, and her wide eyes remained intent on mine.

Le Monstre smiled, though it seemed to stretch his mouth painfully. "Indeed. Let me introduce you to Kiera, then. The poor child is Irish and German in extraction; she was born fighting and will, I suppose, go to the grave that way. Kiera, this is...Amelia Stone. I loved her once."

"*Non*. That was not love, but use and abuse. I was a fool to ever believe it."

"*Non*," *le Monstre* echoed softly, and the sure ground I stood on shifted beneath my feet. "I was a fool to abuse you, Amélie. I was a fool to take from you what I did, and to shatter what we had together in the way I did. I learned much in the fire, *ma chérie*. I have hoped all these years to see you again, that I might say I was sorry."

My stomach twisted with disbelief and rage. "Sorry? *Sorry*, Gabriel? *Sorry* for destroying my family, for murdering my father and reducing my mother to a shell of herself? *Non, mon ami*," and I spat the word *friend* with all the contempt I could muster, "you do not get to be *sorry* for that. I meant to kill you that night and I only regret that I failed."

"I regret," *le Monstre* said with sonorous clarity, "much."

Again, Knapp— *Non*; I would think of her as Kiera, a softer and gentler name that suited the tremble that again shivered over her skin. She had fought me, perhaps, but I would have done no less in the days that Paul-Gabriel Laval held me in his thrall. She had fought and she had failed: I had escaped with the crown, and I knew too well the price of failing *le Monstre*. My parents had paid that price and, through them, so had I. But it was no easy thing to escape his grasp, and few could claim the incentive I had had. If she could not fight her way free, then I would fight my way in, and rescue her from him. "Regret all you like," I said through bared teeth, "but expect only a few short days in which to revel in those regrets. I will not allow you to walk away again."

Le Monstre's gaze slid sideways to alight on Kiera. She could not see it, but I could: the challenge, the amusement. "Not even if I have something you value to trade?"

The threat hung between us like a darkness, thickening the air and engendering rage in my throat. But then as if the miasma was real, *le Monstre* brushed it aside with a stiff motion of his right hand. "*Non*," he said more gently. "It is hard, Amélie, not to be fed by your anger. Not to play to it, as I once would have. I am no longer the man you remember. My regrets are real, as is my—"

"Pain?" I said, when it seemed he would not.

"It is constant." With small, controlled actions, he

lifted both hands to his head, and there unhooked some sly fastener that freed the pig-iron mask from his face.

The crowd encircling us could not ignore that, no matter how hard they tried. Nor could I, and my breath rushed out as did all of theirs: a circle of silence began with me and rippled across the whole of the opera house's lobby, broken only by the faint hiss and swish of silk and satin brushing against itself as patrons turned to look.

It did not matter to him that they looked; it only mattered that I did, and—like them—I could not look away. Fire had ravaged his features and the healing had not been kind. On the cheek he showed to the world, the scars were faint and silvery. With the mask full removed, I could see that he must have protected his face with his arms: that was the width of the barely-scarred skin, narrowing as it crossed his face toward the temple. Around it, red weeping scars and lumps of flesh were left where beauty had once reigned. His hair was not burned away, though I suspected a wig rather than his scalp having gone unscathed. The revelation of bone-deep lashes across his face was more than enough; he did not need to show how the fire had bit into his skull as well.

Kiera, who must have seen his true face before, kept hers averted; around me, soft gasps and louder cries of horror sounded as men and women alike turned away from the ruin of an angel's gaze. Only I, who had condemned him to this, could not allow myself to look away, much as I might wish to.

Unmasked, his eyes were depthless and full of stories. I might have expected rage and hatred; instead I saw compassion and regret, an awareness of tragedy. I could not read those things on his twisted features, but nor could I read anything else: it was all in his eyes, and too much of it at that. He did not ask for forgiveness with that quiet pained gaze; instead, he offered it, and like a drowning man reaching for land, I wanted to claw at it.

I could not look away, but I could steel myself: stiffen my belly and tighten my thighs and proclaim *non!* within the confines of my own thoughts. I did not regret, *could* not regret, although in my peace of mind I had thought and wished him dead, not burned and in everlasting pain. I was not, I hoped, that cruel, even toward *le Monstre* who had so shattered my own life. "I do not need your forgiveness, Monsieur Laval. I do not want it."

Even as I spoke I knew my own words for a lie; no one who called herself human could look on that ruined face and not wish that somehow the tortured soul within might find it possible to forgive the one who had so disfigured him. But he lowered his gaze, accepting what I said before lifting his eyes, still so richly green, to mine again. "And if I were to beg yours?"

Seventeen years. The span of my life, doubled since I had last seen this man. My mother, long since recovered; my father, long since dead. My choices now could not affect them, though I did not want to forgive him, even with a lifetime between us. Perhaps my hatred should have run its course in that time, but it bubbled deep within me, bound inextricably with the love I had once had for this man.

And yet I had done him as much lasting harm; perhaps more, as my mother's pain had faded and my father's ended, while Paul-Gabriel Laval lived in eternal torment. I could only believe the regret in his eyes, and I could not deny the awareness within them that he had greatly been the orchestrator of his own dreadful fate. Filled with shame, I was finally forced to avert my gaze.

When I did, *le Monstre* replaced the mask using the same small, controlled actions with which he had removed it. "It is too much to ask," he said then. "I would not cause you more pain, Amélie; I have offered you enough of that in this lifetime. *Merci, ma chérie,* for speaking with me. That is a gift I cannot repay.

"Kiera," he said and drew her away, back up the stairs. The crowd opened for them again, leaving me to stand alone in a circle of awe and fear until finally the lights dimmed to announce the next act.

20

For all of Josephine's beauty, I could not watch her in the second half of her performance. My attention strayed time and again to *le Monstre* and to his companion, who looked so frail and young at his side. Her frailty was an illusion; that I knew, having been the recipient of more than one blow from her small fists, but I could not shake the idea of it, knowing as I did how easy it was to fall under Paul-Gabriel Laval's spell. More than once I caught her looking my way in turn, as if I were a kindred spirit, perhaps one of a few truly able to understand her precarious position.

Le Monstre himself never looked my way, though I did not know what measure of willpower that cost him. It may have been none at all: Josephine may well have commanded the entirety of his attention without fail. She was, after all, the reason we were all here. It was only a shame that I could not properly enjoy the richness of the show. Even her final aria passed me by: the sudden swell of ovation and the roar of admiring voices took me by surprise.

It happened, though, that because of that surprise, it was myself alone whose attention was drawn not to the stage at Josephine's moment of triumph, but rather to the audience, who stood before their seats as one, waving, cheering, clapping, shouting —but not moving, and yet there were men in the aisles, sweeping toward the stage with far less subtlety than the fascist incursion of the night before.

Uniformed police, led by a man with a captain's ranking on his hat, charged through the theatre, making rings around the seating sections with their bodies, the better to keep barely aware patrons confined. Their protests began to rise only as police blocked their view of the stage, but redoubled as they realized they were reined in. Excitement, rather than anger, seemed the emotion at hand; this was, to the theatre-goers, precisely the encore they had hoped for to the previous night's performance. Shrill voices exchanged theories as women clutched each others' arms and men puffed up to establish themselves as persons of authority. Had I not suspected the police's motivations, I might have smiled at the crowds; but my focus was not on them, but on my old rival, the green-eyed monster.

He alone remained focused on the stage, where, at a glance, I saw Josephine standing in pique, with arms akimbo and her fine features caught between aggravation and amusement: surely no other diva had had *two* performances interrupted in such outrageous ways. It would sell papers, and that was publicity better than money could buy. Assured that she was well—if moderately infuriated—I looked back to *le Monstre* with such will in my gaze that it seemed he tore his attention from Josephine under a compulsion. It was not a quick thing, the finding of my gaze with his own, but when he did he offered that terrible, twisted smile before he spoke.

I could not, in truth, have heard him, and yet I saw his lips shape the words and heard them whispered in my ear: Je t'adore, Amélie, but you should never have returned to Paris. Most of all, you should never have interfered with Josephine Baker.

No sooner had this little warning faded than a hand landed firmly on my shoulder. Suspecting foul play, I instantly came to my feet, catching the wrist of my assailant and twisting it as I turned.

To my dismay, it was a small, balding man with a pinched expression beneath his glasses whom I had in my grip and had driven to his knees—Robert Langeron, Prefect of police. I released him swiftly and yet too late: he came back to standing, his face burgundy with anger, and snarled, "Madame Stone, I name you a collaborator with Nazis and a threat to the peace of *la Ville-Lumière*. You are under arrest as an enemy of the state!"

By this time every eye in the theatre was on me: I could feel the curious gazes prickling my spine. A palpable excitement hovered in the air, as if the flimsiest of excuses was all that would be necessary for chaos to break loose. Bearing this in mind, I drew a slow breath and spoke clearly as I raised my hands to shoulder level. "Prefect Langeron, *pardonnez-moi* my rudeness in seizing you. Had I known it was your august self I should never have reacted in such a way."

Though I knew it for puerile drivel, a touch of his florid coloring faded at that. I offered a winsome smile, wishing again that I wore an opera gown; innocence was more easily feigned in elegant clothing than in duds that had clearly already seen a fight or two—or more—in their time. Still, unless Professor Khan was to develop a time machine whilst fiddling with other sciences, I would have to keep the cards I had dealt myself, and took comfort in knowing that at least I had freedom of motion in my fighting gear.

But a fight was the last thing I should engage in here. I had already undermined Langeron with my decisive response to his approach; now it was necessary to be agreeable and respect his authority above all else, at least while we remained in public. To do otherwise would be to invite the certainty of arrest and face no chance for extradition until it was far too late for Josephine and Kiera both. "*Bien sûr,* this must only be a misunderstanding, but I will go with you gladly, Prefect, to sort it out. Your duties as the protector of this city are paramount."

I could barely contain a sigh of relief as his anger faded under the onslaught of my sniveling admiration; had he retained ill humor I did not know what I would have done, as I had already reached the limits of my ability to pander to his ego.

"We will go to the station," he announced loudly enough for the entire theatre to hear, but as luck—or devilish fate—would have it, I had an admirer in the audience.

"No!" that worthy bellowed. "That's Amelia Stone! I was here last night! I saw her fight the Nazis herself, holding a dozen of them off with a wooden sword and a whip! *Mon dieu,* the legs on that woman —!" Raucous laughter met the last exclamation, and while I would have far preferred him not to say such a thing, it would have been better had he said *only* that, and not flown in the face of the police chief's procla- mations. But he had, and other voices rose to carry the banner he had flown, supporting me, claiming that they, too, had seen my antics the evening before. Indeed, it seemed that there was nary a man or woman in the audience who had not attended the previous night's performance as well. Their enthu- siasm became pushy, but the rings of police held firm, not quite pushing back.

Langeron had become purple again, his accusa- tions of my faithlessness booming out over the crowd. They grew more virulent, ready to be part of the events surrounding Madame Baker, and I, concerned for their safety, cried out, "Fear not, fellow citizens! We all must realize this is a misunderstanding and best concluded out of the public eye by such wise minds as our Prefect! My faith in his decisions is—"

A strange contraption flew into the air from the

opposite side of the theatre, its little propeller buzzing so loudly that it silenced all of us into peering curiosity. No bigger than my doubled fists and quite round, it glittered dully, like pitted iron, and dangled from the wildly rattling propeller as if it might fall at any moment.

When its lower hemisphere dropped two inches, every living being in the theatre surged back, our gasps drowning out the propeller's song for an instant. Half a dozen tiny nozzles protruded from within the ball, which now proved to have a second smaller ball inside; this was what the nozzles were attached to.

A fine mist hissed from the nozzles and drifted down over the audience's upturned faces. Too late I realized its source and flung my arm over my face, taking care not to inhale the falling Emotion as I shouted, "Cover your faces! It's a trap! Don't breathe it in!"

My words were nearly incomprehensible; I shouted through leather and my elbow alike, muffling my voice so thoroughly I ought not have bothered. With a heartfelt apology, I turned to the man beside me and whipped his cummerbund away, wrapping it over my own face to make a more reliable filter. Even as I did so, more of *le Monstre*'s devilish contraptions flew into the air, releasing I knew not what, but could guess as the audience began to tear itself apart: Distillations of Panic, Rage, Disgust, and Hatred. Gentle women who had never thrown a fist in anger in their lives unleashed fury on one another; men who had bottled up the horrors of the Great War found sudden release in bashing into one another until some few of them fell to the floor sobbing.

"*Amelia Stone!*" cried a great and terrible voice; a voice I had once known to rise and fall in pleasure, to murmur laughter and love. Sick and saddened and enraged all at once, I saw *le Monstre* on his feet, a dreadful contempt and satisfaction on his stricken features as he thrust a gloved finger at me. "*Amelia Stone is your enemy!*"

As if experiencing a great release, the whole of the audience surged toward me, eager to rend what had been defined as evil. Those in my box clawed at me, fingers catching in the sturdy leather of my coat and reassuring me finally that I had chosen well with tonight's attire. It was with apologies that I struck each of my box-mates down, singular blows to the jaws that caused their eyes to swim in their heads before they fell back into the comfortable large chairs of the box seats.

Only the Prefect did not attack, though when I faced him again I finally saw what I should have noticed all along: the redness of his face, the blood-shot lines of his eyes, the heaving breast. He was not his own man, but rather *le Monstre*'s, poisoned already by some Distilled Emotion. Obedience, perhaps; I had tasted that one myself, and knew the futility of fighting against it. I clapped him on the shoulder and squeezed. "No hard feelings, *mon ami*; we have a common enemy, and I would beg that you listen to *my* orders, not his. Think for yourself, Prefect: that's all I ask of you." I did not know if such tactics would work, but Langeron's eyes cleared and I sagged with gratitude. "Cover your face, Prefect, for our enemy poisons the very air."

As I had done, he made free with another man's cummerbund whilst I returned my attention to the snarling crowds. The first of them were nearly upon me, agile and determined creatures climbing the very walls to have their chance at me. Loathe to do them harm, I scrambled backward, searching for a means of escape. Unfortunately, I was in the same box I had been seated in the night before, and its curtain ropes had not yet been replaced. My options were dire: retreat, which left Josephine to fend for herself, or throw myself into the fray and render as many of the opera patrons unconscious as swiftly and gently as I could.

Retreat was truly no option at all. Cursing *le Monstre*, cursing myself for allowing myself to be swayed by him even for a moment, I sprang forward, intent on fighting my way through to him.

Even as I leapt, so too did another: across the theatre, Kiera, in her delicate green gown, did as I had done the night before, and struck free a rope from her box seat curtains. In the same moment, she snaked a hand into *le Monstre*'s fine coat and withdrew a vial, which she dashed to the floor as she swung wildly across the theatre's stalls. To the patrons, she shrieked, "Fire! Run for your lives!"

A tremendous number of them did, pushing and shoving, climbing over seats, all with terror written on their features as they rushed for the doors. I wondered what emotion she had released. Fear, perhaps, or Belief? Whatever she had chosen was effective. More effective than her attempt at escaping *le Monstre*. She lost her grip on the rope and tumbled to the ground with a cry of desperation: "Amelia! Amelia, *save me*!"

21

I could no more deny that call than I might deny the pull of gravity itself. I did not think, only acted. I sprang over the climbing bodies of Parisian noblesse, sliding down the slippery silk of evening gowns and, I feared, exposing more of a lady or two than they might have wished, as my weight pulled at fabrics not intended for use as climbing materials. I landed in a sea of bodies, all of them reaching upward to rend me. Their waving hands provided a kind of rolling platform which I squirmed along until wiser minds prevailed and lowered both their hands and myself. Although still reluctant to damage ordinary, if bewitched, citizens, I also could not move forward without decisive action. I persevered until an enterprising soul struck at my makeshift mask; then, unwilling to risk inhaling the terrible Distillations that affected them, I permitted myself to unleash the skills I had obtained in fighting over the past decades.

A cleverly aimed blow could knock a large man to

the ground and take several of his compatriots with
him: that was my method of dealing with the horde.
Entangled they fell and all too often—for them if not
for me—entangled they remained, their normal
tendencies at war with the compulsions of *le Monstre*'s
potions. I did not know how long the philters might
remain effective, but had to trust that it would be too
long for me if I was not hasty.

Fortunately, Kiera was handy with her fists as well,
and far more profligate with them than I chose to be.
She appeared to be a whirlwind of green silk, devastating all who came near her. In moments, we stood
back to back in battle, struggling to work our way out
of the elixir-enraged crowd and, I slowly realized,
entirely failing. "There are too many! We'll never
make it out this way!"

"I can't go back to him!" A sob broke in the young
woman's throat, though she swallowed it back again
with as much courage as anyone might show. I sent a
quick look toward the box seats. *Le Monstre* stood alone
there, watching the chaos below him. Watching Kiera
and myself, his protégée and his tormenter, fighting
together. I saw the fury it caused him written in the
thin line of his lips and in the fierce grip he held on
his silver-headed cane. I saw too what else he
watched, and how it brought him pleasure even in the
midst of his rage: the audience's tide, swelling back
toward us. We were doomed if we could not retreat,
but there was nowhere to fall back to, nowhere—

Nowhere save a literal fall! I spun and seized
Kiera's arm, dragging her with me even as we strug-

gled against our opponents. "The orchestra pit! Enough fighting, let us—" I ducked as I spoke, and a broad-shouldered man punched the man behind me in the jaw. A roar of outrage rose up, Kiera and myself forgotten as fresh enemies were presented. We crawled through a tangle of legs, applying judicious elbows and once, memorably, a ferocious bite when a woman's heel landed sharply on Kiera's hand, pinning her in place. Kiera looked not at all apologetic as the woman above us howled, and we scurried onward, myself with less difficulty than Kiera, whose evening gown was not meant for crawling in.

My plan seemed shrewd enough until the very moment I boosted Kiera over the orchestra pit wall and swung down myself to face no fewer than thirty black-tuxedoed men with an awe-inspiring assortment of weapons, ranging from tubas to a violin of such lustre I knew at once it was aged beyond price. The fool swinging it at me lacked the sense to be grateful when I seized not it, but his arm, and wrested the violin away to hide it safely beneath the conductor's stand. This, *bien sûr*, brought me within range of the conductor's baton, which was a deadly enough thrusting tool without his sudden drop into a flawless fencing stance, the baton held as an *épée* might be. I briefly regretted having hidden the violin, but fell back on practicalities: the violinist had a bow as well. I leapt back as the conductor struck, offered a sincere apology to the first violin as I introduced my elbow to his temple at high velocity, and snatched his bow as he collapsed.

The bow had a few inches' reach on the baton; the conductor, a few inches reach on me. We were perfectly matched for distance, but mindless rage drove him whilst I remained in full command of my faculties. A slash; a parry; a thrust; a quick series to the four and the six, and then I stepped inside his guard, and with as much heartfelt apology as I had offered the violinist, I cracked the conductor across the jaw and stood above him as he fell.

The full component of the orchestral unit fell upon me then, and I knew despair, for thirty men was more than I could best when I started at the bottom of the pile. And yet I could not surrender; it was not in my nature, though as I kicked and struck at the weight of bodies, it seemed that there would be no shame in yielding if I must. My punches became weaker; the power of my thews, uninspiring. The press of bodies above me became overwhelming, and I wished only to succumb that I might rest a while. I had fought long enough and hard enough; it was all I had done with my life already, and we Centurions would live a hundred years or more. I writhed at the bottom of the orchestra pit, coiling my hands over my head and praying the world would slip away.

A blood-curdling scream rent the air, so tremendous that it lifted hairs on my nape even through the muffling burden of so many men. It rolled on and on, waves of sound that came from above with such vigor as to sway me from my stupor. I dared not imagine what tortures awakened a cry of that nature, but no creature on earth could be deserving of such terrible injustice. I unwound, not to fight but to catch a lapel and roll in what small space was afforded us: in a moment, the bassoon player was beneath me and I above him, the position compromising should anyone see it in our dark dance. A knee caught my cheek-bone, sparking stars and pain in equal parts, and in a fit of pique I seized the knee and began to crawl up the body it was attached to. Above me, the screams continued, urging me to move more swiftly, a task easily accomplished as I approached the top of the dog pile and fewer bodies pinned me down.

A man flew off the top of the pile as if he had grown wings, and in doing so, exposed my eyes to the brilliance of stage lights and a sight like nothing I had ever imagined: Cleopatra, Queen of the Nile, standing barefoot atop a roiling pile of tuxedoed men and screaming, screaming, screaming, whilst a green-gowned young lady seized a flautist and threw him away, too.

Josephine's screams stopped the moment I appeared. She bent, offering me a hand, and with great strength hauled me from the squirming hill of men. It all but dissolved beneath us, not quickly, but surely. In seconds we three stood back to back: *la grande dame, l'ingénue,* and myself, *la combattante.* I drew in a deep, preparatory breath, and in that moment realized my mask had been torn away and that a miasma hung around me: foul air, tasting of Despair. *Le Monstre*'s aim must have been flawless, to break a vial of the stuff near me as I fell beneath the oncoming orchestra. But now I knew the sensation of crumbling courage was not my own, and I could rally against it.

From the corner of my eye, I saw a man lift his hand to strike at Josephine, and flung myself between them. She was brave and her voice had brought me back from despair, but I did not believe her to be skilled in the ungentle arts of fisticuffs, and trembled at the thought of injury coming to her for her boldness in helping me.

But it was not my speed or determination that saved her. Rather, a cultured shout carried over the whole of the theatre with as much conviction as Josephine's singing; a shout from a voice I knew all too well.

"STOP!" cried *le Monstre*, and every soul in the theatre obeyed his command.

22

In that moment of stillness, new elixirs rained from the air. My first breath was of Relaxation; the next, of Calm. Knowing their potency, I retained my own fighting awareness, but the war-like atmosphere faded in seconds, rendering much of the Parisian upper class shaky and confused. In the audience, men and women began helping one another to their feet. Mumbled apologies filled the room, and the excitement of realizing that they had all participated in mad conflict was muted by the civilizing emotions drifting through the opera house.

I alone looked to *le Monstre*, but his gaze was for Josephine; I understood then, and almost sighed at the constancy of the man. He would not risk that voice, not while she had the crown; not when he had no one to replace her with. She had thrown herself into battle on my behalf, and so the battle had ended.

Well, I was not one to miss the opportunity. Turning, I shouted, "Prefect Langeron! *Lui là-bas! Voilà l'homme que vous cherchez!*" and pointed ferociously toward *le Monstre*.

En vérité, I half expected him to whisk his cloak up and disappear in a flash of smoke; when he did not, a soft laugh escaped me. I, too, had been taken in by *le Fantôme de l'Opéra* charade, just as Josephine had. But *non*; he only stood and watched as police swarmed his box and put him under arrest. I assured myself of Josephine and Kiera's safety—both were well, if wide-eyed with excitement—and excused myself to speak with Langeron, who, glowering, marched *le Monstre* down from his box seat via the stage and then through the theatre, making certain that he might be seen by all as a reprobate and a scoundrel. Men and women alike drew back as *le Monstre* passed them by, now feeling free to exhibit the revulsion and fear they had quelled in our meeting during the interlude.

Langeron bristled with defensiveness when I caught them just outside the theatre doors, as if afraid that I would name him a fool for having been a patsy in *le Monstre*'s schemes. But I spoke with a degree of truthfulness when I clasped his hand: "We have all been victims of this creature's nefarious plans, Prefect. Be wary of him even yet; he has controlled us before with elixirs of emotion, and will seize the chance again. For my own part, I will try not to draw your attention again."

"That would be..." Langeron searched for his phrasing long enough that I had plentiful time in which to supply my own guesses at what he might prefer to say. "...ideal," he finally concluded, more kindly than I might have anticipated. Then, with greater ferocity, he added, "Stay away from Madame Baker, Mademoiselle Stone. I will not have the jewel of Paris harmed on my watch."

Le Monstre locked eyes with me, and for an instant I thought humor danced in their green depths. "That, sir, is one thing I believe we can all agree upon. Amélie, I look forward to seeing you again."

"At your trial," I snapped, though even as the words flew free I knew them for wishful thinking. *Bien sûr*, he smiled, that tight and uncomfortable stretch of skin that was my legacy to him, the smile of a burning man, and a worry churned my belly as Langeron escorted him away. I could not help myself, and followed them through the doors of the opera house, watching as the chief gave *le Monstre* certain admissions for the ungainliness of his gait, even catching him when my fallen angel lost his footing and slipped.

The coldness of certainty swept me too late; as I rushed forward, a vial crashed at my feet, cool vapors rising to Stun me. My limbs became thick and useless, my heart a heavy dirge in my chest. I could not move, could hardly feel; it was much the same sensation as I had experienced in the horrifying moment of discovering that Paul-Gabriel and *le Monstre* were one and the same. Agony beat inside my breast, and though I saw, as if from a remove, that *le Monstre* waved another vial under the chief's nose and moments later shook his hand and walked free, I could do nothing to stop it, not even voice so much as a protest.

I knew not how long I remained there, but when at last the trance passed I stood alone on the wide curving stairs, the opera house quiet and dark behind me, and the streets empty of anything but starlight.

23

I sat on the opera house steps, allowing myself a moment of weariness. Again and again *le Monstre* thwarted me; again and again I left him free to harm others. There could be no more of this. Somehow I must find and stop him, even if the cost should be the highest there was. It had not occurred to me to go into the flames with him, seventeen years earlier; now I wondered if there was any other way to hold him in a trap.

But I could not allow myself to wallow. Rather, I must plan. I must be as conniving as he, and use what resources I had to hand. Khan was in Paris and others might be found in London or Berlin, for if I could not conquer *le Monstre* on my own, there was no shame in calling on my Centurion companions for help.

With a sigh, I stood again, dusting the seat of my jodhpurs as I did. To my surprise, someone spoke behind me: a sultry warm voice I knew well, but had not expected to hear in the darkness. "Amelia?"

"Josephine." I turned, unable to contain my smile, though in many ways there seemed little enough to smile about. "I thought you were gone."

"We waited for you." Clad all in black, she stepped free of the shadows beneath the opera house angels, and from my stance a few steps below her, I could almost fancy that their wings sprang from her own spine, unearthly creature that she was. I imagined that, could I only hold still enough, could I only wait for the right moment, she might spring upward into the sky, vast wings carrying her aloft, and that in a moment of grace she might extend her hands to me and I might fly with her, unburdened by the duties of the earthbound.

Instead, slowly, her few words caught up to me, and I said, "We?" dumbly as Kiera Knapp came from the shadows as well. Though I took care not to let it show too obviously, I felt my shoulders slump, and knew a thin, sour humor that I had imagined Josephine might be mine alone for some little window of time.

Kiera, though, did not simply step from the shadows: she flung herself from them and into my arms with such strength that I stumbled backward upon catching her. Like a child seeking reassurance, she buried her face in my neck and sobbed. Startled, I held her, then gently set her on her feet. "Easy, child. You are free of him now."

"How could you bear it?" The words burst from her like sobs, tears flowing over her cheeks. "How could you bear to face him again? How could you stand to offer me help, when I fought you with tooth and nail? How——"

"How," I interrupted, oddly charmed by her histrionics but mastered by curiosity, "did you survive that fall?"

The girl dashed tears from sad wet eyes to no avail; they rose and spilled over again as she sniffled. "A parachute beneath my overcoat, of course."

"*Bien sûr.*" Had I worn one, the whole of the previous night's activities—had it only been the night before? Too much had happened in so little time, though that was usually the way of things—had I worn a parachute, the whole of the plane fight might have been less alarming. No wonder she had seemed so fearless as we fought.

That, perhaps, and being spurred by the greater fear of returning to *le Monstre* a failure. I sighed, and Josephine took it as her cue to lead us. "Let's go to my apartment. I don't think Amelia's had any sleep in the past two days, and she should be at her best for the race tomorrow."

I groaned. "Josephine, we should go to—to my mother's, or my hotel. Not your own home, where he may be lurking in wait..."

"Amelia," Josephine said with strange gentleness, "do you really believe that if your *monstre* wanted to find me, going anywhere with you would hide me well enough? Let's at least be comfortable and eat a little something. After that you can argue about where we all should sleep."

My gaze sharpened on her expression, which

altered from pure innocence to sparkling wickedness inside a blink before she slipped her arms through mine and Kiera's both. "Come along, girls. Entertain me as we walk. We all know what he is to me; tell me what he is to you."

I was not, at first, certain to which of us she spoke, but Kiera's helpless gaze peered around Josephine to plead with me, and so, reluctantly at first and then with the relief of confession, I answered, for I knew that the brief response I had given her in Khan's offices was insufficient.

The length of my tale took us from the opera house to Josephine's apartment, though the word did a disservice to the premises. I did not believe any other flat occupied the top floor in the building she had taken; it was all hers, and as sumptuous as one might imagine. Furs, not carpets, sprawled across floors; splashes of color in art and fabric; warm lights making deep shadows of doors opening onto unlit rooms.

From one of the darkened rooms came a cheetah, padding silently across the soft floors, its golden, round-eyed gaze intent upon Kiera and myself, not as though we were welcome, but as if we were likely meals. Its pointed, shifting shoulders were higher than my knee and its casually lashing tail the length of its body. My heartbeat slowed, a curious and deadly calm taking me: for all that she was Josephine's pet, the cheetah had been known to attack, and I would have only one chance to defeat her should she pounce. I was not afraid, but my hand went to the knife at my thigh in a prudent, preparatory gesture, and I tucked Kiera, whose whole body trembled, behind me for safety.

The beast paused, one foot lifted, and met my gaze squarely. We stood, two predators, waiting on one another, until the cheetah yawned suddenly, its mouth peeled back from its lips to show deadly fangs and a curling pink tongue. Then as if it had never intended anything else, it changed course and slunk to Josephine, its diamond collar visible and glittering against spotted yellow fur as it turned aside. She sat and it joined her on the couch, one massive, clawed paw resting possessively on her thigh. It yawned again, and settled its chin on one leg, and though its eyes slitted shut, I could not shake the feeling that it watched me with dubious intent.

"Chiquita," Josephine said fondly, and scratched the great beast's head as if it was nothing more than a house cat. "She likes you," she said, primarily, I felt, to me, as Kiera was scuttling to a chair at a safe distance and drawing her feet up from the floor. "Most people are afraid of her and she pushes them around, but she respects you."

"As I respect her." My voice, while it did not shake, was somewhat deeper with emotion than was usual. I restrained myself from clearing my throat as I, too, took a seat and tried to look as composed as Josephine was.

The sofa I'd chosen was softer than I'd expected. I sank in, suddenly aware of a certain weariness, and chuckled as I righted myself. "Your home is beautiful, Josephine."

"*Merci.* I can see all of Paris from these windows." She gestured, and though most of the windows were gauzily curtained, the glimmering outline of the city still shone through, faint lights turning hazy with a mist that threatened rain. "But go on. Finish your stories of *le Monstre*," she said to Kiera, who, nervously watching Chiquita, crept from her chair to the other end of my sofa, as if my nearness gave her strength to speak.

"I'm less than Amelia was to him," she began. "Only a stray found on the street. I was his project, to see if he could train an eloquent voice from out of an urchin. I adored him," she said bitterly, "until I realized he was testing his elixirs on me too. But by then my loyalty..." She laughed, though it was a sound closer to tears. "My loyalty was his. He had taught me to fight and said I was so young no one would see me as a threat. The perfect *femme fatale.* I thought we were as one, he and I, until... The *Führer* has a fascination for the occult, you know. Monsieur Laval and I were searching for the crown, but so was he. We reached it first, but only just, and we didn't have enough elixirs with us to turn all of the soldiers' loyalty. Laval took the crown and gave them me as a promise he would exchange the crown for me when he was done with— with you, Madame Baker."

"Exchange the crown?" I asked incredulously. "*Le Monstre* intended to give it up to the Third Reich?"

All at once a fierce hope came into Kiera's eyes

and she extended her hands toward me. "You see? You don't believe it either! Neither did I. So I made my own bargain, Amelia. I had to, you see? To make certain the *Führer* believed I was loyal to *him*, so that if *le Monstre* betrayed me, as I feared he would, I would still have a place *somewhere*, with someone. So I told them where to find the crown, the one time and place I was certain it would be."

"Opening night of *La Reine du Nil*," said Josephine dryly. "Because you couldn't know where he would hide it, but you would certainly know where I was performing."

Stalwart and unashamed, Kiera replied, "It was a good plan," before slumping as she glanced toward me. "I didn't expect you, though. When I realized I no longer had the *pschent*, I crawled back to him, claiming I had evaded Nazi clutches while they fought for the crown. They already knew its power, of course, so it wasn't difficult to persuade him they had deduced when and where it would be used without my assistance."

"But why return to him?" Josephine asked in astonishment. "You might have been free of him forever."

Kiera looked upon Josephine as if the singer was an innocent, then turned a bleak gaze upon me. "Have *you* escaped him?"

I could not help but look away. I had escaped, yes; I had thought him dead and I had left to explore the world, but even rumor of him drew me back to Paris, and now that I knew he still lived—"*Oui*," I replied quietly, "and yet, *non*. In a way I never have, and perhaps I never shall."

"You see?" Kiera asked Josephine. "So I saw no point in trying. Not until the *Opéra*, when I met Amelia and for the first time thought beyond the depths of his betrayal, and my fear. Alone, I knew I could never be free of him, but if I joined with you, Amelia, if we worked together——!" Kiera seized my hand in hers, holding on as though I had become the sole lifeline tethering her to a world she dearly desired.

It could not be said that Josephine lacked sympathy for either tale, but neither could she hide amusement as Kiera clung to me. "Such stories call for a drink," she announced, and, with Chiquita trailing after her, she rose and called for servants to bring refreshments. She paused, though, as she returned to her divan, and bent to murmur in my ear. Her teasing tone as she whispered, "You two would make a charming couple, Amelia," caused me to suspect the entire activity of calling for drinks had merely been a ploy to allow her to speak to me in so intimate a fashion, and *en vérité*, it was all I could do to not redden.

She chuckled at my discomfiture and trailed a fingertip across my shoulders as she returned to her seat. I did blush then, seeking anything of safety to feast my eyes upon; I found Chiquita, whose round golden gaze was intent on mine, as if she could read my mind—or, perhaps, simply as if she still thought I might be a suitable snack. My lip curled in response

and Chiquita yawned extravagantly, then found somewhere else to look herself.

Josephine watched this entire exchange with a
poorly hidden smile, though Kiera, still clinging to
me, seemed not to notice it at all. I could not think
that the girl's intense bond with me was in any fashion
romantic, no matter how secretly pleased Madame
Baker was by my distress at the notion. Had I not
been so taken by her, *sans doute*, I would not have been
so uncomfortable, but as I could not look upon
Josephine without heart-palpitating admiration and
an intensity of emotion unusual to me, I found the
entire situation disquieting.

As if quite satisfied she held the whole scenario
well in hand, Josephine accepted a drink and edible
tidbits from servants who appeared to think no more
of visitors in the midnight hour than they did of the
languid cheetah sprawled across the full length of a
couch. Once the servants had left us all with sustenance and libations, Josephine pushed Chiquita aside
and sat again; the cheetah thumped to the floor with
the gracelessness and expression of a much smaller
cat upon whom such indignities had been heaped,
and began to wash herself with offended ferocity.

It broke whatever tension had built, even Kiera
biting back giggles, and for some little while we were
old friends, exchanging stories that had nothing to do
with green-eyed monsters or *Opéra*, but were only tales
of past absurdities and embarrassing moments, each
trying to top the other, as might happen on any late
and rainy night. At one point, well into her cups,

Josephine stood on the couch and sang us an aria of conquest with such bravado that we wept tears of laughter; Kiera, wiping her eyes, wheezed, "No wonder he wants you, Madame Baker. I heard you sing tonight—last night—whenever it was!—with the power of that crown, and wanted to fight for you then. An aria like this, calling us to arms. It's as well you don't wear the crown now, or we might well rise and fight even Chiquita for you!"

"Nonsense," Josephine said with smug pleasure as she sat again. "It's my voice that swayed you both now and then; the crown I wore last night was only a costume piece. The real one has been secreted away by Amelia and her friends. I need no such props, Kiera. I am the voice of this age."

Kiera clapped both hands against her mouth, an action of pure childish surprise. Above her fingers, green eyes widened; through her fingers, a whisper emerged: "You *fooled* him? You fooled *le Monstre* with your performance tonight? Oh!" She turned to me, seizing my hands again as tears of relief sprang from her eyes. "Oh, Amelia, I admit, I've still been afraid, tonight. He knows so much and always seems to be ahead of everyone else. I've felt like this is only a respite, like it's going to end at any moment, but, oh, if he *can* be fooled, then maybe I really am safe! Maybe everything really will be all right!"

"I promise it, Kiera." I drew the girl against my side to kiss her forehead in reassurance, as if she was indeed the child she struck me as. As if she was the girl I had once been, but graced with escaping a dire fate moments before it closed around her forever. I knew such sentiment was a folly, but it was too easy to see myself in her, and I wished to be her protector.

It was not, however, as simple as that. With a deep inhalation, I said, "But there is something I must ask of you, Kiera. You have been his companion these last years, have you not? You know his plans and you know where he now hides."

She lifted her head, eyebrows furrowed in surprise. "Yes, of course. Why—oh," she said much more softly, and a shudder coursed through her. "Oh, yes, of course. I'll bring you there."

"Where is there?" I demanded with quiet urgency. "You are tired, and I should make haste. If I can go myself, I will."

The address she named sent a thrill of disbelief through my bones. "*Non*," I said almost before the number, much less the street name, had passed her lips. "*Non*, Kiera, I know that house. It lies abandoned, decaying. He cannot be there, hidden in plain sight."

"But he is," she protested in surprise. "Why can he not be?"

"Because it was his home with me," I whispered. "I know that house, Kiera. I have searched it every time I have visited." Except this time: I had not yet been there, in the few days since I had come to Paris. "There has never been any sign of him."

Sympathy and a sudden understanding lined her young face. "Now I understand. Now I know why we only ever approached from below, and almost never entered the house itself. There are rooms beneath, Amelia, a safe space while the building above goes to rot. He has lived there as long as I've known him."

A curse escaped me as my fists clenched. "Is there a way in from the house itself?"

"Through the wall behind the cooker," she replied. "I'll show you."

"*Non.* If I know where to look I can find my own way. There's no need for you to risk yourself again, Kiera. The intelligence is all I need."

"Thank you." Kiera's gratitude might have broken my heart, had she not relaxed suddenly, as if all tension had finally been taken from her. With its disappearance, welcome sleep could finally claim her. Her head tipped over and a small snore escaped her; I looked up, struggling not to laugh, to see Josephine with just the same struggle written over her own face. The singer touched a finger to her lips and, silently, stood to collect Kiera's legs while I gently hoisted her torso. Together we carried the girl to one of the bedrooms and tucked her under the warmth of a duvet before tiptoeing out again.

"Well." Josephine met my eyes directly as we closed the door on Kiera's sleeping form. "I believe that settles the matter of sleeping arrangements for the evening."

Regretting it with every fiber of my being, I whispered, "I believe it does," and left her to sleep alone in her own bed while I stole into the night to catch a monster.

24

E ven in the desolate ruin of Paul-Gabriel's old
home, stepping through its front doors carried
the scents and sights of memory. It did not matter that
cobwebs danced in the breeze as I pushed the door
open, nor that the magnificent curtains were tattered
and fell in ruins toward the sitting room floors; to me,
the dust and muck were hardly there at all, and the
curtains held in warmth and love, only allowing the
outside world glimpses of it as they swept by.

Stained glass windows, covered in filth, now let
only the faintest glimmer of streetlights glow across
the once-handsome parquet floors that were dull
and caked with dirt. To my mind's eye those colors
were still rich enough to dip my fingers in, and so
deep that I thought I might savor a taste should I
then touch my fingers to my lips. The light no
longer reached the broken stairs that I had once girl-
ishly run up and leapt on the bannister to slide
down; now I would not dare to risk even the stairs,

far less the shattered spines of the bannister. I
lingered in the doorway, seeing and not seeing, and
my feet took me toward the stairs and the pathways
I had most often travelled when I lived here. This
had happened before, on the other occasions I had
come searching this house for signs that Paul-
Gabriel had lived, or had not; it meant a slow wend
across failing floorboards, cautious investigation of
dust-filled rooms.

But never before had I entered with the knowledge of where to look. Kiera's words guided me away
from the familiar spaces I was inclined to. Instead I
followed halls I knew but had rarely visited: the wash-
room, the scullery, the kitchen, and there, though it
seemed to me that the dust had gone undisturbed
since my last exploration here, years ago, I found the
secret door that I had missed.

It was not, as I might have suspected, part of the
servants' halls, but the entirety of the cooker wall that
swung away: a passageway so vast it must have been
built with the house, and used at great risk when what
now held the dilapidated stove had instead been a
hearth with roaring fire and heavy pots sloshing from
iron yokes. Today, with those fires long since cooled,
there was no such risk at all. I stole through dark
passageways, unwilling to kindle a light for fear of
warning *le Monstre*, should he still be within these
hidden walls. I did not expect him to be: only a fool
would sit and wait when his second-in-command had
sided with his enemy, and my angel had never been a
fool. That appellation was mine alone. But still, I

moved silently through the dark, using my fingertips to guide me, and did not risk a light.

The walls were of smoother stone than I expected. They had been carefully hewn and cared for, and when I found a doorway, it was framed by polished wood, as any doorway in a house might be. I tested the knob and found that it turned both easily and quietly. I slipped inside, pressing it closed behind me, and stood for long moments in the darkness, listening for the sound of breathing other than my own.

There was none to be heard. With exploratory fingers, I searched out lights, and was astonished to find the room fitted with electric ones. Their illumination showed me a bedroom, well kept but ordinary, its interior decorated in such a way as to suggest it had been Kiera's room rather than Paul-Gabriel's. I turned the lights off and moved on, discovering another bedroom, a kitchen, and—finally, in the largest room of all—a laboratory that appeared to have been hastily emptied.

Scraps remained: notes pinned to corkboard on the walls, pieces of metal that I fingered absently whilst rifling through the notes, familiar glass vials that lay broken and empty on the floor. The floor itself was of soft, untreated wood; there were worn paths in it around tables that contained stains and scars from whatever experiments had been done upon them. I treaded the paths as if they might somehow show me *le Monstre*'s daily behaviors, or explain to me the inner workings of his mind. Instead, twice they led me to a wall, which I, bemused, turned away from as I continued my search of the laboratory. The third time a worn path led me to the same spot, however, a spark of wit awakened in me and I realized I was, in fact, being shown something of my adversary's daily activities. Suddenly eager, I searched the empty wall, hoping for some brick or bulge that would allow me egress to another secret tunnel, as the one in the kitchen had offered me. I pressed each inch of the broad surface, my fingers flying over it delicately but swiftly, and when the telltale click finally sounded, I leapt back with pleased anticipation.

The wall did not swing away, though: it dropped downward smoothly to reveal a shallow curved space behind it, into which numerous shelves were set. These shelves contained stacks of paper, many of them weighted by pieces of metal or large empty glass vials. For a few seconds I merely stared in astonishment, but a smile of understanding pushed surprise away. *Le Monstre* had emptied his laboratory and made his escape, but he had left this alcove untouched, trusting that it would not be found. Indeed, had he not visited this space so often that the tender wood had been marked by it, I would not have. Hardly aware I spoke aloud, I murmured, "*Merci, mon ange,*" and withdrew several stacks of paper to spread on the tables.

It was at once clear that most of them contained schematics for dreadful machines and notes on dangerous ideas. It was equally clear that most of them would be of interest to Khan but were beyond my limited knowledge of—or interest in—alchemy and science. None-the-less, I rifled through them, searching for any more personal notes that might suggest where *le Monstre* could now be found, or how I might later apprehend him.

Instead I fell upon pages of schematics I *could* comprehend: various designs for armor, some as crude as a medieval knight might wear, others so form-fitted that on paper they appeared to be like a second skin. The only thing they all had in common were spaces at the thigh, hip, and arm that were clearly meant to hold vials of *le Monstre*'s elixirs: cutaway drawings showed the intubation the wearer would undergo.

I did not need to read the notes written in a cramped hand alongside these sketches to suspect what *le Monstre* intended, but their words confirmed what I imagined: he dreamed of an army of soldiers reliant on and slaves to his elixirs. They would be unable to refuse a command, unable to even think of doing so, under the compulsion of Obedience or Fear. But *le Monstre* wanted more; he wanted his soldiers to be unstoppable, and needed more than the elixirs to accomplish that. He envisioned armor, but armor unlike anything the world had ever seen: fitted, light, unbreakable, able to resist even a bullet wound. Thus far, though, the right formula to create his magical metal had eluded him.

Inspired by curiosity, I withdrew one of my pistols and cracked its butt against one of the metal shards I had taken from atop the papers. Rather than reverberate as I expected it to, the metal shattered into thin deadly blades. Pistol returned to its holster, I collected one of the shards and fingered it thoughtfully as I pored over the sketches. If this metal was as close as he had come, his armored soldiers were many years away from success, but the idea of them was alarming. I left the laboratory and found, in Kiera's room, a small but sturdy canvas bag. Upon returning to the laboratory, I stuffed all the papers and several pieces of the brittle metal into it the bag. *Le Monstre* would no doubt have copies of his notes, but if he did not, taking these would set him back even farther—and Khan would be fascinated by them.

There were no other stretches of worn floor leading straight into the walls, neither in the laboratory nor in any of the other rooms, now that I knew to check. I hesitated a little while in *le Monstre*'s lair, but, unable to think of a way to find him now, and dearly wishing for a few hours' rest before dawn, I retreated to Josephine's apartment, where I stored the bag of notes under a pile of pillows Chiquita called her own. I myself was pleased to take, for the brief time that I could, advantage of the sleeping arrangements offered earlier by *la grande dame.*

25

The race itself was hardly the thing; despite its adventures the day before, my Indian was in good repair, and thanks to *their* adventures, my competitors were decimated, though I was relieved to see Stringfield astride her blue Harley again. My concern was for the Italian, Bernardo Viccini, whose hard eyes and lean body vibrated with more intensity than the day before. When Signor Panterello appeared to remind us one final time of what we raced for, Viccini leapt forward, hands clawed as though he would throttle the slight inventor as he screamed, "Where is it? Where is the motorcycle? What have you done with it?"

I seized his collar, wrenching him back, and pulled his face close to mine. "Your master will not be pleased if you destroy the maker of his coveted engines, *idiot*. The machine is safe and Signor Panterello must remain that way too, or I'll know who to finger for it."

The Italian youth turned a look of such furious betrayal on me that it seemed the race would indeed not be the thing at all. We were nearly at fisticuffs in the predawn light, and though I spoke Italian, his outrage was so great that I doubted anyone could discern actual coherence from his guttural sputtering. I could not help but notice, though, that beneath his leathers he wore the military black shirt favored by Mussolini, and I looked forward to the opportunity to teach him a lesson or two about the errors of supporting dictators.

I wanted nothing more than to forget all for the duration of the race, to enjoy the wind and speed and think nothing of *le Monstre* or stolen motorcycles or fascism. It was not, of course, to be. I could not ride without worrying for my competitors, without watching for traps, without wondering if Josephine would again, against all common sense, wait at the finish line, though I had left her sleeping in her apartment in the morning twilight hour. I thought of Kiera's pale-faced bravery and prayed I might whisk her away from Paris and *le Monstre*'s influence before he entangled her again, as he had entangled me. She had done a great deal already, offering me what she knew of his whereabouts, and I did not want to fail her. I thought of my mother's thinness, and wondered briefly, terribly, if there might be a Distillation of Health in *le Monstre*'s hidden lair, and whether I was craven enough to make use of an evil creature's potions for what I believed to be the benefit of another.

I had, in my musings, stopped racing: I sat idle on a bridge, heedless to the other bikers sweeping around me in a wide V, a formation made necessary by the fact that I had, unbeknownst to myself, half turned back, as if I meant to return to Josephine's apartment with all haste and beg to know if Kiera was aware of Distillations of Health or Energy.

But ahead lay another injustice, one perpetrated by a dictator and a fascist, and one in whose pursuit my friend Khan had nearly bankrupted himself; I could not in conscience abandon that task even if my heart pressed me to deal with *le Monstre* once and for all. Cursing softly, I set the Indian back on course. *Le Monstre* had waited this long. He could wait another hour for this race to be won, Panterello protected, and Khan repaid with the knowledge of Panterello's engines, worth more to him than any gold.

I had lost significant ground with my ponderings; the bulk of the pack was ahead of me now, spitting water, grime, and stone from their back tires. Pebbles pelted me, some hard enough that tomorrow I would find bruises, and more than once I failed to move forward because the muck on my goggles had to be cleaned before I dared risk a chancy passage. At times I fit myself into spaces too small for belief, jostling my fellow riders until they gave way and I slipped through; twice, I chose the wet depths of a puddle in order to pass on the inside. One by one, muddy colors were left behind, until there were clear streets and the echoes of only one or two motorcycles ahead of me— Stringfield and Viccini, unless I'd missed my count in passing them. The race would be down to we three again, and of us, only I had enough of a lead to take both third place *and* the prize. Thrilled by the knowledge, burning with the spirit of competition, I gunned the Indian and rushed forward in pursuit of my opponents.

I was wholly unprepared to spin around a corner some half-mile ahead and to find them blockading the narrow street together, their bikes wheel-to-wheel and their resolved faces turned toward me in anticipation. I knew instantly that they would not flinch; that I could not run at them and trust them to twitch away at the last moment. Nor was there any sort of incline, not so much as an out-of-line cobble, whence I might leverage the Indian over them. They had chosen their trap well, for my strength, while considerable, was not enough to drag the weight of an entire motorcycle into a leap without some form of assistance.

For the second time in two days, I could not stop quickly enough. I saw; I judged; I lay the Indian down, shouting pained curses as I slammed over cobblestones at great speed. The Indian spun and clanked, garnering as many bruises as I did, and for that these two miscreants would pay, even if I held one in great admiration not two minutes earlier.

With myself no longer aboard, they *did* step aside to allow my battered bike the remaining space it needed to slow and stop, and then as one, Stringfield and Viccini dismounted and strode to me as I too thudded to a painful stop.

Stringfield arrived first and crouched, hands

dangling between her knees. Before she spoke I twisted my aching body upward and drove a knee toward her temple. She, somehow not expecting that I might defend myself, did not defend *herself*, and fell with an expression of pained stupefaction. I checked her pulse as I came to my feet; it beat strongly and steadily, assuring me I had probably done no permanent damage.

That, at the moment, was more than could be said for the consequences I suffered for her actions. There was not an inch of my body that did not pound with agony; I was more badly hurt, by a considerable measure, than I had been by going into the fire yesterday, and then all I had needed to do was snatch a man from certain death. Now I was obliged to do battle with a lean-bodied military man whose fitness, at the moment, was of considerably lesser question than my own.

From what he no doubt imagined as a safe distance, he said, "Signora Stone," but whatever threats might have followed were silenced by my shoulder burying itself in his gut.

Viccini flew backward under the power of my forward drive, grunting in pained astonishment as we both hit the cobblestones, myself atop him with fists already flying. My punches lacked their usual power, muffled as my hands were in gloves, but anger and pain drove me, as did a string of invective that poured from my lips. I had thoroughly questioned Viccini's heritage and was well into a line of suggested perversions when it struck me—perhaps an unfortunate term—that the man was not fighting back. That, indeed, he held his arms crossed over his face and through them shouted pleas that, whilst I bellowed, were utterly futile. When I at last briefly ceased my shower of blows, he dropped his hands to cry, "The black shirts, Signora Stone, the black shirts!"

"*Oui*, I know, you fascist dog, but you will have no more of Panterello's inventions—"

"*Non, Madame Stone!*" he shouted in quite good French, "*Les chemises noires!*" and thrust a pointing finger behind me.

Though it was an old and known trick, I could not stop myself from following the line of his finger, as, behind us, dozens of motorcycles spun and wheeled at the corner, intent on thundering down the racetrack we were sprawled across. This was no surprise; I had, after all, only passed them moments ago. I was on my feet, running before any further observations made impact on my mind. My first concern was scooping Stringfield, who still lay limp and boneless in the street, to safety; she may have just tried to kill me, but I would not be personally responsible for leaving her to be run over by dozens of tires. Viccini I judged to be breathless but quite able to move aside, which he did. But the racers did not, as I expected, push through. I stood pressed to the side of the street, Bessie Stringfield's weight in my aching arms, and stared in bewilderment as three dozen racers converged on Viccini, trying, by all appearances, to run him down.

With great alacrity he threw himself on his motorcycle, making himself just slightly less vulnerable and, if not precisely more mobile, at least much faster; the pack gave chase while I gaped after them.

Bessie stirred in my arms, then groaned and, as her eyes opened, lifted a swift elbow to crack it against my cheek. Bright pain exploded there and I dropped her with a howl; she rolled to her feet with a furious gaze. "You darn fool woman! We thought you were gone, so we set up our ambush! Now you've left him alone!"

"*Quoi*? What?" The question seemed insufficient to my bewilderment, so I bettered it to the best of my ability: "What?"

"He tried!" Bessie spat in furious frustration. "He tried finding you, honey, yesterday after the race after you went into the fire like that. I mean, he thought you were some kinda fool at first, but then the stories about the opera started getting around and he realized you were Amelia Stone! Nobody else he coulda hoped for more, but you disappeared, and he was left with nobody to turn to but me! Well, never let it be said Bessie Stringfield turned from a fellow man in need, because I've been there, sister. I know what it's like sleeping rough because the world around you won't look at you like you're worth spit, and that boy deserved better. We all deserve better."

"Miss Stringfield, *s'il vous plaît*, I don't understand—"

"Well, of course you don't, haring all over the place after fantastical monsters when there's real ones right here in Paris today!"

The very sky spun, a dizziness that seemed greater than the sum of the beating I had taken. "Surely you do not speak of *le Monstre*, Miss Stringfield...?"

"I'm talking 'bout the black shirts, you darn fool!"

I was unaccustomed to feeling so slow; it was as if, although we shared a mother tongue, Madame Stringfield and I were actually speaking entirely different languages. Given the number I *did* speak, I began to wonder if I had somehow lapsed into one she did not know. I spoke carefully, making sure the bulk of the words were English: "*Oui*, the blackshirts, of whom Viccini is one, trying to retrieve Panterello's wondrous engines—?"

"*Panterello is the black shirt!*" Bessie roared this at me with such frustration and precision that I briefly wondered if this was how Khan felt at all times: as if surrounded by those with less wit, to whom things must be explained in small words and no uncertain terms. For while Madame Stringfield was unquestionably certain in her terms, my mind was slow to comprehend, and a protest sprang from my lips.

"But no, he begged for my help in hiding both himself and the machine. He called Mussolini his enemy and he...but no. I can see it in your eyes now, that the machine is...the machine is Viccini's. But he is so—" Embarrassment flooded me and sharp mockery lit Bessie's face.

"He's so handsome, isn't he? Such a good looking boy, why would he need to be smart, too? Panterello looks like he needs brains to get by, so a'course the motorcycle's his, right? 'Cept it isn't so, honey. You oughta see the underbelly of that bike he's riding in the race today. You wouldn't doubt me for a second, then."

En vérité, I already doubted her no longer. Too late, I turned to look where Viccini had gone; too late, Stringfield's well-deserved sarcasm bathed me. "That's right, honey. That wasn't the racing pack. They've all been picked off. That was a whole platoon of black shirts, and you just let them go after an unarmed man who got left all on his own because of you."

"Why did you cause me to crash?" I asked in dismal tones as my need for action took over. I went to the Indian, righting it and examining it for roadworthiness; it would drive, if not as smoothly as I might hope. "Why did you not take me into your confidence this morning—*merde*. Because I defended Panterello, and you had no other time. But I would have stood with you here—!"

"Look how long it's taken me to explain now, honey, and those sons of guns were right on your tail. Truth is, I didn't even know it was you until you were too close for us to scoot anyway, and you'd already laid that beauty down by that time. An Indian was my first bike," she added with a brief, fond smile. "Ain't no bike but a Harley for me now, but my adopted Irish mama, she got me an Indian for my sweet sixteenth. You should take better care of that baby. Riding it through fires and skidding it over cobblestones, what're you thinking, honey-chil'?"

"That needs must, and that I am near a full ten

years your senior, *honey-child*. Where will Viccini go? Is your Harley well?"

Bessie sniffed, but went to inspect her own bike swiftly and thoroughly. "She's just fine. We said if we got split up we'd double back around to where we started."

"And can he outpace his pursuers?"

Madame Stringfield gave me a look bordering on pity. "Honey, he coulda left us all in gay Paree while he rode to the moon, if he'd wanted to. Only reason he's even playing at making this a fair race is to try an' keep the *Führer* off his fine Italian backside. He'll be comin' round the mountain any moment now."

I swung onto the Indian with an air of determination. "Then we shall fight for him, Madame Stringfield. Why," I added curiously, "does he not simply rebuild from scratch?"

"Panterello's story wasn't wrong," Bessie said as she mounted her Harley. "Gilera got greedy and wanted the plans. Only difference is he wanted 'em from Viccini, not Panterello. And now Viccini's got nothing, no cash, no bike, no way to start again. He says there's a benefactor here in Paris who'll fund everything, but he's gotta get the bike to him."

Her choice of words caused my stomach to feel as though a stone had settled in it. "A benefactor?"

"Some fine rich fella who doesn't race but knows a moneymaker when he sees it, I reckon. Viccini called him a benefactor, sure, and that sounds about right to me."

I had not laid hands upon Viccini's motorcycle,

only seen its fascinating metallic chassis and longed to touch it, but a certainty was rising within me. *Le Monstre* was in search of a compound for his armor; I feared Viccini was about to deliver it to him. "Oh, *mon dieu. Non,* not again. Bessie, no matter what transpires in these next few minutes, do not allow Signor Viccini to bring that motorcycle to this benefactor, for he is *le Monstre,* the self-same *fantôme* you mocked a moment ago and whom I know to be both real and dangerous. I know for a fact he trades with the likes of the *Führer,* so if it is Viccini's wish to keep his inventions from fascist hands, he *must not* deal with that devil."

"I reckon it's too late, honey. Panterello's already looking to make that deal. I hear he's already met with this benefactor."

Cold bit into my guts. For seventeen years, my mother had been a dismissed, if not forgotten, remnant of *le Monstre*'s life—and I, in having brought Panterello to her, might well have led *le Monstre* back to her doorstep. I lowered my gaze, imagining I could see the whiteness of my knuckles through my leather gloves, and spoke quietly. "I will help you dispatch these black shirts, Madame Stringfield, and if I had my preferences I would then round up each and every soul involved in this trickery so it can be set to rights. I will not have time for that, though, and so all I can do is plead that you do not finish this race, but instead take yourself to see Professor Khan at *la Sorbonne.* He knows where the motorcycle is, and in this he will be a friend to you as no other could be. It is for him that I

ride, so he might study and understand the engi-
neering work Viccini has accomplished."

"Where are you gonna be, honey?"

"Settling old debts, madame. I shall be settling old
debts."

As I spoke that promise, Viccini rounded the
corner, leading a pack of Italian black shirts
behind him.

26

I had a knife on my thigh and my guns beneath my leather jacket. I wanted neither, though it would have given me no regret to kill the oncoming men outright. But neither guns nor knives carried the sheer satisfaction of using my fists, and at the moment I was badly in need of satisfaction. I stripped the gloves from my hands as if I had all the time in the world, watching the racers with cool, assessing eyes.

I had not even thought to look before; as they had intended, all I had seen was their colors flying brightly. Now, though, I saw all: they were typified men of the Italian race, most being swarthy with black hair and dark eyes, some with beards shadowing beneath their goggles even though the hour had not yet reached eleven in the morning. They rode well, but they were not experts; had I been less inclined to assign them proficiency in my expectations when I'd ridden through them earlier, I might have noticed that, and deduced some of their hidden truths.

Their colors were gone now, as were other vestments of racing. They still wore leathers, as did anyone who chose to ride fast bikes, but without the colors to distract, the sharp cut of broad military shoulders and trim military waists was quite obvious; it was as well I was generally known for my brawling, not my brilliance. Some of them wore the collars of their jackets open, showing crisp black necklines; some, perhaps emboldened by the belief that they were untouchable, now wore red, white, and green badges visibly.

Viccini shot past me and I gunned the Indian, rising on its footrests to lift a fist and drive it, with all vehicular momentum and personal aggravation, into the face of a banded blackshirt.

He flew backward into half a dozen of his brethren, knocking them askew with a great satisfying clatter, with the scream of engines and the screams of men; many of them would not rise again to do battle with us. With one blow I had reduced our opponents by a sixth. Joy coursed through my veins, washing away the aches and pains of my earlier encounter with the cobblestones. I clenched the Indian's brakes, spinning it in a broad circle; its back wheel became a weapon in itself, clipping blackshirts as I spun. They fell, most of them leaping clear of their bikes, some to the detriment of those nearest to them. I slammed my elbow into the kidney of a rising man; he fell again with a scream and did not try to stand again.

By this time Bessie was in the fray as well, and if she did not fight as well as I, she rode far better.

Despite the rough cobbles, she spun on the Harley's seat, seeming to trust its direction utterly as she punched with both legs and toppled two blackshirts; the farther one's head hit the closest wall with a sound like a pomegranate striking the floor, and blood smeared the wall as he fell. Bessie regained her natural seat on the Harley before he hit the ground.

Above us on the street, Viccini looked back, saw we fought on his behalf, and spun his own motor-cycle so tightly I gasped with admiration. He roared back into the fray, and in seconds every blackshirt bike had been abandoned: there was simply not room enough for our enemies to fight from their vehicles without endangering one another. Though we were less troublesome to each other, our wheels were too tempting a target. A blackshirt kicked a bike sideways, catching Bessie's spokes and seizing the wheel; she flew over the handlebars and for an instant we all froze, watching her arc through the air.

With an acrobat's skill, she hit the cobbles with a shoulder and rolled, coming to her feet with eyes flashing and an eager grin spread across her face. "That the best you can do, boys?"

I feared her courage was bravado; her skill, as far as I knew, was in motorcycle trick riding, not fighting —though while upon the Harley, one was difficult to tell from the other. Still, when a handful of enraged blackshirts bellowed in answer to her challenge, I decided it was they who must first fall. Though fists might have offered the most satisfaction, I was no fool;

my knife flew from its sheath and flew true, striking the leader between the shoulders.

As one, the remaining pack turned back to see who had struck him down, and as one, proved they had not a whit of sense among them—if they had, they would not have returned to me *en masse* to do battle, but instead would have picked off Viccini and Stringfield both. But fortunately for my compatriots, our common enemy concluded that, as the most obvious threat, I must be dealt with first.

We were down a dozen already, but unless I made quick work of at least another dozen, I feared for our chances. Although I was a fine shot, in such close confines I was reluctant to make use of my guns. A missed shot could too easily strike one of my own, or worse, an ordinary citizen. I could not let myself forget that this narrow street in which we battled was home for everyday Parisians, and that only their good sense in remaining indoors kept them from the fray. So it was to be fists and feet in glorious *mêlée*, and as they ran at me I took a moment to assess my situation.

The street was narrow, not ten feet wide; that narrowness meant the abandoned motorcycles lay in heaps and piles. Careful of still-spinning wheels, I raced up the nearest pile and launched myself downward upon the encroaching Italians, striking with both elbows into the joining of necks and shoulders. The two men I struck fell in paralyzing pain, only screams able to emanate from bodies numbed by forceful blows. Now there were only two of Bessie's assailants left, and two could be dispatched with ease. As they dropped, I saw that Viccini's lean body was good for more than fast driving: he ducked a fist with admirable swiftness and came up with a gut punch that crossed the eyes of his assailant. With remarkable efficiency, he then seized the man's head and introduced jaw to knee at great velocity. My heart fluttered with appreciation before I, now confident of his ability to care for himself, returned my attention to the remaining blackshirts and to protecting Bessie Stringfield.

Even as I caught a man's face and slammed his head back against the nearby wall, I saw that Stringfield had found a crowbar and now wielded it to great effect. Only as one man and then another fell did I begin to wonder why *they* did not employ firearms, and could only guess that they had been instructed to a certain amount of discretion in their attempts to seize Viccini and retain the new motorcycle's blueprints. Italian blackshirts firing weapons on Parisian streets would certainly be regarded as an act of war, and I doubted Mussolini was prepared for that. It was to our advantage that no guns were used, for each of us fought with the ferocity of ten, and their numbers fell before us.

It was to my shame, then, that one of the remaining few caught me off guard as I battled another. My opponent was an unnecessarily large man, both tall and strongly muscled, and my only advantage against him was my quickness. Even that proved insufficient, though, as I might as well have rained swift blows on concrete, for all the effect it seemed to have. Should he land a blow it was over for me, and in trying to avoid his ham-sized fists, I did not realize another blackshirt approached from behind. My only notice was that my opponent stepped aside; then I was flung headlong into a pile of motorcycles, upon one of which I hit my head hard enough to see stars despite the safety helmet I wore. A moment later that selfsame helmet was ripped from my head. My giant opponent seized my hair and dragged me bodily to a motorcycle whose back wheel still spun with great enthusiasm. Dizzy and weak, it required all my strength to keep my face from being pushed into the whirling wheel as a large foot pressed itself into my spine and drove me ever closer to ruin.

The sharp, wet sound of a skull breaking gave me an instant's hope, but the great weight on my back continued; in fact, it increased as the giant collapsed onto me. Now shouting with fear and rage, I tried to shake him off, but dizziness still had me in its grip and my muscles were feeble.

As I struggled to remain clear of the wheel, motion caught the corner of my eye: Viccini, reaching past me to thump the motorcycle's casing. Only then did I realize the machine that threatened me was his own, and even with its wheel whipping so close to my face, I admired how the casing parted on a seam I had not seen. Viccini slipped deft fingers between hot pipes to extract and sever—very carefully—a single wire with a pair of pliers he returned to his pocket.

The engine died without a hiss; Viccini stepped over me to put his foot on the tire, causing his boot soles to smell of hot leather and rubber for a few seconds before the wheel ceased its dangerous spin. Then he, with the audible grunting assistance of Madame Stringfield, heaved the giant off me. I rolled to relative safety and comfort, first searching the alley to determine if any of our assailants remained—there were a few running at great speed away from us—and then gazing in thankful astonishment at Viccini and Stringfield. The latter sat, arms looping around his knees and thick black hair falling into his dark eyes. "Now will you listen to me, signora?"

"I believe Madame Stringfield has set me straight on all things related to this situation, signor, and I would like to offer my unstinting apologies for not taking the time to listen to your plaint yesterday when you attempted to approach me. I had painted you with a black brush, and am ashamed. Are you unharmed? And you, Madame Stringfield?"

"Nothing that won't heal up, honey. We'd be a sight worse off if you hadn't come around. How 'bout you? You took some mighty hits there."

I tested a muscle here and there, hardly moving to do so, and found that I heartily wished that I would not have to move again for quite some time. As that was the least likely of possible scenarios, I put the wish out of my mind and said, as Bessie had, "Nothing that will not heal, although I might welcome a shot of something stronger than water to put these aches at ease."

Without a word, Viccini dipped a hand into his jacket and withdrew a silver flask, which he opened and offered to me. I took a draught of what proved to be startlingly fine brandy and, much restored, sat up to admire both the flask and its contents. "*Merci,* signor. I did not expect you to have this."

"It's all that's kept me warm some nights, knowing that my plans have been stolen and are likely to be the engines upon which the next war is driven."

I judged him, my lips pursed and curious. "You are no more than twenty-two years of age, signor. You did not fight in the Great War."

"My brothers, my father, my uncle, and half my village died in it. Besides, must a man fight to dread the thought of his creations driving a war? My machines are for joy, signora, not death. Their engines are meant to drive a man to the greatest speed he can hope to reach, not march him inexorably into bloodshed."

Though I made my living by choosing to fight, I could not help but admire the young man's conviction, and clapped him on the shoulder as I said so. He did not give with the impact; his strength and sense of self were sure. "You remind me of my friend Khan, for whom I ride in this race. You must go to him, signor. He'll offer you the assistance you need, and the materials—"

A shadow crossed Viccini's face and my eyebrows drew down. "Signor?"

"The materials." He hesitated, then seemed to commit himself. "The materials are...unusual, signora. The metal is of my own design, and has been reached through...through a kind of science that some might regard as..."

"As alchemy?" I offered, when he could not.

His posture collapsed, relief warring with embarrassment in his handsome features. "I should have known that one such as yourself would be aware of some of the greater secrets of our world, but I am from a small, superstitious village, Signora Stone. My work would be considered akin to witchcraft by those who love me best, and it has given me a healthy fear of admitting to others where my talents truly lie."

"You have nothing to fear from me," I promised. "And Professor Khan will be eager to offer you whatever materials you need, as well as the necessary workspace and funding." Although, given Khan's apparent state of finances, I was uncertain as to where that last would be procured. None-the-less, not wanting to dishearten the youth, I concluded with, "I have every confidence of it. He knows where the prototype is; all that will be left to me is to arrest that foul fiend Panterello and return the money to the race's backers."

"Or you could win the race," Stringfield drawled, "and give the cash to Bernie here, since that was the deal Panterello set out."

"But Panterello is a villain," I protested, although the idea held merit. "Surely the companies and racers should not be taken in by his antics."

"What's the difference if it's Panterello running the game or Bernie? We all bought in knowing there'd only be one winner. I can't see how it hurts if the proceeds go to the man who invented the plumb thing insteada the folks who were willing to give it up in the first place."

I thought again of Khan's financial state, and the apparent difficulties the Century Club might also be in thanks to his investments, and concluded that Bessie Stringfield might have the right of it. "One of us, then, had best win this race."

"I must first repair my bike," Viccini said without evident regret. "I could win handily, had I not cut that wire to save your lovely face, signora. It must be one of you two. I propose," he added with a wicked twinkle in his dark eyes, "that you wrestle for it."

Bessie and I both laughed, though she held up her hands in pre-emptive defeat. "For your entertainment, honey? I don't think so. It's darn clear Miz Stone here would clean my clock in a fight, fair or not."

"Very well." I stood, and upon doing so, begged another sip of the fine brandy from Viccini's flask. Warmed and soothed by it, I brought the Indian back to life and saluted my two compatriots. "When next we meet, the prototype and the money shall both be yours, Signor Viccini."

27

There were no other racers to catch or defeat, in the end; Panterello's blackshirts had taken care of them all, and my only worry as I roared toward the Eiffel Tower was for the health of all of those who had been waylaid. That and, perhaps, the police who chased me at an ever-increasing distance as I approached the finish line. My exasperation with Panterello's routes and his decision to end the races at prominent public sites reached a peak and I crossed the line well before the noon hour with numerous scores to settle.

I was, rather to my amazement, swept from the Indian and raised on the hands of a cheering crowd whose enthusiasm for motorcycle races appeared to be only just shy of my own. They closed ranks, everyone trying to touch my leg or shoulder or foot, and fully blocked the streets and paths as they did so. Police sirens still wailed in the distance, but came no closer: hundreds, if not thousands, of eager Parisians

were not to be mowed down to scold or even arrest a
street racer. Despite that particular service they did
me, I still called for the Indian, not wanting to be long
parted from it. Finally, both it and I were deposited—
myself by supportive hands, the bike by a boy small
enough to worm through the crowds—in what
amounted to a winner's circle directly beneath *la Tour*'s
center.

Within that circle stood not Signor Panterello,
whom I expected, but rather two persons I did not
expect. The first was Khan, whose presence was startling enough, and from whose hands I received
Hatshepsut's double crown. I stared at it in bewilderment, then transferred that selfsame befuddlement to
Khan, whose deeply lined face wrinkled in concern.

"I had a note," he explained in earnest worry. "A
note in your hand, Amelia, I would swear to it, asking
me to bring the crown here, that you had need of it. It
said to fetch your mother and come here—"

"Maman?" For that was the other unexpected
personage: my mother, looking slight and somewhat
lost amidst the bustle and noise of the racing crowd.
"Maman, what are you doing here? Where is Signor
Panterello? Where is the motorcycle?"

"Signor Panterello went to await the banks'
opening so he could retrieve the cash prize for the
race winner. Congratulations, by the way. As for the
motorcycle..." She glanced at Khan, who let forth a
lugubrious sigh and shook his heavy head.

"Panterello did not, of course, take it with him to
the bank. I doubt the man has the strength to drive

the thing, although that raises the question of how he might design it so successfully—"

"It is not his design," I interjected dryly.

Khan's shapeless eyebrows rose. "Ah. No. Of course not. That explains much. Whose—No; it's not important right now. The point, I fear, is that the prototype was safely ensconced in your mother's garden when Panterello left, and when I came to collect her, it was gone. Only just, I should say; the grass had not yet unbent from its weight even a centimeter, and the garden gate had not yet fully settled closed. I rushed to pursue, of course, but the machine was gone, without so much as a scent of gasoline to follow. So, given the urgency of your note, I returned for Madame Stone and we made haste to the finish line, where..."

"Where it seems we have all been had," I finished slowly. "Panterello absconded with the money, the motorcycle is missing, and someone has connived to have the real *pschent* brought to me. Am I to wear it, do you suppose...?" I lifted it a few inches, the temptation to model it suddenly strong, but my heart missed a beat and I lowered it again. There was only one person who could benefit from my donning the crown, though he had gone to great lengths to rest it on another's head. I curled my fingers against its cool gold, feeling as though the stars and the moon and the sun all pulled me in different directions: Panterello required capture, the motorcycle needed locating, and the single soul whose machinations had guided so much of my life was still at large. Each of these seemed of equal importance, but only one might accomplish two things at once. I took the decision, and tried to banish uncertainty.

"We will find Panterello," I promised Khan. "In the meantime, you must find Signor Viccini, who is with Bessie Stringfield; he is the architect of the missing motorcycle, and though he is loathe to discuss it, he has confessed to me that there is some arcane skill in the mixture of metals he has used. But he may be eager to confess his secrets in your ear, Professor; it is, after all, an extraordinary ear."

"Not at all," Khan said, absently rubbing one of those ears. "It's perfectly normal, for a gorilla. Viccini, Stringfield, Panterello, motorcycle. Have I got it all, Amelia? Very good. Here's your Indian… Good heavens, Amelia, this machine has seen better days."

I sighed and put a hand on the Indian's beaten torso. "As have I, *mon ami.* I could do with a long bath and a gentle touch, neither of which, I fear, are in the cards I hold. I must resume the hunt for *le Monstre.* He must be kept apart from Viccini's metallic compound at all costs, Khan; he has plans for that substance which will bode ill for the world."

Curiosity shone in my large friend's eyes, but I waved it away. "I have his plans and will show them to you at a more opportune time. For now, you might also find Prefect Langeron and suggest he set eyes to searching for Panterello; I'm sure he would be pleased to lay hands on the fellow running illegal races through Parisian streets these past three days."

"I," my mother said firmly, "will attend to that

task. Langeron's heart will seize if our dear Professor approaches him."

"*Faîtes attention*, Maman." I embraced her and she kissed my cheeks.

"You be careful too, *ma fille*." My mother's slight figure slipped easily through the crowds; in moments she was gone and I was left with a twinge of concern that I could not fully place.

Khan placed a reassuring hand on my shoulder. "She has survived *le Monstre* once," he said to me. "Don't fear for her now, Amelia. She's stronger than you imagine."

"I can't help it," I said, petulant with worry. "She's my mother."

"And you are in every way her daughter." His smile ought to have been fearsome, exposing the great incisors that it did, but to me it was welcome and heartening. On rare impulse, I embraced him as well, then climbed aboard my Indian, leaving a discomfited, yet pleased, gorilla behind.

The crowds parted for me as they had not for my mother, but then, I was on a motorcycle and she had been afoot. Even so, I could not gain speed until I was well away from *la Tour*, and then I was glad that the police were still enmeshed in the crowds there, else my journey might have been more brief than I had intended.

In truth, I had no leads save the fact that *le Monstre* was drawn to Josephine Baker, and so it was to her side I intended to return. He would in time come to her; it was a matter of patience, and of hoping that her voice would lure him before Viccini's fascinating patents did.

I was not yet partway to Josephine's apartment when another motorcycle leapt from an alley, its engines so quiet I did not hear it until it was on top of me, a phrase of striking accuracy: the machine's bulk soared above me, sailing in front of me, and I realized its downward trajectory would smash it on me only a few yards hence.

In that same moment of realization, I saw that it was Viccini's prototype, and that *le Monstre* himself rode it. His wicked black cloak opened like a raven's wings, his dully masked face looked down at me, and a vicious grin split the ruin of his mouth as he saw that it was I below him.

I could not say which of us twitched the wheel, which of us brought our collision course out of align- ment; I knew I did, but it seemed to me that even as he flew above me on black wings, so too did he, somehow guiding Viccini's creation away though it had no traction in the air. However it came to be, he landed in parallel with me, and with the lightness of a bird; the motorcycle seemed to absorb the impact as if it was irrelevant. *Le Monstre* roared ahead at great speed, giving me a clear look at the machine's broad back tire, which gripped so much road that it must by itself throw the motorcycle forward more quickly than my Indian could dream of, never mind the engine, which I now imagined must be made of stardust to rise and fall so lightly.

He could have lost me in moments; he chose not

to, and instead led me on what seemed a merry chase, but swiftly became clear as the most direct route into Montmartre, where I had not been in many long years. There, he slowed and stopped the great roaring motorcycle and turned to me with challenge flashing in his vivid eyes. "I can go no further, Amélie, but you can."

"Why would I go further when my quarry lies here?" I was off the Indian and of a mind to fight, all my pains and aches of earlier now faded beneath the excitement of facing my enemy.

Le Monstre wore no helmet. Had he one, removing it might have been the dramatic gesture he wanted, but he did not, and so the vigor with which he tore the pig-iron mask from his ruined face spoke of baring the very ruins of his soul. He had been hard enough to look upon in the opera house; here, in fresh daylight in the brilliance of the noontime sun, he was a wound to be cowered from. It was only pride that kept my spine straight as I gazed upon his burns a second time.

"Because you mistake your quarry today. On any other morning, perhaps, you would be right, but not this day, Amélie. Forgive me, but I had to lead you here." He extended his ungloved hand to me; between two fingers he clasped a folded piece of paper.

No cloud came to cover the sun, no rain fell to chill my skin, but I was cold suddenly, so cold that I hardly trusted myself to take the paper from him. My trembling fingers brushed his and I could not say if the shock was electric or ice.

The note was simple, the handwriting plain: Bring the crown to the Moulin Rouge or Baker dies.

That the paper did not tumble from my shaking hand was a wonder; that Paul-Gabriel Laval's face was strained with pain, an even greater marvel. "You," I said after some small silence of terrible length. "You sent Khan the note in my handwriting."

"The elixirs, *ma chérie*," said my one-time lover. "They contain much of you; an Essence of Amélie gave even these warped hands the skill to mimic your letters."

"But how did you know the crown was with him?"

Momentary disdain replaced the agony on his features. "*En vérité*, Amélie, did you think you could fool me? I saw her sing on opening night; the power she commanded the second night was tremendous, but it was mortal. That was not Hatshepsut's crown, and you would not be so foolish as to leave the crown in your own surrounds, could you avoid it. I inquired and learned soon enough that your fellow Centurion was about; to whom else would you turn? It was all too easy, *mon amour*. Loathe me if you must, but do not underestimate me."

I flushed, though whether with anger or shame even I could not say. "And the motorcycle. You followed Khan to find it. Why?"

"I needed speed, stealth, and a certain way to garner your attention." He pressed a hand over his heart, mocking himself; mocking me. "There was an infinitely small chance that you could resist only me, but never that you would ignore both of us together."

"Infinitely small," I agreed under my breath, and stared again at the note, then down the street that led so soon to the infamous dance hall. To that distance I spoke, as if I might deny the presence of my partner in conversation if I did not look at him. "You have the motorcycle's speed and the knowledge of where she is," I said slowly, and in the end, had to return my gaze to him. "Why can you go no further? Why call me to your aid?"

Paul-Gabriel's smile was thin and bitter and full of truths he did not care to acknowledge. The grace of his unburned hand was immeasurable as he gestured with long fingers toward the melted, lumpy mass that was his face, and his voice, when he spoke, was that of my long-ago lover's: soft, poignant, sweet. "Because Christine does not love the Phantom, *mon amour.* She only pities him, and hates him. *Oui,* I could be the hero for her, fight the battles she needs fought, but to do so I would have to come into the light, and you know best of all that I was always a creature of shadows."

I did not want betraying tears to stand in my eyes; I closed them, willing the heat away, and instead wetness rolled free. "You were the sun, to me."

"No." With my eyes closed, the touch of his fingers against my cheek, brushing away tears, was the touch of my lover, unscarred, unstinting, unkind. "No, Amélie. You were the sun, as you have always been, and the best I could do was stand where you shone, and pretend. Go. Shine for my angel of music; show her the way, as you might once have shown me. Let me orchestrate from the shadows, where I belong; let me listen to her sing, and let me fade away forever."

"But you will not, my Gabriel. *My* angel, you will not; I know that already." My eyes had opened as he spoke; he smiled now as my tears dried, and slipped his mask back into place.

"No," he agreed softly. "I will not. And neither will you allow her to die, no more than I could, and so our game will begin again, Amélie, but not today. Not today."

It was the bright daylight of noon; there were no shadows in which to slink away. I blinked once, loathing the weakness of sorrow, and when the blink ended, *le Monstre* was walking away in the sunlight, not a wraith, not a phantom; just a man.

28

I did not look back, once I mounted Viccini's motorcycle with a pained and regretful glance at my beaten Indian. But I would need speed and lightness—and, in sharp truth, desperate curiosity held me in its grasp: I wanted to ride the new bike and might well have no other chance. The Indian would be safe enough; I was known in these parts, and no one would abscond with my beloved motorcycle—or if they did, they knew I would come for them.

Viccini's bike was impossibly light for its size, and with the wide tires gripping the stone, I could not help but feel that their rubber made up most of the vehicle's weight. I tested the brakes, which required only the lightest of touches, and then, with glee, I let the machine go.

It leapt forward like a cat, like a living thing with will and intent of its own. I laughed with a splendid reversal of emotion, letting memories of *le Monstre* flow away for a little while as I hunched low behind the glassy windshield and reveled in how the wind cupped around me. If I had cause for regret, it was that there was only a little distance to traverse; I was not more than a handful of short Parisian blocks from the Moulin Rouge, and Viccini's bike deserved a much more thorough maiden voyage under my guidance. But even if I had not known Josephine's life hung in the balance, an acrid scent was filling the noontime air, and the fear of fire would have driven me not away, but toward, the source of the smell.

No one, I thought as I approached, no one would be so foolish as to set the Moulin Rouge alight, though ugly streaks of smoke were rising in that area. Then I thought again: no Parisian, perhaps no Frenchman, would do so, but I knew already that it was not only *le Monstre* who sought the double cobra crown; so too did the *Führer*. Whilst I knew no stories of Mussolini holding the occult in fascinated regard, it was not impossible that he too might desire an object said to give command over all of ancient Egypt. Still, I believed brownshirts to be more likely than black, and, as I burst through the gates at the Moulin Rouge, I was not disappointed. Within the courtyard were the elephant, the empty stage, and what seemed at first glance to be an extraordinary number of Nazis. I careened past them, joyous at the motorcycle's so-quiet engines that allowed me to approach unexpectedly. I raced to the courtyard's far end and whipped the motorcycle back to face them whilst I took in the situation.

The Moulin Rouge's titular windmill stood above

the garden entrance, and Josephine Baker was trussed to one of its red sails so thoroughly I doubted she could easily draw breath. Ropes wound from her shoulders to ankles; below the ropes dangled bare feet; above them gleamed bared teeth, for—perhaps anticipating delight from her screams—they had not gagged her. If so, their hopes were for the moment dashed; never in my life had I seen a woman who looked less inclined to scream in fear than did *la grande dame* now.

It might well have been wisdom that stilled her screams, though; a pyre of pallets propped against the entrance's foot burned sullenly and smoked profusely thanks to the previous night's rain, and that smoke rose inexorably toward Josephine. Screaming would mean drawing more of that blackened smog into her throat and would risk damaging her astonishing voice; even in the midst of danger, she behaved as though the show would go on.

And go on it would, had I anything to say about it. My first business was to free Josephine before smoke ruined her voice; my second was to deal with the Nazi scourge.

There were over thirty, now that I had a moment to count: an unnecessary number, given that their enemy numbered two, and one of those was bound to a windmill's leaves dozens of feet above the ground. But then, I had bested half a dozen of their biplanes by myself; perhaps they were wise to be overprepared. With that in mind, I spun the motorcycle to a stop, offering them the broad side of it—arrogant, perhaps even foolish, but also suited to proving myself unconcerned about their superior numbers—and spoke. "Josephine, I shall be with you in a moment. Fascist dogs, this is your opportunity to run. I will not stop you."

One or two shifted as if they might like to accept that offer, but quelling glares pinned them in place and, as a whole, a certain readiness came into the troops. "*D'accord*," I said beneath my breath, "we will do this the difficult way, then."

I gunned Viccini's motorcycle with the full intention of launching myself and the bike straight into battle. Its size and speed would stand me well against so many opponents; should it come to the worst as I fought my way to Josephine, I could always lay the motorcycle out and take many of the Nazis down at once. It would, of course, be my final choice, for I had no wish to damage the prototype—but it could, if necessary, be rebuilt. Josephine Baker could not.

"*Wait!*" A voice broke through the ranks; a voice which told me I had not, after all, seen everything in my sweep of the courtyard. I killed the motorcycle's engine, which, though in itself not loud, left an echoing silence in the courtyard; a silence which allowed footsteps to reverberate, and for the quick shuffle of bodies parting to sound loud as a windstorm beneath the turning wheel of the *moulin*.

Clad once again in Nazi uniform, Kiera Knapp strode forth from behind the troops with her chin lifted high and a light of madness in her hazel eyes. "The crown, Amelia."

I admit to my astonishment without shame; even then, gaping at her, I could not entirely believe that she was not somehow being forced to this. With this in mind I said, "Kiera?" in honest bewilderment. "Kiera, *ma chérie*, you are free of him now, you do not need to..."

"Free?" she demanded incredulously, then laughed. "My God, Amelia, just because you might have crawled back to him doesn't mean you should believe that anyone would. I haven't been his creature since the moment he left me with the *Führer*'s troops. It was the chance I've been waiting for, after *years* of playing my part—"

"Years?" I echoed, and this time it was I whose incredulity could not be contained. "Kiera, you are no more than half my age, a mere child! You cannot have waited years for anything! Stop this nonsense immediately, Commander Knapp; you are better than this."

"I'm better than *you*," she corrected with a sneer, then half-turned away and withdrew from her waistband not a standard German pistol, but a snub-nosed flare gun, which she pointed directly at the wooden sails of the *moulin* above us. "The crown, Amelia," she said softly, "or I will set the windmill itself alight, and you can fight my men while wondering which will take your darling Josephine first, the smoke or the flames."

With dreadful slowness I came to understand that she was quite sincere and also, it seemed, quite mad. I had seen her as a reflection of myself, a child who

needed protection; I had admired her for her bravery
in telling me where I might find *le Monstre*. I wondered
now if she had slept at all the night before, or if she
lain awake until I had come and gone again, and then
stolen Josephine in order to further her own nefarious
plans. I could not, as of yet, imagine her ultimate
design, but if in her determination she was willing to
lie down with the *Führer*, no good could come of it for
anyone.

Carefully, although with no intention of giving in
to her demands, I dismounted Viccini's motorcycle
and lifted my hands. "The crown is tucked into the
back of my coat, above the waistband. I will loosen
the waistband and remove the crown." A full half of
that claim was true: the crown *was* at the small of my
back, but it was the guns I wore beneath the coat that
I wished to lay hands on.

Kiera uttered a warning sound and gestured with
her flare gun; no fewer than five of her troops immediately stepped up to me, loosening my jacket's belt
themselves. The crown fell before they had time to
discover my weaponry; its heavy, swift fall caused a
dive and scramble, as if they hoped they could catch it
before it hit the cobbles.

With a kick, a knee, and an elbow I felled three of
them before gold smacked against stone; the fourth,
distracted by my swift actions, made the error of
looking up in surprise rather than pursuing the prize.
I dispatched him with a powerful fist to the chin just
as Kiera began to comprehend that her plans had
gone awry. She cried out in anger and the flare gun

fired. For an instant we were all transfixed by its trajectory, the stream of smoke its red glare left behind before it struck not, *grâce à dieu*, Josephine herself, but the sail beside her. That wood, ever turning, was drier than the pallets at the windmill's foot, and after a few seconds of smoldering, flames caught and began to burn.

Josephine, who had up until now been so resolute, screamed in terror, and to that accompaniment, mayhem was unleashed.

29

I no longer cared about the crown. My only concern was reaching Josephine before flames bit into her skin, smoke stole the breath from her body, or fire wrecked the *moulin*'s integrity and dashed her beautiful form to the cobblestones below. To this end, I scrambled upward, searching for any bit of leverage I might attain. Nazi troops, trying desperately to please their mistress by presenting her with the coveted crown, assisted me in this by flinging themselves bodily upon the crown and dismissing me almost entirely. One or two unlucky fascists encountered me instead of the ever-growing stack of men, but I struck them down with ease as I ran for the windmill.

Slowly burning pallets would never take me high enough on the *moulin*'s sides, even if I could climb them without turning myself to a cinder. There were no stairs circling the windmill's exterior; to reach it one must go inside the garden entrance, or use a ladder. The entrance was, of course, littered with smoldering pallets; those I had knocked aside in my impetuous entrance had been replaced. Now, as if sensing my need and hastening to disoblige, those pallets finally burst into full and enthusiastic flame.

"*Amelia!*" Josephine's shriek shivered the *moulin* walls. Disregarding all personal safety, I tore at the pallets, flinging burning chunks of wood aside, a feat I could not have done if I did not wear leather from head to toe, and one which, despite the leather, I was not eager to be long at pursuing. Acrid smoke stung my eyes. I tried not to breathe it in, but it was hard going, and holding my breath made it all the more difficult. Only one thing lay in the fire's favor, which was that those Nazi troops who could not hope to reach the crown also had no interest in trying to reach me. I blessed their lack-wittedness, for my back certainly made an open and appealing target, but not one of them thought to make use of their sidearms. By this I concluded they were young and green; the *Führer* would not, I thought, use inexperienced troops in his next occultish venture, though I could see that this might be considered a proving ground.

Fortunately, they seemed to have nothing, as yet, to prove. Coughing and weeping from the smoke, I finally broke through to the entrance and found the door within—infuriatingly—locked.

It was also wooden, and my temper had reached its limits. With a shout that came from my belly, I delivered a side kick with the hard heel of my motor-cycle boot and was rewarded with a sharp, deep crack from the wood. My second kick was no less resolute; this time, splinters shattered everywhere and the door moaned its way open. Snarling with success, I leapt the kindling and low-licking flames to enter the *moulin*, and was surprised to encounter no resistance within. *Le Monstre* would have left men to burn in order to stop me; I had expected the same of Kiera, whom I was now willing to paint as a villain. I took the stairs three, then two, at a time, as the effects of smoke inhalation slowed but did not stop me. They could not be permitted to do so; the marvelous Madame Baker's life depended upon it.

That there was a second door at the top of the windmill, also locked, was an insult nearly too great to be borne. It was far more fragile than the exterior door; a running crash led by my shoulder splintered it and I was through, into a haze of orange smoke and terrified screams as the windmill's sails swept by me.

I knew nothing of windmill construction save that there had to be *some* kind of turning device at the center of the sails. Lacking time to consider, I stripped my leather coat off and threw it into the guts of the thing; the machine groaned and tore, my jacket strained and blackened, and the whole of it shuddered to a reluctant stop. Triumphant, I spun to receive Josephine's accolades, only to discover I had stopped the sail with its precious cargo at the highest point of its circle. Josephine's screams had stopped, but not out of admiration: she glowered at me through the smoke and demanded, "Now what?"

"I suppose, madame, that now I scale the tower to save the—"

"If you say witch, I'll bite you when you get up here."

Grinning, I examined the predicament I had put us both into, and swiftly devised a plan. Though one of the sails was alight, it was not the nearest-most to me; the nearest one, pointing nearly directly downward and equally directly below Josephine, was thus far in perfect condition and—as they all were—made up of three increasingly small wooden segments lashed together by struts, nails, and wire. It was of no particular consequence to climb these like a ladder, although the intensifying smoke made breathing and seeing increasingly more difficult. I paused at the gears, wondering if I might somehow rescue my jacket, but it was not to be; it lay stretched and mangled, brown leather smeared with black tar or smoke, with metal teeth jutting through it hither and yon. With a regretful sigh I bade it farewell, and completed my climb.

In mere moments I was nose-to-nose with Josephine Baker, who now, evidently confident of rescue, showed no signs at all of fear; indeed, the expression in her eyes might well be called a challenge. "Well?"

I slipped the knife from my thigh-sheath and spun it in my palm, knowing quite well that it was folly to show off in such a precarious position and yet unable to resist under her expectant gaze. One of her immaculately groomed eyebrows flickered upward as I took knife to rope and with swift, certain slices reduced her bonds to so many bits of string.

She could not help but fall forward; there was nothing but myself between her and the ground below. I spun the blade back into its sheath and caught her with one arm, trusting the strength of the other to hold us to the *moulin*'s sail. "The queen," I said then, and earned the grace of her slow smile. "I believe, madame, that I have scaled the tower to save the queen. Now if your majesty will be so good as to embrace me so that I might carry us down again...?"

"My majesty would be delighted," purred *la diva*, and for a heady moment clung to me so closely that the scent of her perfume was more intense than the stench of the fire.

It was at that moment, *naturellement*, that my beleaguered jacket gave way and the red sails of the *moulin* began again to spin.

30

Josephine shrieked, not in delight; the sound, so close against my ear, sent a ringing through my skull and a pain behind my eyes. Through gritted teeth, I suggested, "Perhaps not quite so loudly, my queen," and her quick gasp was of embarrassed apology. Then, no longer given to play-acting, I commanded, "Hold tight," and obeyed my own instructions as the sail began its downward arc.

It was not impossible; it was not even particularly difficult, save that we had been upright at the apex of the wheel and would necessarily be upside-down at its nadir, which hung over open ground and fire rather than the small walkway around the *moulin*'s top. Alone I could have managed it without a second thought; burdened, however gloriously, by Josephine, I was obliged to strain myself somewhat. "Wrap your legs around my waist, Josephine, and bury your face in my shoulder. Do not let go or look until I tell you to."

"You're going to do something mad, aren't you?"

she asked, but, somewhat to my surprise, did precisely as I requested. With her thusly attached, I gripped the sail's upper lip and swung us to its backside, putting us that much closer to the approaching *moulin* floor. Josephine looked up; I snapped, "*Jojo!*" and she buried her face against my neck once again.

I could not allow us to be turned entirely topsy-turvy; it was critical to leap free at just the right moment, before gravity made the task all the more complicated. I watched, counting the seconds, and when I judged the moment right, thrust away with all the power at my command, leaping the small but deadly distance.

Josephine screamed in my ear again, an outburst silenced by dint of my landing atop her with a fair amount of force when we crashed to the walkway floor. Her eyes bulged and I rolled away, but the damage was done: she could not inhale again until the last wheezes of air had escaped her diaphragm. When she did once more breathe in, it was a tremendous, gulping gasp that ended in a squeaked demand: "*Jojo?*"

A chuckle ran through me. "I thought the liberty of such an intimate nickname might be permitted, given your legs were wrapped around my waist, madame. Forgive me if I overstepped my bounds."

"This time," she squeaked, still not entirely at ease with the breathing process, but a shred of humor was visible in her eyes and she managed to waggle a finger at me. "This time, Madame Stone." Her third gasp for air righted her somewhat and, pressing a hand to her belly, she worked her way to her feet. "Tell me, *Amy*, how are we going to get out of here? Oh, your face." Despite the recent blow to her diaphragm, a broad, full laugh pealed from her. "All right already, people do call me Jojo, but I can tell nobody's ever called you Amy in your life. Still," she said, impish and delightful, "given that I had my legs around your waist, *mi ami*, I think I've earned the liberty."

I could not retrieve a semblance of neutrality no matter how hard I struggled for it; Josephine, laughing again, seized my hand and pulled me toward the door I had broken down. "Your face will freeze like that if the wind catches you, and we're on a windmill. Come on, Amelia. Save me." Her laughter suddenly disappeared. "And finish that betraying little beast called Kiera."

My own amusement vanished. I put myself in front of Josephine, showing her how to fold her arm over her face to slow the inhalation of smoke. She bestowed upon me a look that implied my wits were duller than usual, and slid the knife on my thigh from its sheath. She slashed the skirt of her dress, creating two masks in a matter of seconds. Still with the same look, though now tinged with fondness, she restored the blade to its sheath, tied the mask around my face, and murmured, "Madame *Voleur*," with obvious delight before making use of her own mask.

I murmured, "I am only a thief if there is something I might be permitted to steal," and then, both pleased at her perspicacity and exasperated at my own lack of it, I added, "What, no water to douse these fine masks in? Madame Baker, I fear you are a merely adequate sidekick."

She kicked me in the side as I began my way down the stairs, a blow with enough force to make me stumble, but more, to make me laugh. "I deserved that."

"You deserve a considerably more thorough tongue-lashing, but under the circumstances I'm afraid it's going to have to wait." Her tone was so arch I dared not look back for fear of blushing when I met her eyes, but I turned my head enough that she could see the shape of a smile spreading across my face, even masked as I was. I reached for her hand; she put it in mine, and together we hurried down the stairs, grateful that the *moulin*'s walls had not yet begun to give way to the fire.

We burst forth onto a scene of chaos. I had expected that Kiera, the crown safely in hand, would be well gone. Instead there seemed to be a *bataille royale* going on over the crown itself. Some number of the fascist troops appeared to be loyal to Kiera, as evidenced by the protective stance they had taken up around her. Others, perhaps more ambitious, seemed to have concluded that they themselves might rise in the ranks should they be the one to present *der Führer* with the *pschent*. All of this I surmised by the fact that the battle was pitched, that some men still wore their armbands and others did not, and, most especially, from the greedy bellows that emanated from the struggling troops.

"Stay here," I commanded Josephine, and flung

myself toward the bottom of the writhing pile of men, hoping my slighter frame might allow me to squirm my way in and seize the crown from an unlucky pair of hands at the heap's center. Instead I had no more begun my attempt when, from the top of the mountain, came a huge roar of satisfaction. I withdrew in time to see the double cobra crown arc through the air to be caught in Kiera Knapp's confident grip.

To my surprise, she did not jam it onto her head immediately, but rather dipped her hand into the breast of her long black jacket, whence she withdrew a vial. Smiling cruelly, she lifted it high, cried out, "Hunt well, my dogs! Amelia Stone is your prey!" and dashed the vial to the cobblestoned earth.

The familiar reek of Obedience rose up. I held my breath, grateful for the mask that still clotted my senses, but as one, the Nazi troops turned from inflicting damage on one another with the clear intent of instead taking out their aggressions upon my own unfortunate self. I struggled to see where Kiera's path took her as fists began to fly at me until, incensed, I roared, "*Out of my way!*"

To no one's astonishment more than my own, the obedient fascists fell back, making a pathway. Laughter stuck in my throat. "Good. Sit down and stay still until someone of authority gives you other instructions." With my pursuit thus stymied and, in the distance, fire bells ringing to assure me that the *moulin* would be saved in short order, I sprinted after

Kiera, only to be arrested by Josephine's eager call: "Amelia! Amelia, wait!"

Astonished, I turned to find the singer racing after me. Dizzy with delight and dismay, I caught myself on Viccini's motorcycle and put a hand out to Madame Baker, who caught my fingers in her own and breathlessly insisted, "I'm coming with you."

My knees knocked in one part wishing and in one part trepidation. "Josephine, *ma chérie*, I admire and adore you; your bravery is without question and your wits sharper than nearly anyone I know. But you are not, as I am, a brawler, and where I go now, what I must do next, are not places for you to go or things for you to see. I beg you to heed my pleas and remain here, in safety."

"You've got to be kidding, Amelia! Miss out on the final act after all of this? Not a chance!"

My very soul slumped as she spoke the protest I had feared she would. "Josephine, listen to me, *s'il vous plaît*. If any harm should come to you I could never forgive myself, but more than that, even, if any harm should come to you, then how could the show go on? Paris needs you, *ma chérie*; your audience needs you. We all need one such as you to show us the depths and trials of life in such a way as we can bear them; you are a muse, *mon amour*. Do not deny us the triumph of your voice rising above all this madness to show us the light." Had I been ever so slightly bolder, I might have kissed the full softness of her lips then, for she was never so lovely as she was then, gazing upon me, soft with pleasure at my words.

But I did not kiss her, and was to regret it forevermore, for the passion and romance of the moment passed and her mouth quirked in amusement. "Nice try, Amelia, but—"

Knowing it was both unforgivable and for her own safety, I spun her from me, unbalanced her over the seat of Viccini's motorcycle and left her for the fire brigade to find, tidily tied there with the remnants of the rope that had bound her to the *moulin*.

There was not a soul native to Paris who did not know that beneath the city was a riddle of catacombs and tunnels that led as far as forty miles afield. There were few, indeed, who had not searched out some spot through which they might enter and explore that endless maze, and some few who had of course never returned. The chambers beneath *le Monstre*'s warehouse lair had touched on them; it was perhaps inevitable that he had run to them seventeen years ago when the flame had driven him to madness. It was equally inevitable that I could never have found him in them; their twists and turns were too many, and so the fox need only stay one corner ahead of the hounds to survive.

The fox which now led me beneath the city was fleet of foot and driven by righteous fear of her pursuant, but that, I thought, was not truly what drove her underground. She had the *pschent*; there had to be some greater plot that I did not yet see that

moved her to bring it into the catacombs instead of to
der Führer, though I suspected Kiera had no more
loyalty toward him than she did for *le Monstre*. Something else was afoot, and I gave chase with an energy
fueled by fury; whatever the purpose of her plot, I did
not care for being its mark.

It was in part this blind rage that sent me into the
first trap; had I been properly wary, I might have seen
the signs of it in the way Kiera leapt nimbly from one
stone to another, almost dancing, but in my anger I
saw her lithe motions as mockery, proving that she
was not afraid of me after all.

I might also have blamed the light: though it was
midday above the streets, below them there were only
sudden pools of striated daylight where grates above
showed promises of the upper world. Between those
pools, limestone walls bounced and reflected some of
their light, and Kiera, who had always intended to
retreat into the catacombs, had a lamp; it made her
easier to follow and yet dangerous to lose, for what
light she brought was nearly all I had. Without the
shining beacon of her lamp, it was at best dusky,
hardly showing the pitted walls or the shadowy inhabi-
tants therein. I was grateful for that: I did not need the
leering faces of the long dead to add to my disquiet.
As it was, the scent of damp and decay brought back
far too vivid memories of the day I had discovered my
parents bound to the Emotion Extractor chairs.

Oui; it was memory, more than anything, that let
the first trap close around me. So embroiled in past

emotions was I that I did not think to echo Kiera's dancing steps, only charged forth like the bull in the china shop, and was nothing but purely astonished when the floor itself crumbled beneath my feet.

There was a word for these holes: *oubliette*, a place where one threw people to forget about them. Most oubliettes, though, were only that: a hole. But some more enterprising soul had thought to litter the floor of this one with four-foot spikes, all sharpened to a razor's edge and of such strong material that it was the falling stones which shattered further upon impact, and not the spikes that dulled or fell.

I leapt, knowing that the breaking stone beneath my feet would never support a jump as lengthy as mine must be. Nor was I wrong: most of what I accomplished was laying myself out so that when I fell it would be my belly that struck the spikes, thus ensuring a long and painful death. But a few pillars remained amongst the shattering floor, those few points upon which Kiera had danced her weight, knowing that they were safe. My fingertips clawed one of those pillars and held me; I swung into it with great force, knocking the wind from my belly. Like a child clinging to its parent—or like Josephine Baker clinging to me so recently I could still taste the scent of her perfume—I wrapped my legs around the pillar's narrow width, and told myself the sounds escaping through my teeth were whines of exertion, not whimpers of terror. After a moment I found that my arms, too, were wrapped around the pillar and hugging it with such strength that it was a wonder it did not fall to pieces in my grasp.

I could not go down—the floor would make a pincushion of me, even if I controlled my descent; a sneeze or a misstep and slip would spell my doom. Nor, it appeared, could I go up—the grip I held on the pillar would not be loosened for love or money, neither of which was in abundance to tempt me into seeing if I was wrong.

It would be an ignominious death, clinging to a pillar until I rotted. With a sigh that I chose not to think of as frightened, I pinched my thighs together one whit more tightly and, thus secured, convinced my arms to scoot up a mere quarter-inch or so. It required several iterations of these minute movements to move my arms high enough that I could then tighten them and in turn loosen my legs, scooting myself up some infinitesimally small distance. By the third or fourth cycle I had grown bolder and also, perhaps, much more aware that Kiera's departure meant the light was gone, and I was beginning to imagine the things that might crawl out of the dark. Whilst I might normally consider myself fearless enough to face all comers, the scent-borne memories of the place reduced some part of my soul to the quivering fear of a child: of the child I had been when I first faced *le Monstre*. I simply did not wish to be alone in the dark in the catacombs; my nerves were not prepared for that, even if my fellow Centurions might scoff.

It was thus with some haste I finally flung one arm

over the pillar's top and dragged myself up to balance precariously upon it, and it was only then that I began to appreciate the true difficulty in which I now found myself.

Kiera's light was gone entirely; only the fact that my eyes had slowly adjusted to the faint glimmers from above allowed me to see at all, and then, not well. Well enough to know—to almost sense—that there were other pillars upon which I might balance, but far too poorly to judge the distances to them so that I might leap free of this predicament. Above me the curved, carved tunnel roof offered no assistance. I could perhaps create some sort of swinging mechanism with the leather gun holsters secured around my torso, but there were no visible hooks from which I could dangle and swing. My choices were to go down to the spine-ridden floor and search blindly for a way up the far wall, or jump.

With a roar intended wholly to drown my own fear, I leapt before I could think on it further: toward the left, and forward, trying to recall in my mind's eye the steps Kiera had taken as she danced through the death trap. My feet hit squarely. Scarcely able to believe my own good fortune, I leapt again, this time surging to the right—and this time I was not so fortunate. My right foot landed hard on a pillar's edge; my left, not at all. My right ankle twisted and so did I, too frightened, too desperate, to even scream. My right arm, flailing as I fell, caught the pillar's flat top; so too did my jaw, which snapped shut hard enough to cause stars in my vision. Before I could stop moving and think, I called on desperate strength and hauled myself upward. The very moment my feet were under me, I crouched, turned to face the way I believed I had been traveling—in the dark, after the fall, I could no longer tell—and with a prayer for wings, jumped.

A coward dies a thousand deaths, they say, and a brave soul, but one. In that leap, I was a coward, imagining every iteration of pain that I might soon face; pierced through the eye, the kidney, the stomach, the lung—all the worst ways to die by piercing came to me, but I could no more alter my course now than I might change the path of the sun in the sky.

I hit solid stone, rolled, and came up against a wall with such force that dust shook from above and coated my gasping face with the detritus of dead men.

32

I was not dead; this was chiefest amongst my blessings. I was also in the dark, alone, and without any notion of where I ought to be. Silence was my only companion, and no matter how intently I listened, I could not discern the distant echo of Kiera's footsteps. My choices, though, were simple: go on in the darkness or go back. The latter was no choice at all, nor would it have been had I an easy way to cross the broken floor again. It was onward, as always; onward through darkness and silence, with my fingers stretched to brush both walls so I might find side passages, and each step taken slowly so I would not plummet should another pit open beneath my feet.

Even in the depths—and we had gone deep before the trap had opened on me—even in them there were ways to guess at direction: the sound of water flowing, or the slightest breeze. I cursed my foolishness in having not stopped for a torch, but it was too late for regrets; instead, I did the best I could, scenting for a hint of human sweat and pausing, when I reached passageways, to gently investigate the dust on the floor, brushing my fingers clean after each examination so I might have some chance of telling whether Kiera had passed this way before me.

Thrice I found passages where the dust, sometimes fingertip-deep, was broken. Thrice I followed those passages, hoping that if they did not lead me to Kiera or *le Monstre* they might at least take me to an inhabited site within the catacombs, and that from there I might find my way back to the surface. I began to believe I could see again: that the white sparks in my vision, born of the eye's desperation for information, were in fact light that could guide me. Unwisely emboldened by this illusion, I began to walk more swiftly, though my belly was tight with apprehension each time my foot touched the ground. Once in a while I encountered a loose stone and kicked it forward, listening to the clicks and bounces as if they were sonar, telling me where I dared or dared not step.

In time, this intense listening suggested to me that there was more space above my head than there had been, as if the catacombs rose up in cavernous arches. I breathed more freely for a moment, but found the sound disturbed my efforts at navigating like a bat, and returned to the slow, shallow breaths I had unconsciously adopted. In that very moment, I perceived the faintest whistle of rapidly disturbed air, a sound so unlikely that I fell to the floor, not even knowing why. Doing so saved me from certain death: a boulder as broad as the tunnel whizzed over my spine. It swung back again a moment later, its breeze riffling my hair. Physics demanded that it would at some point stop; if I remained where I lay, I would be trapped beneath it, perhaps not crushed but certainly unable to move. As it swung a third time, passing behind me again, I crawled forward on my belly, staying as low to the dusty ground as I could. Each swing came faster, the pendulum's arc shortening, but when it groaned to a stop I lay some yards beyond its weight, still on my belly and gasping at the nearness of my miss. I rolled onto my back, staring sightlessly at the high ceiling, and suddenly grinned.

I had not yet gone astray, it seemed; there would be no need for traps if there was nothing ahead of me to hide. Heartened, I all but leapt to my feet, but in the swiftness of my actions thought I heard something, and went silently still.

German voices, some distance behind me, shouted orders to one another with no evident fear of being overheard. They were pleased with themselves; they had passed the pit trap without injury, by which I surmised they must be carrying appropriate materials to deal with the catacombs as a whole: rope, picks, grease—a dozen possible items, but most importantly, *lumière*. I suddenly wanted light so badly it became a taste in my mouth, bright and clean after all the dust I had breathed in.

I remained where I was, heart palpitating as I considered my options. They would soon encounter the boulder that blocked the passage. I darted back to examine its shape with my hands: round, as I had suspected; if it had been squared to the passage, I would not be standing there to tell my tale. I knelt, gauging the distance between the rounded sides and the catacomb walls. *I* could fit through if I had to—if I had grease, and perhaps applied it to my bare skin, and then had a certain lack of regard for the condition of that skin once I had squirmed through—but anyone larger than me would have great difficulty. There were bound to be youths amongst the troops, though, and it was possible that a narrow-shouldered young man, necessarily lacking my own attributes, might fit more easily than even I. Thoughtful, I backed away from the boulder once more and stood quietly, listening to the Nazi approach and garnering what knowledge I could from the scraps of conversation that floated toward me.

Their loyalty to the *Führer* had outweighed the elixir of Obedience; that, or a single vial broken among so many had simply lacked the strength to keep them in rein for long. They were more interested in obtaining the double cobra crown than in arresting me, though I imagined they would regard me as an entirely suitable secondary prize.

Exasperation rose in the voices when they finally reached the boulder that separated us. A brief discussion took place, ending as I hoped it would: with a youth ordered to strip down and squeeze through; they would then pass him a light and he could investigate some small way ahead to make certain the path was clear and that they were going the right way. Smiling in the dark, I moved far enough away that he could come through unimpeded, and even found myself in some sympathy as he grunted and cursed while wiggling through.

At what must have been the very moment he completed the passage, he demanded, "The torch! And my clothes, for God's sake, my clothes!" in near-panic-stricken German.

Laughter bounced around the boulder and the torch was passed through before his clothes, which he was obliged to request again, in a far politer tone. My grin was as broad as his superiors', though I did not allow myself the luxury of actual laughter. He sighed in relief as the clothes came through and, foolishly, set the torch down beside himself, pointing *toward* the boulder, not away from it. While he pulled his trousers on and sat to don socks and boots, I crept up behind him silently and laced an arm around his throat, squeezing with all due strength; within seconds he fell unconscious without ever having made a sound. I laid him out quietly, collected the torch, and paused briefly to examine his build: slim-shouldered indeed, and altogether too much of a youth to suit my fancy, although his sleeping face was handsome enough. Feeling lighthearted, I blew him an apologetic kiss and, now able to see clearly, broke into a swift run. It would be a minute or more before his comrades even began to suspect something was wrong, and, I trusted, considerably longer before they were able to do anything about it.

I considered, briefly, the possibility that they might carry demolitions with them, and dismissed the concern: the risk of bringing the entire section of catacombs down upon themselves was too high when the goal was merely pursuit, not survival. I, at least, would not choose to risk that level of action unless I faced otherwise certain death. Breaking the boulder to bits with pickaxes would be far more time consuming, but much safer. I believed I had earned myself a long head start.

It came as some surprise, then, when several minutes later, explosives rattled the entire catacomb system. Dust and stone rained on me from above and I turned to stare back into the pale darkness with genuine astonishment, and a hope that the poor boy I had rendered unconscious had awakened and moved away before a boulder was demolished on top of him. I had no sympathy for the Nazi cause, but a half-naked boy lying beneath rubble was a person, not a cause, and worthy of justice.

This, though, was not the time to see how badly used he may or may not have been. I turned again and continued my journey, able now to follow foot-steps and see the passages Kiera had chosen. Behind me, newly motivated troops moved swiftly to catch up, and whilst the narrowness of the catacomb tunnels might offer me sufficient advantage to defeat so many, in this particular case I preferred not to fight.

Armed with a light, I saw the third trap before I triggered it, and, toothfully pleased, darted past the danger point to set it off myself: a severed rope allowed another massive boulder to roll entirely free. I stood near the top of a slight incline; the boulder picked up speed almost immediately, rumbling and crashing loudly as it bounced toward the Nazi troops.

Shouted orders echoed along the passageways, followed by high-pitched squeals as men threw themselves into the cut-out tombs along the catacomb walls and, I imagined, embraced Death far more literally than they might ever have hoped to. I resumed my own journey with a florid bow that I thought would please *le Monstre*'s theatrics; he had, after all, been the architect of my escape from these pursuers. I listened as I climbed, and after some time, heard the boulder grind to a halt. There would be some men on my side of it, but many more would be trapped on the far side. If fortune favored me, none of them would have explosives left, so that those few who followed me, if they did, could be dealt with easily enough when the time came.

The air's texture changed as I hurried forward: warmth came into it, and the lightest scent of well-oiled machinery. Triumph clenched my gut and I broke into a run, following the warmth and increasing smells of humanity, eager to lay my hands upon Knapp and end this farce for good. Those behind me were forgotten; all that mattered now was Knapp, and in her aftermath, *le Monstre*. Justice would at last be mine.

33

I flung open the rotting wooden door with, I admit, some expectation of becoming the main player upon the stage; Josephine's dramatics, it seemed, had infected me. But no sooner did the door crash against its stone setting than I realized I was, *en vérité*, the very least player upon the stage, so unexpected were the other actors.

The room's size put *le Monstre*'s old lair to shame; it very nearly put the opera house to shame. It was not a place of rot and damp, but rather a clean and modern laboratory, with curved, plastered walls painted soothing cream that brightened but did not blind as electric lights reflected off their smooth surfaces. Betwixt the light settings were steel cabinets set into the very walls; their glass-doored fronts showed row after row of beautifully colored liquids, arranged in dizzying arrays. These were the elixirs, and their clever cabinetry no doubt helped to keep them cool so they would not spoil. A full quarter of the walls were taken up by these units, and I knew a moment's horror, wondering how many innocents had fallen to fill *le Monstre*'s vials.

But if I was the least player, the cabinets were the least of the setting. Around them, also set into the walls, stood chambers no more than a hand's-width apart from each other. Each of these chambers was coffin-shaped and primarily made of a door; large handles intersected the midpoint of each. But at chest height, rising to the top, each chamber also had a window, within which much steam and colorful lighting could be seen. I did not know, and did not *want* to know, what lay within them. There were easily two dozen of those chambers, perhaps more, and anything within was likely to spell a certain doom for the solitary Centurion who had chosen to throw herself into this fray.

A host of lesser things—tables, beakers, papers, desks, and the like—made a smaller circle within the great shape of the room. But other than a brief awareness that many of the items displayed upon them could be used as weaponry, I did not take much notice of them, for within both concentric circles were the two people I pursued: Knapp and *le Monstre*, who stood locked in a struggle unlike anything I had ever expected.

He fought to wrest the double cobra crown from her grip; *she* lashed and fought and bit in an attempt to reach a great red-topped plunger that fed innumerable tubes running from beneath the plunger's table to the windowed chambers all around the room. His strength was terrible, the power of a madman, but he was crippled by his burns. She was weaker but, it seemed, also taken with the strength of madness; as his burned hand lost its grip on the crown, she swung it with remorseless violence, impacting his head with such force I flinched with it.

So too did *le Monstre*, but ill luck held for Knapp: she had taken him on the masked side, and though the ringing of two metals clashing reverberated in the room, it only stunned, rather than felled, *le Monstre*. But that was all the time she needed; with both hands, she threw all her weight onto the plunger, which shuddered as it sank.

Liquid of such bloodlike hue coursed through the tubes that I watched in fascinated dread to see what would happen when it reached the coffin chambers. But as suddenly as the blood flowed, then so to did another color, and then a third, and a fourth: elixirs, then, not blood, but they could mean nothing better as they rushed toward the chambers.

Le Monstre howled protest, bringing my attention and Knapp's back to him; this time when Knapp hit him with the crown, she directed the blow to his unprotected cheek and sent him into a collapsing spin. He fell and did not rise again, though consciousness was still his own and he did not cower before her; my angel had never cowered in his life. When he spoke, his cultured voice could not quite hide his honest confusion, though he did a better job of it than any save a trained performer like Josephine might have managed: "Why? Or, why now, as I am now certain you've intended this for years, perhaps since the beginning...?"

"Don't you know?" Knapp bent, though she never came close enough for him to seize her and gain the advantage. "*Don't you know who I am?*"

The strangest, most gentle smile I had ever seen on his face touched *le Monstre*'s lips. "Of course I do. You have the look of your mother. You always have. You could not imagine I regularly selected waifs from the street to raise, Kiera. I had forgotten," he confessed, so softly I found myself straining to hear. "I had forgotten, in my pain and rage, that you had even come into this world, until I saw you by chance one day. I began this project then," he said with his gaze going to the now wildly steaming chambers. "I began it because I could not bear for you to look upon my ruined face and to see the fear and revulsion in your gaze. I wanted to be beautiful again before I confessed the truth to you, though it now seems you've known it all along. Amélie," he said, so unexpectedly and clearly that even I startled, as though I had forgotten I stood witness to this strange scene.

Kiera, it seemed, had not known at all; her startlement was far greater than my own, and turned at once to blackest rage. She fell back from *le Monstre* with a stride or two toward me, then stood trembling in one place, unable to decide where to first unleash her fury.

My angel, *le Monstre*, stood when she stepped away, and with careful motions I knew so well, tidied his cuffs, his collar, and brushed imagined dirt from his trousers before speaking again. "Amélie, in a few moments you will have done the maths, and although it will make no difference to you now, I would like you to know that in all the ways I did betray you, this was not one of them: I knew Kiera's mother before I knew you, though Kiera was born in the time we were together."

"But her surname is German," I said in perfectly foolish astonishment, and cringed to have even entered the conversation, when silence would have been all the wiser. I did not think I felt betrayed; I was too surprised for that, and too embarrassed that I had missed what—in truth—did not seem at all obvious, even now.

"My stepfather's surname," Kiera spat. "He married my mother, ruined though she was, and he taught me to fight, so that when they died I was able to care for myself until I worked my way under *his* wing. Yes," she snarled at the now immaculate *Monstre*, "I knew. I always knew, and all I ever wanted to do was destroy you. But then you had *this*!" She flung her arms wide, embracing the whole of the room. Paul-Gabriel and I both tensed subtly, watching the crown in hopes that it would fly free, but *non*: she kept it tightly gripped in one hand. "All of this, and once I understood, I knew I could live forever once you perfected it. I have been waiting, *Father*, so that on your day of greatest triumph I could take it all from you! The crown. *Baker*. Your lust for *les divas*, for the purity of their voices, is pathetic. When you traded me to the *Führer*'s men, I knew the time was right; with their help I could be certain you would be left to die with nothing."

Her mouth curved into a cruel smile. "And then who should come back but Amelia Stone, for whom you spurned my mother. I could not have asked for more. Now you will die here together, and I will make certain that it is in flames."

With thunderous clanks the coffin door handles disengaged, and from the opening doors stepped dozens of men with the perfect, unspoiled features of my childhood angel, *le Monstre aux Yeux Verts*.

34

"Paul-Gabriel, what have you done?" The question barely passed my lips, but his rough laugh said that he had heard me. Like me, he could not take his eyes from the copies of him. They were perfect, and yet not; those beautiful faces were not as I remembered him from my youth, charming and clever, but rather they began to distort and contort with the blackest of emotions: hatred, rage, envy, fear. All they lacked was the will to act, and not one of us thought, in those first stunned moments of their lives, to command that will. I was too awestricken, too horrified; Kiera too enamored; and *le Monstre*, too filled with pride.

"They were meant to be filled with Obedience," he replied nearly as softly. "They were meant to be sculpted, perfected, until I could distill all that was my own essence, and with the crown, command them all to take that essence and become me. I have spent a lifetime creating these elixirs, Amélie; did you never wonder why? I have always meant to rule, though for a time I despaired of it; the burns," he said, as if those two words were enough, and *en vérité*, they were: he had led as much with his beauty as his wicked wits and cruelty, and to have one of those weapons stripped away must have seemed like the end of everything to him. I had *meant* it to be, and I still found no regret within myself for that. He was a vile criminal, and I would loathe and love him in equal parts, perhaps forever, but I would also not hesitate to strike him down a second time.

"But then Kiera came," he murmured, "and I could not face her, not with this face. Not as a father, and so I devised another plan, and realized I could do more than rule: that I could live forever. I have spent years growing these doppelgängers, years developing armor that might protect their fragile bodies against all weaponry. I am so close on both counts: I have spoken already with Monsieur Viccini, and today I felt the pliable power of his new metal beneath my hands. Had you not come, Amélie, then Josephine might have sung me into one of these bodies and I, embraced in unassailable armor, would have sought you out."

A coldness settled in my belly, a spectre of the shock that would have been. I could almost feel it, the numbness of my body, the thickness of my hands, the slowness of my thoughts, if my angel had appeared before me again, whole, handsome, *young*: younger than I had ever known him in life. The ease with which he might have then dispatched me was laughable, if imagining it turned me so thoroughly to ice. "For revenge."

"For forgiveness." A kind of laughter rode his reply, and he completed it swiftly: "The armor, in this case, would be to protect me long enough to beg that forgiveness, *mon* Amélie."

Fire came as fast as the ice had, thawing me, heating the cold humors and finally breaking the doppelgängers' spell: I was able to look away from their many perfect faces as I growled, "Do not presume, Paul-Gabriel. Do not even dare to ask."

He looked at me, smiled, and opened his hand, his gloved hand, to show me the doppelgängers. "I dare," he said, and the charm, the sweetness, the cajoling, was gone from his voice, leaving only the merciless monster I knew him to be, "I dare *everything*, Amelia Stone, and I dare it most of all with you, who took everything *from* me."

"Not everything," said Kiera, whom I had almost forgotten, and who lifted the crown of Hatshepsut high as I looked to her again. "She left you *me*, Father, and now all that was yours, is mine!"

The crown fit upon her skull as if it had been made for her; it had fitted Josephine that way too, and I wondered if there was some occult spell that molded it to the skull of its wearer. This frivolous thought occupied me as I sprang forward, forgetting *le Monstre* in my haste to silence his daughter before she spoke. I was too late, of course; I knew even as I leapt that I ought to have made use of my pistols. Her voice was great and terrible as she cried out, "Slay them, *les monstres*! Slay them both!"

Where Josephine had wakened adoration through her skill as much as the crown, Kiera simply demanded power from it. Her demands were met: presence rippled from the crown, smashing through each of us as a physical force. I was thrown back, so great was the *pschent*'s magic; *les monstres*, as she called them, had no chance at all. As one they became mad things, driven by her command and by the dark emotions that had wakened them. One fell upon me with inhuman speed, his teeth bared as if he would, dog-like, rip my throat out. It was only the reflexes of a lifetime spent fighting that brought my hands to his nape and jaw in time to snap his neck before he tore into me.

As quickly as that, *le Monstre*—the *true Monstre*, my angel—seemed to die at my hands, and a terrible joy filled me. There were so many more to enact vengeance upon; it was as if I had been offered an unexpected gift. Greedy to claim it, I came to my feet again.

A second *monstre* came at me; my intentions of laying waste to him were thwarted only by another pair of hands seizing me and flinging me halfway across the laboratory. I slammed through one of the glass-doored cabinets and slid to the floor, soaked by a medley of brightly colored liquids.

Freshness surged through me, washing away all the aches and pains of the past few days, and deep rage came with it. The latter might have been my own

untempered spirit; the former was without question
the power of an elixir, perhaps of Resilience. For the
first time I not only understood, but appreciated, the
usefulness of *le Monstre*'s experiments, even as I
disgusted myself by doing so. Each emotion was so
intense, so refined and focused, I could not say if they
were mine or not, but they made me feel powerful,
and so I chose not to question their origins.

Two of *les monstres* converged upon me, each
seizing an arm and a leg both, and pulling. A scream
tore from my throat as Fear coursed through my veins
as well, a thousand other imagined horrors adding a
pain no less real as *les monstres* pulled at me. Left with
no other limb to use, I flung my head sideways,
hoping to shatter some vial that might wipe the terror
from my mind. A sweet scent arose and Peacefulness
washed over me; my muscles relaxed and even the
agony of being pulled apart seemed remote and
unimportant.

Without warning, one of the two *monstres*
screamed, then fell forward, narrowly missing me as
he collapsed. The other dropped me while I turned a
lazy gaze upon the fallen *monstre*, no more than mildly
interested to see that a knife—no, a scalpel—
protruded from his spine. Above me, to my disinterest,
the other *monstre* died as well, and in nearly the same
moment a vial crashed beside my face, releasing
bright blue liquid that smelt of Ambition. My
lethargy passed and I surged upward, trying to escape
the effects of other elixirs.

A hand thrust itself into my view: *le Monstre*, his

fingers still gloved, his silver-headed cane in his strong hand. I seized the offering without allowing myself to think. He pulled me to my feet and for a moment we were as we had been a hundred times, a lifetime ago: face to face, nearly lip to lip, his green eyes intent on my brown. Were it not for the pig-iron masking half his face, I might have been able, in that moment, to forget, but it was not to be. It was never to be, and the faint quirk of his lips, the slightest twitch of his eye, said that he knew it too.

He released me and spun; in the blur of black cloak and speed, he withdrew a sword from the cane and flourished it against the oncoming doppelgängers. I could not help but laugh: the theatrics of it were flawless, and I had not anticipated them. I seized my knife from its thigh-sheath and settled in beside him, and then—as we moved deeper into the room to pursue a common quarry—at his back, as if we were old friends fighting familiar battles. He, with his height and his sword, struck high; I, with my litheness and speed, went low, and together we circled, back to back, cutting down all who threatened us. There was a terrible, heart-soaring glory to it; I could have fought at his side forever, and again could not tell if it was the elixir's magic working in me or a long-buried truth surfacing. I was not certain it could not be both.

Above the sounds of *les monstres* fighting—not just us, but each other, in their eagerness to reach us— Kiera's raging objection rose: "She is your *enemy*! You should have finished her, Father!"

"The enemy of my enemy is my friend," *le Monstre*

called to his infuriated daughter in a voice danger-
ously near to laughter. "We do not fight for each other,
ma fille, but for survival. I believe you may trust that
we will turn upon one another the moment these
other concerns are dealt with. It would, after all," he
said more softly, to me, "be a shame to allow our story
to end any other way."

"*Ça, c'est vrai,*" I muttered, "as I have already tried
once to end it that way, and have no intention of
being cheated again."

"I should have corrupted you, Amélie, instead of
playing with you. We would have been unstoppable."

"I would rather have died." Thankfully, at that
moment *les monstres* ceased their in-fighting and turned
all their attention to us, bringing a welcome and
abrupt end to the discussion. We turned again,
slaughtering copies of a familiar face, until a hand
grasped my ankle and pulled me backward. I fell with
a shout; *le Monstre* drove his sword down, piercing the
doppelgänger who had seized me, but we were parted,
and though I came to my feet and continued the
battle, I could not again reach Paul-Gabriel's side.
Still, our enemies were fewer; we were individually in
less danger than we had been, or so I thought.

I did not correctly perceive Kiera's path as she,
too, worked her way through *les monstres*, pausing to
whisper to each of them as she went. Too late, I saw
the circle opening around *le Monstre*, leaving only
enough doppelgängers to distract him; too late I realized that circle was closing around me. I fought wildly,
but their purpose was no longer to kill, but to subdue;

as I reached for my last weapons, they seized my arms, my legs, even my head, with a hand held firmly over my mouth. I bit and screamed regardless, struggling with all my strength, but there were a dozen of them to my single person, and I could do nothing as *le Monstre* dispatched the last of his opponents and swung, triumphant, to face the next comer.

Kiera met him on the empty floor in an embrace that buried a knife in his belly.

35

"*A*nge!" Too late, *le monstre* whose hand covered my mouth loosened his grip under the rending of my teeth; too late, the lover's name burst from my lips. *Le Monstre*'s gasp was audible in the following silence, his astonishment pure even on his scarred and ruined face. He fell back a step from Kiera, body bent around the pain, hands shuddering near the knife's hilt. It could not have been long, and yet it seemed like only a heartbeat shy of forever before he lifted his gaze, first incredulously to Kiera, then, slowly, as if knowing it to be the last thing he would do, to me.

His eyes seemed to be all green, endlessly green, dying green, when I looked into them. He did not speak, only extended one hand—leather-clad, blood-slicked—toward me, and then silently, easily, fell backward into death.

Les monstres released me, which could not have been their orders, but even for the newly born, to see their progenitor fall must have been a great shock; they could not have helped but notice that their faces were his. They might, for all I knew, have been wakened from time to time in the past, so they might know the face of their creator. Whatever the reason, I was freed, and stood, one woman amongst many men, all of us alike in our loss.

I did not know what I felt. The elixirs staining my clothes offered many choices, alternating with each shift of my body and wrinkle of my shirt: shock, sorrow, anger, fear, disbelief, but all of it weakened by a great emptiness inside me that seemed the only real emotion of my own. I had meant to kill him, *bien sûr*; I had tried once before, and raged at my failure, and yet there was no gladness in me to see him fall. Perhaps it was that I had been cheated of his death; perhaps it was that I had so long defined myself by the hunt for *le Monstre aux Yeux Verts* that without him I did not know who I was.

Perhaps it was that hate only burned so deep when it was born of love, and that the ever-kindled fire of hatred could not help but also keep the flames of love ignited. My center; my *heart*, was broken, bitter and ironic as I knew that to be. I took a breath, perhaps the first since Paul-Gabriel Laval had fallen, and with that breath I *hurt*. Not just my heart, my chest, where my breath stabbed like knives, but in every part of me, so shockingly that my fingers curled with it; my muscles tightened and I bent as if I, too, had been cut through with a blade. The second breath was no better, save that it hurt so badly that in order to encompass it and survive I was forced to straighten, to stand tall and let agony course through the whole of my body. My feet ached as if the task of standing on them was too much to bear, and yet I could not allow myself to fall as *le Monstre* had done; not yet and, I knew as deeply as I felt this pain, not ever.

Without my conscious command, my feet took me a step forward; without deliberation, I spoke a single, uninflected word: "Kiera."

She whirled toward me, a maniacal grin dying on her face as, unhurriedly, I withdrew one of my pistols from its holster, aimed, and without hesitation shot her through the heart.

36

I had not forgotten my pistols; I never forgot them. I had delayed with them deliberately, not because I preferred the intimacy of fists and knives, but because once fired, bullets did not return; guns did not reload themselves. I often carried some small amount of extra ammunition, but it was in the coat that had been thrown so carelessly to the *moulin*'s gears; I had a dozen bullets, no more, and I had not, until this moment, felt the need for them was insurmountable.

The sound might have shattered the laboratory walls; it certainly shattered *les monstres*' numb composure. It hurt my ears, but no more than I already hurt; it was strangely easy to stand and watch Kiera as wetness bloomed on her brown shirt.

Her astonishment was, if anything, greater than *le Monstre*'s had been. Her lips parted, eyes wide, as if surprise was far greater than pain. As her father had done, she looked down; as he had done, she curled

her hands to her breast. She crumpled then, falling
down, not over, and her blood spread across the
polished black marble floors to meet her father's. The
pschent, the coveted double cobra crown, fell away and
rolled across the floor.

As if madness had taken them one and all, *les
monstres* let forth sobbing howls and as one rushed
wildly for the crown. Not wanting to hurry, not
wanting to move at all, wishing only to stand and
absorb all that had happened as I waited for the pain
to fade, I was obliged instead to act swiftly. The
pschent's curious shape gave it a particular trajectory,
and it was little effort to anticipate where it would
most likely roll. I went there whilst *les monstres* followed
where it had been, and I collected it just before the
most fortunate of the remaining doppelgängers laid
hands upon it.

His lovely face contorted in a snarl and I, for once
having no heart to fight, jammed the cursed crown on
my head and snapped, "*Arretez-vous!* All of you, stop!"

An ease of leadership that I had never before felt
washed over me, replacing even the bone-deep ache
of loss. "Stop," I said again, more wearily, and one by
one they did, to once again stand as if lost and undi-
rected. I wondered if they had minds of their own, or
were merely empty vessels to be commanded. The
latter seemed likely, though perhaps if given a life
outside their coffin-like chambers they might grow
into individuals with thoughts and hopes of their own.

I swayed, wondering too if that was what I
intended for them. There were no more than a dozen

left; *le Monstre* and I had been thorough in our house-cleaning, but a dozen men with the same face would be at best difficult to hide and at worst impossible. A dozen identical men without a hint of native intelligence amongst them would spawn wild stories of being raised by wolves, or apes, or perhaps even tales of the truth, if anyone was left who could recognize *le Monstre* in their fine features. And yet I could not in conscience strike them down when I was not fighting for my life; they had done nothing save carry out the orders they had been given, and lacked the experience to have judged those orders as ethical or immoral.

Khan would better know what to do; I would command them to remain and find my friend, whose wisdom I trusted. Between us all, the Century Club could make lives for *les monstres*—and watch over them to see that they did not become as their progenitor had been.

"Amélie."

The sound of my name was so weak that had there been any other noise in the room I would not have heard it. As it was, I thought I imagined it before realization seized me and I whirled, falling to my knees at *le Monstre*'s side. "Amélie," he said again, and I could neither deny nor regret that tears once more stung my eyes. He chuckled, though it must have cost him an enormous amount; his pale face whitened further, and blood trickled from his lips. "The crown suits you."

I lifted my hand to throw it away, but with a shocking surge of power he caught my wrist, though he could not then control the descent of either his hand or my own. "No. No, Amélie. Amélie, will you not...sing me to sleep? It has been so long...since I heard you sing."

"I do not sing any more, angel."

A different pain crossed his face, a pain somehow more real than the agony of death drawing him close. "Because of me. That is...my worst crime. Do not give up song because of me, Amélie. Do not let me take that joy from you."

My own low chuckle broke free. "Paul-Gabriel, *mon ange*, if you truly believe that to be your worst crime..." I could go no further; a litany of his crimes and their magnitude would do nothing, and I lacked the rage to try to hurt him now.

"Kiera?"

"Dead."

He nodded, but closed his eyes, as if I had, after all, pained him greatly and he could not bear to look on the world with that knowledge of it. "Another crime," he admitted after a moment. "There are many."

"Do you repent, Gabriel? Shall I call a priest now, at the end?" He was no more religious than I, but the question curved his lips, which somehow seemed worthwhile; somehow I did not wish to see him die in sorrow. And because of that, all unintending, I began the whisper of a song, a thing from the summer we had shared together. I remembered the words with dreadful clarity, as I could remember each hour of that time, and so, it seemed, did he, for he smiled again, and in a few shuddering breaths, went still in my arms.

The words I half whispered, half sang, broke as his weight pulled me toward the gleaming floor. I bowed over him, still trying to sing, and only lifted my eyes when the laboratory lights began to pulse and the air to swirl. Vents opened, drawing the air in, and in moments the looping tubes and coiled metals began to burble, as though extracting something from the air. I stared upward, dry eyed and heaving rough breaths between each phase, before a wild and terrible understanding swept me.

Snatches of Josephine's final aria came to me and I gave them full voice to see if my belief was true: a note, then two, sung aloud. My voice was rough and unpleasant; I had not lied to *le Monstre*. He was the last audience I had ever sung for, and to lift my voice now was not a farewell, but a momentary madness. Cleopatra had sung for the loss of Egypt; I sang for the loss of innocence, and if my song was broken, there was no one here to hear me. No one save *les monstres*, whose own madness was born of their creator's, and who were as enthralled by song as he had ever been.

Liquid began to form within the tubes: silver drops, trembling as they coalesced. A sob caught my throat, tearing the aria apart, but as my voice failed, another one joined it.

For several seconds I could not sing even if I had wanted to, instead staring confounded as Josephine Baker stepped through the laboratory door and gath-

ered the threads of my shaking song to lift them
upward with the grace and power that was hers alone.
She smiled at my expression, and as if carnage and
death did not lie all around me, crossed the laboratory
with her gaze locked to mine and her voice never
faltering. When she reached me, she took my hands in
hers and nodded once, an offer of encouragement, as
she brought the aria to higher reaches.

I did not know how the next note escaped me; it
was not through thought or deliberate effort, and it
sounded more of a frog's croak than a song. But it was
a sound, and it required breath, and between those
two things it made the next one easier, and the one
after that easier still. I could remember the melody, if
not all the words, to the final aria; with Josephine's
guidance I did not need the words. As if she lent me
the strength to say a proper *adieu*, my singing
improved. I remembered the lessons Maman had
taught me—the way to breathe, the carriage of a
trained vocalist. I was still rough, but my voice was a
not-unpleasant counterpoint to Josephine's as, hands
held tightly, gazes locked, together we reached for the
crescendo, found it, and collapsed into a trembling
and exhausted embrace in its aftermath.

Only then could I look upward, there to see what
I had suspected: that the tubes were filled with silver
liquid that bubbled and streamed within them.
Josephine glanced upward as well, then turned a
curious look tenderized by concern upon me. "I was
right," I whispered. "He improved his emotion
extractor until it could draw emotion from the very

air. I will have to check the opera house catwalks; I am certain they must be littered with contraptions like the one above."

"What did we sing into it?"

I replied, "Farewell, I suppose," before I remembered the *pschent* upon my head and touched it wearily. "Or perhaps commanding presence. That, after all, is what this is supposed to convey, and no one doubts you bear it within yourself, Madame Baker."

The unlikelihood of her arrival here finally came back to me and I frowned, my confusion renewed. Josephine's gaze brightened, anticipating my question, and said, "You shouldn't have told them to wait on a person of authority, Amelia. Not when, as you've just said, I have a commanding presence myself."

"You—but—you—you didn't, Josephine!"

"Oh, but I did. I had to abandon them at the second boulder," she said with a wild, pleased smile. "They went back for explosives, but I slithered through and came for you. I'm afraid my influence will have waned by the time they reach us, though. We'd best flee."

My eyes were dry, but my voice was strained: "Josephine, are you telling me that—"

Neck and neck, shoulder to shoulder, men in shirts of brown and black burst through the laboratory doors and fell upon us all.

37

I cried, "Fight! *Les monstres,* fight for your very lives!" even as Josephine, outraged, demanded, "Where did the Italians come from? It was only the Germans, Amelia, it was—!"

From the fascist faction's midst swaggered Signor Panterello, whose small stature allowed him to slip through the struggling soldiers with relative ease. "You did not imagine I would let you go after so thwarting my plans, did you?"

"The motorcycle, Josephine, where is it—?"

"Khan—!"

All was well, then; freed from the fear that Mussolini had acquired the beautiful bike, I could turn my disgust and loathing upon the thieving Signor Panterello, at whom I purposefully strode. "I imagined never to see you again, Panterello, but it seems you are even less clever than your larcenous ways suggested. If you were wise you would have taken the money and run—"

"When I have a platoon of soldiers at my back? I'm not afraid of you, Stone—"

"You should be."

It had been no time at all since *le Monstre* had fallen, since I had killed Kiera in a strange and terrible justice for his death. In that tiny space of time, I had known agony and ecstasy, but neither had offered the sweet simple release of action. Panterello did not speak again, for I had forgotten I wore the crown, and my word was law; he had not been afraid, but now he was, knees locked and eyes popping as I stormed toward him. It was not a fair fight, nor did I care; in a moment I was upon him with one fist seizing his shirt as the other struck his jaw in a mighty, silencing blow. He fell without protest and I turned to the nearest doppelgänger, thrusting Panterello's limp form toward him. "Carry him out of here," I ordered. "Bring him to the police; tell them he is the instigator of the street races and that he is a gift from Amelia Stone. Then go and live your life, *mon*—" I seized upon the word, reluctant to name a freed man *monster*, and instead substituted, "monsieur. Be a good man; that is all I ask of you. Now go!"

L'homme, for I would not now allow myself to think of him as a monster, gazed at me with astonished, beautifully green eyes, then snatched Panterello from my hands and ran, not toward the door through which fascists poured, but another egress I had not previously noticed. Josephine, who had wisely remained behind when I strode into the fight, watched him go, then turned to me with wide eyes. I pointed imperiously, but it appeared the crown did not work with silent commands; the corner of her mouth turned up and she deliberately located a still-upright laboratory bench and sat upon it, waiting on and challenging me.

There were a dozen doppelgängers and at least four times that number of soldiers; I weighed the balance and found the lives of *les monstres* worth less than that of Josephine Baker's, and with some, but not debilitating, regret, began my retreat. Gunfire was not yet in play—there were too many soldiers still forcing their way through the narrow door to have begun shooting—and I chose not to introduce it, merely forcing my way back through the growing crowd until I broke out of its back and pursued Josephine.

She had left the bench and stood in front of one of the unbroken cabinets, its door open as she took great handsful of the vials and stuffed them into unlikely locations: her bosom, her waistband, even her garters. When I came to her side she smiled brilliantly at me. "These are the potions he was using, aren't they? I thought they might come in handy."

I could not argue, and seized as many of the vials as I could, filling my pockets and my waistband until they overflowed. Then, with a glance back at the erupting battle behind us, I caught her hand. "I would like to propose something to you, my queen."

Josephine's sultry smile slipped over her lips and she purred, "Oh? I await your proposal with bated breath," causing me to regret the prosaic nature of my suggestion: "I propose we run, Josephine."

"Oh." Her smile turned to a laughing pout. "Yes, that might be a good idea."

Hand in hand we fled the laboratory after *l'homme* I had set free; behind us, gunfire echoed, and I knew we had not bought ourselves as much time as I might have hoped. When the shots behind us stopped, so did I, though I urged Josephine onward. "Go, *mon amie*. Let me deal with these ruffians."

Josephine instantly released my hand and took a dozen running steps before whipping back toward me, fire flashing in her eyes. "You used that crown on me!"

I clapped a hand to my head, surprised to find the *pschent* still there, and said with genuine remorse, "Forgive me. I did not mean to."

"Then take it off!"

"And carry it how?"

Unable to find a satisfactory answer, she changed the subject: "How many shots have you got?"

"Eleven," I replied reluctantly. I could see already where her argument would lead, and I had very little ground upon which to stand against it.

"And how many vials?"

"*Je ne sais pas*, Josephine. Perhaps two dozen?"

"And how many Nazis are there?"

"Nazis? Two dozen." I gave a pedantic sniff and felt I had earned the dour look Josephine bestowed upon me. "Blackshirts and brownshirts both, I don't know. Forty, or as many as fifty."

"And so with eleven bullets and two dozen vials you intend to defeat fifty men singlehandedly? I don't think so, Amelia, and we're wasting time standing here when we could be running. Let's go!"

Able to argue—able to win, no doubt, as I still wore the crown—but also reluctant to lose her in the catacombs, I succumbed to Josephine's demands. "You can always order them to run the other way if they catch us," she said breathlessly as we loped down a well-trodden path together. The idea had merit, though as the first bullets zinged behind us I wondered how I was meant to command metal to stop its flight through the air.

I did not have to, of course. I shouted, "Cease fire!" in a carrying voice and in three languages; immediately the bullets stopped, and, with a flash of childish delight and hope, I called, "Stop chasing us!"

We ran without pursuit for almost a minute; then footsteps began to pound behind us again. "Stop following us!"

Once more they stopped. By the fourth iteration of such commands, laughter, bordering on the hysterical after a day of too-high emotion, was breaking from my chest. "What else can they be doing?" Josephine asked. "Chasing, following, pursuing, hunting...stop running!" she suggested, and I echoed that order back in a powerful shout.

The footsteps faded again, but in no time the echoes began in a quick-time march. Exasperated, I stopped trying to vary my commands and instead rifled through my pockets, examining the vials of emotions as we ran. "Hatred, Fear, Despair—"

"That one will be of use." Josephine seized it from

my hand and flung it behind us; it crashed upon the stones and splashed free, causing me to be grateful for the general lack of breeze in the tunnels.

"Good Nature—" She seized that one as well, while I fumbled through the remaining vials, trying to separate the dangerous from the helpful. "Lethargy, Peacefulness—" We left behind us a trail of elixirs wafting in the air, and the sounds of pursuit grew less and less alarming. "I have no more to dissuade them," I finally said. "We'll have to fight those who remain."

"You can fight. I'll throw my own elixirs." Josephine dipped her fingers into her bodice, retrieving a rose-pink bottle. "This one has no label."

"Best not to risk it. There can't be that many of them left." I took her vial and tucked it into my pocket with the other dangerous items as I turned to face the last few of our enemies who had fought their way through the clouds of emotion elixirs.

The men who came toward us had all masked themselves by covering their faces with a jacket or a sleeve. When they saw us making our stand, they cast away those masks in favor of seizing their weapons. I pressed Josephine against the wall and, trying to provide some cover, began to fire my own pistol.

My aim was true; most of my bullets met their mark, and several of the fascist dogs fell to the catacomb floors to join the dead who already lay along these halls. The rest scattered, pressing themselves to the walls, and Josephine seized her chance, leaping out to throw her brightly-colored elixirs. *Her* aim was true as well; one vial broke against a black-shirted shoulder and the Italian's eyes rolled up as Calm overtook him to such a degree that he could no longer stand. The man nearest him mellowed as well, then sank in shoulder-shaking sobs as Resignation landed on the floor before him and did its work.

"With these I could be the greatest actress in the world," Josephine whispered to me; despite the predicament, I once more could not help but laugh. Her ambitions barred none, and I loved her for it, a thought which brought heat to my cheeks. She hugged the wall again as one of the fascists began to fire wildly at us, clearly hoping for luck rather than trying to aim. I fired back and missed, and then my pistols were empty. I turned to Josephine, guns dangling from my fingertips in a display of uselessness before I tucked them back into my holsters. She sorted swiftly through her remaining vials, muttering dismissals of most, and finally selected one of pulsating red. She held it up, winked at me, then screamed, "*Mon dieu! Amelia, she is dead!*" with such conviction that I clutched my own heart, wondering if I had been struck and simply had not yet noticed.

Without hesitation, two men raced down the hall toward us: two and no more; we had conquered the rest. Josephine, still screaming, turned toward them as if they were her salvation. I saw sly cruelty sluice across the face of one before Josephine threw her final useful vial with both speed and accuracy. It broke to pieces on the catacomb floor before them, and the two men stumbled, then turned and seized one another in a passionate embrace.

Josephine's screams turned to surprised laughter, trilling through the catacombs. "That was Romance. If I'd known it worked that well, I might have kept it! Quick, before it wears off!"

Hand in hand, laughing at the nearness of our escape, we ran through the catacombs and out into the bright Parisian afternoon.

38

Some number of the orchestra still sported bruises; I could, even from my box seat, count the ones that I had laid upon them. Their instruments seemed particularly out of tune to my wincing ear, though the damage to them had of course been repaired, or the instruments replaced, by now. Only the first violin still held what was certainly his original instrument, and, as if he knew both that I was there and that I had taken some special care to ensure the instrument's survival, his gaze sought mine across the distance, and he smiled.

His eyes were blue; I looked away regardless.

Inevitably, perhaps, I looked to the box across from mine. It was more than empty: it was blackened, crepe laid over the seats, the doors sealed. They called it *la boîte du fantôme* now, the phantom's box, and until superstition passed or greed prevailed, I imagined that it would remain unused. Still, I could not help but search its depths as if I half believed a dead man might somehow be hidden in its shadows.

"You're early, Amelia." My friend Khan's deep voice filled the whole of my own box, and I turned my profile to him with a smile.

"*Oui*. I wanted to watch everyone come in. You are looking very well, *mon ami*." And he was: his fur gleamed and the nails of his enormous hands, always well manicured, had an especially careful sheen. He wore a kilt as always, but tonight's was made of heavy raw silk dyed a forest green, and sported a thick silken belt so deftly twisted and pinned in place with a huge gold brooch that the entire ensemble could only be called formal wear. I stood to embrace him and kiss his cheeks, awed as always by the careful return of affection from a being whose unattended strength could crush my bones without thought.

"*Merci*, although I fear I am somewhat lacking in comparison to yourself, dear lady. Amelia, you are very nearly...Josephine, tonight."

The corner of my lip curled and I turned in rueful amusement to display my gown, which was the color of, and littered with, rubies. "She dressed me, I'm afraid. She has been, for the evenings. What do you think?"

"That she understands that neither of you are shadows of the other," Khan said with unexpected acumen. "Tonight you are made in her image, though I've seen you together in the city during the days this past week, and she's often chosen to dress as though she's been made in yours."

"*Oui.*" I sat again, gathering the splendid and ridiculous skirt in my fingers, then smoothing the shimmering fabric between them, though my gaze was for the yet-empty stage. "Rather more glamorous, but *oui*. The jodhpurs...suit her."

"Amelia," Khan said dryly as he sat beside me in a chair that creaked and protested at his great weight, "I am an ape, and disinclined to find human women, no matter how remarkable, to be enticing. However, I believe I would not be sentient if I could not see, and say, that any article of clothing that encases Madame Baker's backside so splendidly is barely done justice by the phrase *suits her*."

To my relief, I laughed: I had not known if laughter was in me tonight, the final night of Josephine's performance as Cleopatra. "I strove for discretion there, Khan. I will take your response as meaning that I succeeded."

"You have been," he said with great gentleness, "very discreet, Amelia. Tonight is her last performance."

For the third time, I said, "*Oui*," but because we both knew that a question lay within his statement, Khan waited on what more I had to say. "You said it very well, *mon ami*. We are not shadows of one another. We each cast too much light, and might illuminate each other, but...she cannot be Amelia by day and myself Josephine by night. Our lives are too different, and neither of us will give up that which we thrive upon. For Josie, it is the stage, for me..." I opened my hands, releasing the fabric and displaying the old bruises and faint scars upon my knuckles. My nails were not as elegant as Khan's: even polished, they showed the nicks and chips that came from my way of life.

Khan covered my hands with his own, warmth pouring from his skin to mine. I met his solemn gaze, then smiled in gratitude as he murmured, "I am sorry, Amelia."

"*La belle et la bête*," said another familiar, friendly voice, and Khan and I both stood to greet my mother as she stepped, smiling, into our box. "Khan, Amelia. You are a fairy tale together."

"*Pas du tout, madame*," Khan disagreed. "Fairy tales are built of the dangers in the night and the fear of power, especially powerful women. I should say that together Amelia and I are what fights the fairy tales."

Maman pressed a hand against her chest and smiled through a shine of tears in her eyes. "A much better story. Besides, as the old lady I would no doubt be cast as the crone or wicked queen, and prefer to be only the brave heroine's mother. Thank you for inviting me tonight, Amelia. I've wanted to hear Josephine sing on stage."

"*Bien sûr, Maman.* I'm glad you could join us. That dress," I added in admiration, and, just as I had done, Maman spun in pleased delight, showing the flare of a kick-pleated skirt and the swing of a low-cut back that showed her figure to great effect.

Khan caught her hand to steady her when she wobbled too far, and her "*Merci*" was for both of us as she sat on my far side. "And where is our fourth?"

"Here, signora." Bernardo Viccini, stupendously handsome in a short-waisted, long-tailed tuxedo, his over-long hair tucked into a tidy curl at his nape, stepped into the box as well. "Madame Stone," he said to me, nervously, "I'm afraid I'll embarrass you here. I've never been to the *Opéra*. What if I fall asleep?"

"Then I shall kick you," Maman replied serenely. "You won't fall asleep, Bernardo. No one could sleep through a Baker performance."

"Signora," Viccini said ruefully as he took his seat beside Maman, "the truth is I don't think anyone could sleep though any adventure your daughter is present at."

"I am not dressed for adventure," I told them in a tone that could not be dismissed. "There will be no adventures tonight. There have been quite enough of those for one brief performance run."

"Speaking of performance," Viccini said, leaning forward that he might see Khan clearly, "your suggestions to improve the engine's performance were just what I was looking for. The new metallic compound has always been superior to the heavy steel of older bikes, but..." He carried on, and though on nearly any other night I would eagerly attend to the design and development of a new, faster, lighter motorcycle, tonight my gaze drifted again to the filling audience.

A dead man did not sit in the box across from ours; nor did his youthful doppelgänger enter the theatre, though I looked again and again for those familiar features. *L'homme* had indeed delivered Signor Panterello to the authorities; the thieving fascist was now imprisoned for endangering the public with his races and soon would see charges of fraud, for the race's investors had all demanded their money back, only to find it had disappeared. Panterello would not see the light of day as a free man for a long time, if ever; *l'homme* had fulfilled his task well. I prayed he would also do as charged and live a good man's life—and *en vérité*, that he was *not* at this, Josephine's final performance in *La Reine du Nil*, boded well on that account. I could not say why I had, even so, hoped to see him.

Attuned as I was to the slightest motion on stage, my gaze was first to the curtains amongst those in my box seats; the curtains shivered and rose, and for the next hours we were captives of Josephine's voice, myself most of all. I watched her, memorized her, burned each motion and vocal triumph to memory, and if I wept at times, I was not the only one. Even Khan was not immune to her talents, and Viccini most certainly did not sleep. From time to time, Maman clutched my hand, and I held hers just as strongly, understanding the envy and admiration that had to consume her.

But it was all nothing to the final aria; as that song began, it was as if Josephine had not even been present until then. For all of her strength, all of her power, all of her presence up until the last piece, she might have been a child singing rhymes on a street corner, compared to the raw emotion, stripped free of any pretense, that came into her final song.

This, the last performance of her dying aria, was not sung for her voice master, nor for *le Monstre*, the creature her voice master had truly been. It was not sung for the people of Paris; it was not even sung for herself, when it might well have been, a triumphant finale in which her own glory was paramount.

No, it was sung for me, to me, a farewell, and she made no pretense of it being otherwise. The aria was not presented fully to the theatre, but instead she turned toward me, made each dying gesture to me, for me, and for all the people in the opera house, the song was for my ears alone.

I did not know that I had come to my feet until my fingertips brushed the box seat's railing; I did not know at all that hundreds of eyes were on me, enraptured by a song of love and loss even as they wondered at the story Josephine truly told with her voice. I did not even know that a quick-thinking stagehand had directed a spotlight onto myself and dimmed the rest of the lights, so that we were in truth alone in pools of light in the darkness; to me it was that way anyway, Josephine Baker the singular light in my world, her song all the sustenance I might need.

Its ending was a shock, the reverberations of her voice leaving a most perfect silence: no sound from a stunned patronage, no music from the awed orchestra, no song from Baker's lips. She waited; oh, she waited, knowing with flawless certainty how long she could hold them in the silence, and in the moment before it broke, she spoke a single clear word—and spoke it in French, to be certain her audience would understand: "*Adieu.*"

Then I knew I stood in a pool of light, because the stagehand killed it, leaving me in darkness, leaving Josephine the sun for all the patrons, and as she turned back to them, her hands raised in glory, such sound burst through the theatre as to shake its very walls.

I fell a step back, a marionette with my strings sliced, and even so, a breath of laughter escaped me at the perfection of her performance. No one could ask for a more magnificent farewell; no farewell, so staged, could be taken as anything other than final. Nor could any ordinary mortal hope to overcome the depths of emotion displayed by such a goodbye; it had been a gift, a terrible gift, for it had confirmed where her strongest affections would always lie. I had known, *bien sûr*, but I was left now with no pretense to survive upon.

I pressed my hand against Khan's shoulder as I left the box, assuring him that I was well; then, alone in the theatre halls, hurrying through opulence to leave this place before the audience swept out to find the woman to whom Josephine Baker had sung, I took from my bodice a vial. Rose pink, sweet smelling liquid sloshed within; the very vial I had taken from Josephine in the catacombs, knowing it then for what it was and seeing greater use for it in the future than in the fight at hand.

I did not breathe it in, but drank it, so that its

powers might imbue my very being, and upon the curving steps of the Paris Opera House, like a glittering glass slipper, I left love behind, transformed forever to an abiding fondness. Fondness softened the edges of regret, and if I dashed tears away, so too did I smile at the memories of the past two weeks, and smiled more broadly yet as I struck out into the Parisian night with one certainty in mind:

Adventure awaited!

EPILOGUE

Dying lights spat along the ceiling, illuminating tubes and cords that twisted amongst each other like lovers. They overlooked wreckage when they shuddered to life: cabinet upon cabinet of fallen glass, their contents spilled into indistinguishable browns on the blood-slicked floor. Laboratory equipment ranging from tables to beakers lay broken and overturned with bodies flung across them in haphazard ways.

A dying man shuddered on the floor, then heaved into consciousness with a cry. His fist, gloved in leather, slammed against his chest; a vial shattered there, driving glass through the fine silk and linen of his suit. The pain was nothing; the pain was unnoticeable beside the pierced agony of his belly. What mattered was the scent that rose up, like honey and steel, sweet and unbreakable. It saturated his lungs and filled his pores: *will*, Indomitable Will, the most precious elixir he had ever extracted. It had come from a woman—from *the* woman, his partner, his nemesis, his love. Never in all the years of his life had he encountered such will; he had carried a vial of it by his heart for all the years since it had freed her from him and it would now drive him beyond the possible, beyond death's grasp itself.

He could not move: every part of him knew that, but the Will pounding through him demanded that he move anyway. One hand twitched, then clawed at the blood-drenched floor. It found purchase: a man's leg. He grasped it, pulled himself over onto his belly, and found himself gazing into his own face, wretched with agonizing demise. A roar burst from him and he crawled rapidly over that body, over another. Over a third, this one a girl, his daughter, whose face was a rictus of surprise even now. She had killed him; that knowledge fueled his Will, and he dragged himself onward. Past the laboratory tables, past the broken cabinets of elixirs that no longer mattered. Only the will to survive mattered; that, and one other thing.

The wall was seamless; it took knowing the precise location to apply pressure to break it open, and that could not be done from the floor. He lay on his belly, bleeding, gasping, and thought he could not do it; *her* will sneered and drove him to his knees and then, hoarse with ragged screams, to his feet so bloody fingers could lean heavily against the catch.

He fell when the door opened; fell through into darkness that flickered once or twice as low lights over the bed began to respond to his presence. He could hardly see, blackness taking his vision, pain and blood loss taking his strength, but he didn't need to see. The bed lay three paces from the door; the whole of the room had been designed as a small, contained space. Elbow over elbow he pulled himself forward, finding the bed by falling into it, for he had always known that if he needed it, he might not be able to crawl up to a height; better to have it on the floor, where, once in its confines, he could roll onto his back through force of will. *Her* will. He threw the mask away, threw the wig away; he would not need them after this.

The nodes were difficult to place, with bloodless trembling hands, but like everything in this room, they had been prepared for the worst imaginable scenario. They did not have to be perfect; they only had to stay attached to his burned and terrible skull, and the sticky paste within them made certain they would. With the nodes in place, he allowed himself something like a rest: his hands fell, but they fell to the switches he must pull—even the need for a moment of recuperation was planned for, allowing him to continue with the inexorable change as his ability to carry on failed. He pulled the switches, tensing his slashed belly to do so, and cried out.

Her will was fading now; even indomitable will could do only so much with a dying body. But above him shone a single vial of silver liquid, freshly filled: the prize above all, the thing he had begged her for, had tricked her into giving him in their last moments together. Without it, all would have been lost; without it, the last *monstre*, here in its lonely chamber, could not be commanded into life, could not accept the full transfer of a lifetime of emotion and memory that had even now begun. He had to wait, to wait, to wait, until his own sense of self was so faded he could hardly remember who he had been, who he was no longer. Then, and only then, did he trigger the draining of the final vial, the vial of Commanding Presence, newly minted from she whose will drove him on, and with that surge of power, in dying, he shouted a single phrase: "Now *you* are *le Monstre aux Yeux Verts*!"

WITHIN THE CHAMBER, green eyes flew open. A gasp steamed the air, but could not cloud the window made a mirror by light within and none without. A face long forgotten in its perfection was reflected in that mirror: soft black hair growing long and free, thickly lashed green eyes, a deep-set seductor's gaze above a straight nose and cheekbones of razor sharpness. The full mouth curved in a hungry smile, and an intimacy, a promise, a name, shaped the beautiful lips: "*Amélie*..!"

Acknowledgements

I came to reading pulp fiction late, having been inspired to read A PRINCESS OF MARS shortly before *John Carter* arrived on the big screens.

Early in that first book, having arrived safely upon Mars, John Carter discovers the Martians are telepathic. There is a magnificent moment where, with no further ado, the text reads, "Likewise, under Sola's tutelage, I developed my telepathic powers so that I shortly could sense practically everything that went on around me."

Like, that's it, lads. "I, too, developed my telepathic powers." No more worldbulding than that. No more explanation. Just a flat, blanket statement. 'I developed my telepathic powers.' *As you do*.

It was the most amazing thing I'd ever read. I fell madly in love with pulp fiction in that moment. I wanted SO BADLY to write something like that.

And then Evil Hat came along and asked if I'd like to write a pulp fiction novel for their *Spirit of the Century* gaming line.

HOO BOY DID I.

STONE'S THROE is the result of that offer. It is, I feel, reasonably honorable to its pulpy ancestors; I certainly tried, and I hope you enjoyed it!

I'd like to thank Tara O'Shea for the amazing, pulpy cover art that I love so much, and most particularly Fred Hicks for giving me the opportunity to write this book. And, of course, all my love is due to Dad, and Ted, and Henry!

About the Author

According to her friends, CE Murphy makes such amazing fudge that it should be mentioned first in any biography. It's true that she makes extraordinarily good fudge, but she's somewhat surprised that it features so highly in biographical relevance.

Other people said she began her writing career when she ran away from home at age five to write copy for the circus that had come to town. Some claimed she's a crowdsourcing pioneer, which she rather likes the sound of, but nobody actually got around to pointing out she's written a best-selling urban fantasy series (The Walker Papers), or that she dabbles in writing graphic novels (Take A Chance) and periodically dips her toes into writing short stories (the Old Races collections).

Still, it's clear to her that she should let her friends write all of her biographies, because they're much more interesting that way.

More prosaically, she was born and raised in Alaska, and now lives with her family in her ancestral homeland of Ireland, which is a magical place where it rains a lot but nothing one could seriously regard as winter ever actually arrives.

She can be found online at her newsletter, tinyletter.com/ce_murphy, which you should definitely sign up for because it's by far the best way to hear what's out next!

THIS BOOK WAS MADE POSSIBLE WITH THE SUPPORT OF
Michael Bowman
and a cast of hundreds, including

"The Cap'n" Wayne Coburn, "The Professor" Eric Smailys, @aroberts72, @syntheticbrain, A. David Pinilla, Aaron Jones, Aaron Jurkis, Adam & Jayce Roberts, Adam B. Ross, Adam Rajski, Adan Tejada, AJ Medder, AJT, Alan Bellingham, Alan Hyde, Alan Winterrowd, Alex, Alien Zookeeper, Alisha "hostilecrayon" Miller, Alosia Sellers, Amy Collins, Amy Lambzilla Hamilton, Andrew Beirne, Andrew Byers, Andrew Guerr, Andrew Jensen, Andrew M. Kelly, Andrew Nicolle, Andrew Watson, Andy Blanchard, Andy Eaton, Angela Korra'ti, Anonymous Fan, Anthony Laffan, Anthony R. Cardno, April Fowler, Arck Perra, Ariel Pereira, Arnaud Walraevens, Arthur Santos Jr, Ashkai Sinclair, Autumn and Sean Stickney, Axisor, Bailey Shoemaker Richards, Barac Wiley, Barbara Hasebe, Barrett Bishop, Bartimeus, Beena Gohil, Ben Ames, Ben Barnett, Ben Bement, Ben Bryan, Bill Dodds, Bill Harting, Bill Segulin, Blackcoat, Bo Saxon, Bo Williams, Bob Bretz, Brandon H. Mila, Bret S. Moore, Esq., Brian Allred, Brian E. Williams, Brian Engard, Brian Isikoff, Brian Kelsay @ripcrd, Brian Nisbet, Brian Scott Walker, Brian Waite, Brian White, Bryan Sims, Bryce Perry, C.K. "Velocitycurve" Lee, Calum Watterson, Cameron Harris, Candlemark & Gleam, Carl Rigney, Carol Darnell, Carolyn Butler, Carolyn White, Casey & Adam Moeller, Catherine Mooney, CE Murphy, Centurion Eric Brenders, Charles Paradis, Chase Bolen, Cheers, Chip & Katie, Chris Bekofske, Chris Callahan, Chris Ellison, Chris Hatty, Chris Heilman, Chris Matosky, Chris Newton, Chris Norwood, Chris Perrin, Christian Lindke, Christina Lee, Christine Lorang, Christine Swendseid, Christopher Gronlund, Chrystin, Clark & Amanda Valentine, Clay Robeson, Corey Davidson, Corinne Erwin, Craig Maloney, Crazy J, Cyrano Jones, Dan Conley, Dan N, Dan Yarrington, Daniel C. Hutchison, Daniel Laloggia, Danielle Ingber, Darcy Casselman, Darren Davis, Darrin Shimer, Daryl

Weir, Dave BW, Dave Steiger, David & Nyk, David Hines, David M., David Patri, Declan Feeney, Deepone, Demelza Beckly, Derrick Eaves, Dimitrios Lakoumentas, DJ Williams, DL Thurston, Doug Cornelius, Dover Whitecliff, Drew, drgnldy71, DU8, Dusty Swede, Dylan McIntosh, Ed Kowalczewski, edchuk, Edouard "Francesco", Edward J Smola III, Eleanor-Rose Begg, Eli "Ace" Katz, Ellie Reese, Elly & Andres, Emily Poole, Eric Asher, Eric Duncan, Eric Henson, Eric Lytle, Eric Paquette, Eric Smith, Eric Tilton, Eric B Vogel, Ernie Sawyer, Eva, Evan Denbaum, Evan Grummell, Ewen Albright, Explody, Eyal Teler, Fabrice Breau, Fade Manley, Fidel Jiron Jr., Frank "Grayhawk" Huminski, Frank Jarome, Frank Wuerbach, Frazer Porritt, Galen, Gareth-Michael Skarka, Garry Jenkins, Gary Hoggatt, Gary McBride, Gavran, Gemma Tapscott, Glenn, Greg Matyola, Greg Roy, Gregory Frank, Gregory G. Gieger, Gus Golden, Herefox, HPLustcraft, Hugh J. O'Donnell, Ian Llywelyn Brown, Ian Loo, Inder Rottger, Itamar Friedman, J. Layne Nelson, J.B. Mannon, J.C. Hutchins, Jack Gulick, Jake Reid, James "discord_inc" Fletcher, James Alley, James Ballard, James Champlin, James Husum, James Melzer, Jami Nord, Jared Leisner, Jarrod Coad, Jason Brezinski, Jason Kirk Butkans, Jason Kramer, Jason Leinbach, Jason Maltzen, Jayna Pavlin, Jayson VanBeusichem, Jean Acheson, Jeff Eaton, Jeff Macfee, Jeff Xilon, Jeff Zahnen, Jeffrey Allen Arnett, Jen Watkins, Jenevieve DeFer, Jenica Rogers, jennielf, Jennifer Steen, Jeremiah Robert Craig Shepersky, Jeremy Kostiew, Jeremy Tidwell, Jesse Pudewell, Jessica and Andrew Qualls, JF Paradis, Jill Hughes, Jill Valuet, Jim "Citizen Simian" Henley, Jim & Paula Kirk, Jim Burke in VT, Jim Waters, JLR, Joanne B, Jody Kline, Joe "Gasoline" Czyz, Joe Kavanagh, John Beattie, John Bogart, John Cmar, John D. Burnham, John Geyer/Wulfenbahr Arts, John Idlor, John Lambert, John Rogers, John Sureck, John Tanzer, John-Paul Holubek, Jon Nadeau, Jon Rosebaugh, Jonathan Howard, Jonathan Perrine, Jonathan S. Chance, José Luis Nunes Porfirio, Jose Ramon Vidal, Joseph Blomquist, Josh Nolan, Josh Thomson, Joshua K. Martin, Joshua Little, JouleLee Perl Ruby Jade, Joy Jakubaitis, JP Sugarbroad, Jukka Koivisto, Justin Yeo, K. Malycha, Kai Nikulainen, Kairam Ahmed Hamdan, Kal Powell, Karen J. Grant, Kat & Jason

Romero, Kate Kirby, Kate Malloy, Kathy Rogers, Katrina Lehto, Kaz, Keaton Bauman, Keith West, Kelly (rissatoo) Barnes, Kelly E, Ken Finlayson, Ken Wallo, Keri Orstad, Kevin Chauncey, Kevin Mayz, Kierabot, Kris Deters, Kristin (My Bookish Ways Reviews), Kristina VanHeeswijk, Kurt Ellison, Lady Kayla, Larry Garetto, Laura Kramarsky, Lily Katherine Underwood, Lisa & M3 Sweatt, Lisa Padol, litabeetle, Lord Max Moraes, Lorri-Lynne Brown, Lucas MFZB White, Lutz Ohl, Lyndon Riggall, M. Sean Molley, Maggie G., Manda Collis & Nick Peterson, Marcia Dougherty, Marcus McBolton (Salsa), Marguerite Kenner and Alasdair Stuart, Mark "Buzz" Delsing, Mark Cook, Mark Dwerlkotte, Mark MedievaMonkey, Mark O'Shea, Mark Truman of Magpie Games, Mark Widner, Marshall Vaughan, Martin Joyce, Mary Spila, Matt Barker, Matt Troedson, Matt Zitron & Family, Matthew Scoppetta, Max Temkin, Maxwell A Giesecke, May Claxton, MCpl Doug Hall, Meri and Allan Samuelson, Michael Erb, Michael Godesky, Michael Hill, Michael M. Jones, Michael May, michael orr, Michael Richards, Michael Thompson, Michael Tousignant, Michael Wolfe, Miguel Reyes, Mike "Mortagole" Gorgone, Mike Grace (The Root Of All Evil), Mike Kowalski, Mike Sherwood, Mike 'txMaddog' Jacobs, Mike Wickliff, Mikhail McMahon, Miranda "Giggles" Horner, Mitch A. Williams, Mitchell Young, Morgan Ellis, Mur Lafferty, Nancy Feldman, Nathan Alexander, Nathan Blumenfeld, Nestor D. Rodriguez, Nick Bate, Odysseas "Arxonti" Votsis, Owen "Sanguinist" Thompson, Pam Blome, Pamela Shaw, Paolo Carnevali, Pat Knuth, Patricia Bullington-McGuire, Paul A. Tayloe, Paul MacAlpine, Paul Weimer, Peggy Carpenter, Pete Baginski, Pete Sellers, Peter Oberley, Peter Sturdee, Phil Adler, Philip Reed, Philippe "Sanctaphrax" Saner, Poppy Arakelian, Priscilla Spencer, ProducerPaul, Quentin "Q" Hudspeth, Quinn Murphy, Rachel Coleman Finch, Rachel Narow, Ranger Dave Ross, Raymond Terada, Rebecca Woolford, Rhel ná DecVandé, Rich "Safari Jack Tallon" Thomas, Rich Panek, Richard "Cap'n Redshanks" McLean, Richard Monson-Haefel, Rick Jones, Rick Neal, Rick Smith, Rob and Rachel, Robert "Gundato" Pavel, Robert M. Everson, Robert Towell (Ndreare), Ross C. Hardy!, Rowan Cota, Ryan & Beth Perrin, Ryan Del Savio Riley, Ryan E. Mitchell, Ryan Hyland, Ryan Jassil, Ryan Patrick

Dull, Ryan Worrell, S. L. Gray, Sabrina Ogden, Sal Manzo, Sally Qwill Janin, Sam Heymans, Sandro Tomasetti, Sarah Brooks, Saxony, Scott Acker, Scott E., Scott Russell Griffith, Sean Fadden, Sean Nittner, Sean O'Brien, Sean R. Jensen, Sean T. DeLap, Sean W, Sean Zimmermann, Sebastian Grey, Seth Swanson, Shai Norton, Shaun D. Burton, Shaun Dignan, Shawna Hogan, Shel Kennon, Sherry Menton, Shervyn, Shoshana Kessock, Simon "Tech Support" Strauss, Simone G. Abigail C. GameRageLive, Stacey Chancellor, Stephen Cheney, Stephen Figgins, Sterling Brucks, Steve Holder, Steve Sturm, Steven K. Watkins, Steven McGowan, Steven Rattelsdorfer, Steven Vest, T I Hely, Tantris Hernandez, Taylor "The Snarky Avenger" Kent, Team Milian, Teesa, Temoore Baber, Tess Snider, Tevel Drinkwater, The Amazing Enigma, The Axelrods, The fastest man wearing a jetpack, thank you, The Gollub Family, The Hayworths, The NY Coopers, The Sotos, The Vockerys, Theron "Tyrone" Teter, Tim "Buzz" Isakson, Tim Pettigrew, Tim Rodriguez of Dice + Food + Lodging, TimTheTree, TJ Robotham, TK Read, Toby Rodgers, Todd Furler, Tom Cadorette, Tom J Allen Jr, Tony Pierson, Tracy Hall, Travis Casey, Travis Lindquist, Vernatia, Victor V., Vidal Bairos, W. Adam Rinehart, W. Schaeffer Tolliver, Warren Nelson, Wil Jordan, Will Ashworth, Will H., William Clucus Woods...yes, "Clucus", William Hammock, William Huggins, William Pepper, Willow "Dinosaurs and apocalypse? How could I NOT back it?" Wood, wufl, wwwisata, Wythe Marschall, Yurath, Zakharov "Zaksquatch" Sawyer, Zalabar, Zalen Moore, and Zuki.